NO MORE SECRETS

BLUE MOON #1

LUCY SCORE

B*loom* *books*

Cover by Kari March

ISBN: 978-1-945631-37-5 (ebook)
ISBN: 978-1-7282-8262-6 (paperback)

Published by Bloom Books, an imprint of Sourcebooks
P.O. Box 4410, Naperville, Illinois 60567-4410
(630) 961-3900
sourcebooks.com

lucyscore.com

071722

To my brother and sister, the funniest people I know.

Better a warrior in the garden than a gardener at war.
Japanese proverb

1

Summer Lentz hefted her suitcase and laptop bag into the trunk of her snappy little rental car. She paused to catch her breath, grateful for the parking space she had snagged just half a block down from her Murray Hill building.

Every once in a while, her body inconveniently reminded her that recovery was a very long journey.

She took a deep breath of late spring air and resisted the urge to walk back to her apartment to verify that the door that she checked twice before leaving was indeed locked and the stove—that she never used—was off.

It was a week upstate. She'd be back to civilization before she knew it. Besides, maybe a few days without the bustle of Manhattan would allow her to recharge her batteries. Or— she grimaced at the thought——she'd completely disappear from the consciousness of everyone at work. At *Indulgence,* if you weren't there eleven hours a day, you weren't there. The sleek Midtown West headquarters were as glossy as the pages of its magazine. And more cutthroat than a season of reality TV.

Summer had carved out a place for herself at *Indulgence* without selling too many pieces of her soul. Nine months into her promotion as associate editor, things were finally falling into place.

She had upgraded her shoebox studio to a slightly roomier one-bedroom. Her wardrobe had seen a gradual and tasteful edit. The blog that she was so proud of had grown exponentially. On the outside, her social life was a whirlwind of parties, openings, and meet-ups. Though, at times, it was hard to tell where work stopped and life began.

If she could hold herself on this trajectory without any other major crises, she could almost taste a senior editor position in her future.

The phone in her cream-colored Dooney and Bourke signaled.

Summer slid behind the wheel and swiped to answer.

"Are you farm-bound yet?" The deep, smooth voice of her best friend warmed her ear.

"Well if it isn't the famous Nikolai Vulkov. What's the Wolf doing today?"

Niko was second-generation American, but after too much vodka, one could begin to detect the slightest hint of Russia in his bedroom tone. He had a reputation as both a talented photographer and ladies' man, hence the nickname.

When Summer hadn't instantly fallen under the Wolf's spell at the magazine, they had become fast friends instead.

"You sound out of breath. Are you pushing yourself too hard?"

Summer wrinkled her nose. "What are you, my dad?"

"Do not spend this assignment hauling hay bales and tipping cows. You understand me?" he warned.

"Is tipping cows even a thing? I think that's an urban myth."

"Way to dance around the issue, brat."

"I promise to take care of myself. I'll probably be in bed every night by eight." She flipped the sun visor down to check her eye makeup. "I doubt there's any midnight martini special in town."

"Well, while you're there, text me a couple of pics of Old MacDonald and his organic farm so I can start planning for the shoot in July."

"Will do. And while I'm gone, try not to fall desperately in love with any models."

"I can't promise anything. So don't stay away too long. I may need you to vet a Brazilian beauty."

"Never change, Niko," Summer sighed. "I'll see you in a week."

She hung up and plugged the address into the GPS. Just three hours to Blue Moon Bend.

~

HIS BROTHER'S obnoxious ringtone had Carter Pierce straightening from his work and tossing his dirt-covered gloves to the ground.

"What?"

"Hello to you, too." Beckett had his politician voice on, adding to Carter's irritation.

"I'm in the middle of something," Carter said, swiping a hand through his dark hair.

"What are you in the middle of?"

"A field of lettuce. First pickup for the produce shares is this weekend."

"I realize that. I thought we weren't harvesting until tomorrow. Isn't that why I'm spending my entire afternoon with your hairy mug?"

Beckett gave Carter nothing but shit about his beard. His clean-shaven brother didn't understand that after a few years in the military, the choice to sprout facial hair was a special kind of freedom.

"I was checking the irrigation and thought I'd get a head start."

"Well stop starting and get your ass back to the house."

"Why?"

"Check your watch."

Carter swiped a finger over the dirt coating the face of his leather watch cuff. "Shit."

"Better hurry up or you'll give her a bad first impression."

Carter hung up on his brother's laughter, grabbed his gloves and tools, and ran for the Jeep.

The time had gotten away from him, as usual. Knee deep in plants and earth and sunshine, some days he felt as though time stood still. He should have set a damn alarm.

Maybe she'd be late?

He threw the Jeep in gear and hightailed it down the dirt lane toward the house.

It wasn't like he didn't have other things to do. Showing a writer around for a week was yet another responsibility that the rest of his family felt would sit nicely on his shoulders. His mother should be the one holding her hand, letting her pet calves and make garden fresh salads. Or glib-tongued Beckett. He'd give her the idyllic tourist view of the farm and then treat her to candle-lit dinners. Send her back to the city with stories of how romantic Blue Moon was.

But no. It fell on Carter to walk her through life on the farm. And he sure as hell wasn't going to treat her like an honored guest. An extra pair of hands was an extra pair of hands. He was going to put Summer Lentz to work and send her back to Manhattan with the real story on farm life.

He spotted the little red coupe as he shot down the lane to the farmhouse.

Bringing the Jeep to an abrupt halt next to the car, a sense of urgency propelled him out of the Jeep and across the drive. The front door was unlocked, as it always was. Maybe she was inside.

He stopped mid-stride when he spotted her. Her navy button down, with its crisp collar, was tucked neatly into the waist of slim pants the color of ashes. The pants ended a few inches above her trim ankles, most likely to show off the short suede boots with needlepoint heels. Stick-straight hair hung to her shoulders in a silvery blonde curtain. Wide eyes, the color of the Canterbury bells that bordered the flowerbed behind her, peered at him. Her full lips wore a sheen of pink gloss and were parted as if to ask a question.

She looked like one of his grandmother's porcelain dolls come to life. Her small hands were clasped in front of her, spine straight enough to draw a compliment from a drill sergeant.

He had probably scared the hell out of her with his entrance, Carter thought, and stopped his approach.

"Hi."

"Hi." Her voice was whisper-soft with a huskiness that went straight to his gut.

~

THE MAN before her was like no farmer Summer had ever envisioned. His dark-as-midnight hair was shorn ruthlessly short on the sides with more length on top. Beards weren't exactly hot in Manhattan, but his had her questioning why that was. Raincloud eyes held her gaze, and the deep frown that put the line between his eyes had her pulse skittering.

The dirt-streaked Henley stretched across a mile-wide chest, sleeves shoved up his very fit forearms. His legs under the worn, holy jeans were braced as if for battle. She just wasn't sure if it was with her or someone else.

He looked like a model some smartass art director had plunked down in a field to sell jeans or watches. Niko was going to have a field day with tall, dark, and frowny, Summer decided. She wished she hadn't left her phone in the car so she could get a picture of him just like this.

She was already fascinated, and he had only spoken a single word. *This story had just gotten a hell of a lot more interesting.*

"Are you Mr. Pierce?" She started forward, covering the dusty distance between them, her hand outstretched.

He paused for exactly one second before engulfing her palm in his. His grip—and everything else about him—radiated strength. Rough calluses met her manicured, moisturized hand. There was something there. An energy that shot straight up her spine.

"Carter," he said, finally.

"Summer." She returned the pressure of his grip as confidently as she could. In her line of work, everyone was a potential enemy, but Carter Pierce was a different kind of dangerous.

He didn't release her hand, but the frown line gradually dimmed. "Welcome to Blue Moon Bend, Summer.

2

————

*U*nlike its owner, the exterior of the farmhouse was exactly what Summer had expected. The two stories of white siding and windows were capped with a blue metal roof. The wide porch with its natural plank floorboards wrapped around the side, out of sight. White columns held up the roof, and a pair of ceiling fans turned lazily from the varnished ceiling.

Ferns spilled over baskets hanging from the rafters. A quintessential porch swing with faded blue cushions was angled to take in the view of the sweeping expanse of lawn and pasture.

It was a home kept with pride.

"Come on. I'll show you around the house," Carter said, leading the way up the porch steps. She noticed that his dirt-stained jeans fit him just as well from behind as they did from the front.

He pried off his work boots and held the front door, more glass than wood, waiting for Summer to catch up.

She slipped out of her peep-toe booties and after a brief internal debate placed them just inside the front door. She wasn't sure how free range the animals were on this farm or if any of them had a shoe fetish.

The foyer drew an approving eye. Hand-scraped oak flowed from the front of the house to the back. The original layout was intact at the entrance, with formal dining and living rooms to the right and left of the door, but Summer could see the back of the house opened into a large addition.

"Carter, your house is beautiful," she said, examining the staircase with its timeworn treads and steel and cable banister. "It's like this delicate balance of modern and rustic. You'd never expect it from how traditional the exterior is."

She turned to him. Without her shoes on, she had to look up, way up. He was watching her wordlessly, his arms crossed, from just inside the door.

"Mind if I look at your kitchen?" She paused and smiled. "I'm sorry. I'm a horrible snoop."

He shrugged his broad shoulders. "Snoop all you want."

"You're going to regret saying that," she said, arching an eyebrow before she padded down the hallway toward the light-filled kitchen.

Carter followed a few paces behind.

The hallway opened into a bright kitchen attached to an even brighter great room. The wide windows over the stainless apron front sink overlooked a stone barn and what looked like miles of fencing. An island, wide and deep, ran the length of the wall of cabinets and windows, with plenty of space for the six metal barstools.

To the left, the two-story great room housed leather couches, tall bookcases, and a hulking flat screen mounted above a spectacular fireplace. Massive cathedral-like trusses drew the eye overhead, and sunlight poured in through the windows and French doors that lined both sides of the room.

Summer whistled. "This room is twice the size of my entire apartment." She turned back to the kitchen.

"Is it just you here?" The first floor was spacious enough to host thirty with plenty of elbowroom left over.

"Just me." Carter moved around the island to the refrigerator. He tossed her a bottle of water and took one for himself. He frowned at her inquiring stare. "What?"

"I have so many questions already," she admitted, twisting off the cap of the bottle.

"Why waste time?" he shrugged. "Shoot."

Summer took the invitation at face value. She slid onto one of the barstools and clasped her hands daintily in front of her.

"Do you cook? How is your house so clean? Did you design all this? How much land do you have? Do you have help? Do you ever get lonely?"

He was frowning again.

"You're writing about the farm."

"You are the farm."

Carter looked pained. So Summer immediately changed tactics. She waved her hand. "Forget all that. Let's start with something simple. What do you grow here?"

"We've got an orchard for apples in the fall," Carter began. "We also grow just about anything you'd find in a backyard garden. Lettuce, broccoli, radishes, tomatoes, peppers, and sweet corn."

Summer nodded, committing the list to memory. "We?"

He was weighing her questions as carefully as she would his answers, both feeling the other out. He was careful, she noted. Not at all interested in sharing about himself, which was a drastic and refreshing change from her usual subjects. But it wouldn't stand. One look at Carter and his home and she knew there was more than organic apples and acres of sweet corn here.

"I have help," he said, his tone brusque.

Tiptoeing would be key, she noted. "Sounds like a big job. Do you ever get a day off?"

Carter's lips quirked at this. "No. How about you?"

She smiled at the glimpse of humanity. "Not really," she returned. "How many animals do you have on the farm?"

She could see him doing an internal headcount.

"Fourteen, counting the chickens."

"Is that a lot?"

"No. How many animals do you have in New York?"

"None." She had never had a pet. Not enough space, too much travel. There wasn't room in her life for something that needed attention. "I have a plant at the office. It's tended by the building's plant service. How many hours a day do you work?"

"Depending on weather, interruptions, and farm catastrophes... between eight and twenty."

Summer did laugh then. "What constitutes a farm catastrophe?"

"Anything that has the potential to disrupt the regular schedule for more than a few hours." He leveled that steely-eyed gaze at her, and she knew it was a subtle dig.

"Am I an interruption or a catastrophe?"

Carter eyed her up. "That remains to be seen. I'm leaning toward catastrophe."

"Nice." Summer was used to being underestimated. It only motivated her to work harder. She'd change his mind. She wouldn't get in his way, and she would pry everything out of Carter Pierce that she needed from him. She would just have to be careful and use a little finesse.

"How would you describe Pierce Acres? One word," she

asked, purposely turning her back on him to study the view through the windows. She held her breath.

"Sanctuary," he said gruffly. Carter put the water bottle down on the granite with enough force to make her wince.

The unadulterated truth of it echoed in her bones. She didn't know exactly what he meant, but in that one word, Summer knew that the story and this week would be more than she had anticipated.

He rounded the island. "If you're done with twenty questions, give me your keys. I'll bring your bags in and show you your room."

And just like that, sharing time was over. Summer was far from done but bit her tongue on the thousand questions his simple statement sparked. Instead, she handed over the rental car's keys. His hand closed over hers, and again she felt that interesting tingle.

Without another word, Carter stalked down the hallway and out the front door. Summer sighed. Usually she was much better at easing people into interviews. His entrance and the fierce frown on that incredible face had thrown her.

One thing was for sure, there was a lot going on in the fine head of Carter Pierce. She would bide her time and find a way to make the weeklong interview more comfortable for him. She would crack him. She always did.

∽

CARTER POPPED the trunk on Summer's car and put the single suitcase and leather bag on the front porch. At least she hadn't packed her entire wardrobe. It was a point in her favor. He slammed the trunk lid shut and looked around him.

He meant what he said. The farm, with its gentle rolling hills and neatly cordoned pastures and fields, was sanctuary.

His sanctuary. One that had just been invaded by a nosy, appealing woman with Dresden blue eyes. The jolt he felt when he shook her hand had gone straight to his chest like a jumpstart to the heart. It was so unexpected he let his fingers linger on hers when he took the keys just to see if it happened again.

It did.

He wasn't sure if it was just the knee-jerk physical reaction to her or something else. Either way, it was a complication and one he didn't want to make time for. He had worked hard to get himself to a balanced place, and he had a feeling that someone like Summer Lentz could destroy that sweet spot with just a smile from those glossy, full lips.

He'd have to keep his distance there.

Carter decided to buy himself a little more time and distance by moving her car out of the drive and into the garage.

He pushed the start button, and the car and its stereo came to life. She had been listening to classical from a playlist on her phone. It struck deep when he realized it was Beethoven's *Silence*, a personal favorite.

When he had come home from Afghanistan—broken and battered—the wordless symphonies of long-dead greats had soothed and strengthened, restoring his soul as his body healed.

He was a man who believed in signs.

He just didn't know what to do with this one.

3

"Your phone was still in the car," Carter said, pulling it out of his pocket and handing it to Summer who was admiring the dining room table his father had made. "I think you got fifteen texts and emails between the car and here."

"Thank you," she said, smiling up at him. "The magazine never sleeps." She scrolled through her messages. "I can take care of these later."

"I'll show you to your room," Carter said, nodding toward the staircase. He waved her in front of him, and they started up the stairs together.

"You're the first door on the right."

It had been his room growing up. Overlooking the front yard, the large window and sloped porch roof had offered the perfect late night escape for a teenager with secret plans.

The side window afforded a view of the neatly trimmed pasture and the small, bi-level barn. Every Saturday, June through October, Blue Moon Bend's environmentalists, organic-hungry yuppies, and vegetarians descended on the farm and the little barn to pick up their share of Pierce Acres' produce and enjoy a little bit of farm life.

The double bed with its wrought iron frame had been his, as had the writing desk under the window. He put her suitcase on the bed and her laptop bag on the desk.

"This is really nice, Carter. Thank you for letting me stay with you," Summer said.

"Think you'll be able to sleep without drifting off to the sound of traffic and sirens?"

"It'll be an experience, that's for sure," she laughed.

He liked the sound of her laugh and how it filled the room. He'd only recently begun to realize how quiet the farmhouse was at times.

"I'm assuming you'd like an upstairs tour, too?"

"Yes, please," she said, clasping her hands in front of her.

He led her back into the hallway where she poked her head into the bedroom across the hall. It was set up as an office with a desk angled to take in the view of green fields and clumps of forest.

"Is this your office?"

"Mostly. But my mother uses it, too. She's bringing dinner over tonight so she can meet you."

"I'm looking forward to it," Summer said.

"Yeah, well, she may end up interviewing you, so watch out."

"Noted." Summer smiled, her eyes dancing.

"Mom keeps our books and runs payroll. We're thinking about redoing the second floor of the barn next to the house to use as a bigger office. A 'center of operations' as Mom calls it."

"Do you have a lot of people who work for you?" Summer asked as they continued down the hall.

Carter pushed open the second door to reveal the main

bathroom. "Joey and I are the only full-timers. She runs the riding program and takes care of the horses. Then we have a half-dozen part-timers who help out. My brother Beckett—he's coming to dinner tonight, too—gives us some hours every week, and Mom pitches in a lot."

"You have another brother, too, right?"

"Jackson," Carter nodded. "He's a script writer in LA."

"From family farm to Hollywood," she murmured, taking in the wood-framed mirror that hung over dual vanities.

"Does he miss it? Living here?" she asked.

Carter shrugged. Jackson had skipped town the day before his high school graduation, headed for the West Coast and leaving a hole in the family with no explanations or apologies. It was something he knew still bothered them all. Some more than others.

He opened a skinny door next to the tub, stocked neatly with linens and every bathroom product known to man. His mother had gone shopping in preparation for Summer's visit, explaining that women needed more than just soap and toothpaste. "Here's the towels and probably anything else you'll need."

Summer peered around him, and he caught her scent. Something sweet and light that teased the senses.

He took a step back and led her out of the bathroom. "That's another bedroom over there," he said, pointing to the last door on the right. "And this is the master."

He had focused much of the renovation on this room. The existing gabled roof had flowed into the great room addition, which allowed him to add a cathedral ceiling here. Two original windows were replaced with glass doors that opened onto a small but functional balcony facing west for sunset views.

The large bed with its tall wooden headboard faced the view.

The walk-in closet was practically empty. He stored most of his jeans and t-shirts in the center island with its endless drawers and cabinets.

"I've never seen a closet this empty before," Summer remarked. "In fact I've never seen a man's bedroom that was so clean. You don't even have dirty socks on the floor. Army, right?"

Carter nodded and pretended that he didn't hear her reference to other men's bedrooms. He pointed her in the direction of the master bath. "Bathroom's through there."

"Did the military influence how you keep your home?"

"That and growing up with a mother who wouldn't let us leave the house on Saturday until our rooms were clean. I learned very quickly that if it was clean to begin with, I didn't have to spend hours shoveling dirty dishes and laundry. If you maintain what's yours, you don't have to spend as much time putting out fires. Or scraping gum off your hockey equipment."

Summer laughed. "Beckett or Jackson?"

"Jackson."

"Your mother must have some stories from raising you three."

"You'll probably hear every single one of them tonight," Carter sighed.

"I can't wait."

~

CARTER LEFT her in the house so he could finish up some work outside before dinner but not before promising her the full farm tour tomorrow. Summer used the opportunity to set up her laptop and dive into emails and blog comments.

She handled the work-related communications first,

confirming a shoot with a freelancer in Rome for a piece in the October issue and doing a final look at page proofs on an article about a young European designer who was making her big push west.

She texted Niko to let him know she had arrived safely and had not been run off the road by tractors or farm life.

She saved the blog for last. A dozen more followers since she had last checked this morning and several new shares and comments. Her boss, Katherine Ackerman, a senior editor with *Indulgence*, had been skeptical about the value of adding a behind-the-scenes look at the magazine to her blog. But the popularity spoke for itself.

It was the one place where, as long as she adhered to the magazine's strict guidelines about advertisers and designers, she could use her own voice and talk about the things that were important to her.

Summer drafted a brief post about spending the next week at Pierce Acres. It needed art, she thought. She moved to the doorway of her room and snapped a picture with her phone. Downstairs she captured the kitchen and great room in their sunshine and stainless steel glory. In the driveway she snapped the front of the house from a few different angles. The light was getting softer as afternoon gave way to evening, giving the house a cozy feel.

Back upstairs, she tweaked the pictures with filters in her editing apps and then uploaded them to her draft post. She needed one more picture. Her followers deserved to see the striking Carter Pierce. A shot of him on the blog would guarantee fevered interest in the story when it came out in the September issue, she thought with a smile.

Speak of the devil. She heard him on the stairs. A moment later, he was framed in the doorway of her room. His arm rested on the frame, thumb swiping at a streak of dirt on his forehead.

"Hey. I'm going to take a shower. My mother will be here soon to start dinner. I should be out before she gets here, but she's obnoxiously early to everything."

Summer raised her phone and clicked a picture of him. "I'll keep an eye out for her just in case," she said.

"Did you just take a picture of me?"

Summer smiled innocently. "It's for the blog."

He pushed away from the door and stalked down the hall, muttering about blogs and articles.

While Carter got naked, Summer distracted herself by changing into black skinnies and a soft gray tunic with a flattering scoop neck. It was the exact color of Carter's eyes.

She styled her hair into a simple topknot and slipped on ballet flats. Some subtle smoke at her eyes and rose on her cheeks and she considered herself presentable for a casual family dinner.

Summer was halfway down the stairs when the front door swung open.

"Yoo hoo!"

The woman was wrestling a stockpot through the door when Summer got to her.

"Here, let me help."

"I've got this if you can grab the grocery bag out of the backseat," she said with a quick grin. "I'll meet you back in the kitchen for a proper introduction."

Summer hustled outside and grabbed the cloth bag out of the late model sedan. Back inside, she found the woman hunched over the pot on the stove. Dressed in a chunky knit cardigan and jeans, she had dark-rimmed glasses and a blunt bob with streaks of silver that framed her oval face. Trim and fashionable, she was clearly very comfortable in Carter's home.

Summer put the bag on the island.

"Ah! Thank you," the woman said, slapping the lid back on the pot and turning around. "So, you must be Summer Lentz." She extended her hand, and a trio of bracelets jingled.

"I am." Summer took her hand.

"Welcome to Blue Moon Bend. I'm Phoebe Pierce. Carter's mom."

Her grip was just like her expression, friendly and confident.

"Mrs. Pierce, it's great to meet you. I'm so excited to be here."

"Call me Phoebe. And we're excited to have you," she said, digging through the drawers for a wooden spoon. "Spaghetti okay for dinner tonight? It's one of Carter's favorites."

"It smells incredible."

"Pierce family recipe and Pierce family veggies. So where is my handsome oldest?"

"Carter's upstairs taking a shower."

"Good. Then we'll get to know each other before he comes down. Wine?"

Summer grinned. It was going to be much easier getting answers out of Phoebe than her son. She was sure of it. "Sure. Can I help with anything?"

"How about you start chopping for the salad? Pretty much anything you find in the fridge is fair game," Phoebe said, gesturing with a loaf of garlic bread toward the stainless-steel behemoth.

When Carter came downstairs, fresh from a shower, he found his mother and his houseguest chatting and laughing in the kitchen.

"There's my favorite son," Phoebe said, leaning in to kiss him on the cheek.

"That's what she calls us when she can't remember our names," Carter explained to Summer.

She was clutching one of his nicest knives in a white-knuckle grip and focusing on her massacre of a carrot. Anticipating bloodshed, he grimaced and moved in.

He closed a hand over hers clutching the knife. "I've got this. Why don't you sit and interrogate my mother?"

Those long lashes fluttered as her eyes widened in surprise. He knew she felt it too. That zing of current that passed through them every time their hands met.

She had changed and put her hair up, revealing the curve of her neck. Those full lips, painted with a tempting cherry gloss, were parted. The rounded neckline of her sweater would have seemed modest to anyone shorter. But at six-foot-three-inches, Carter was afforded an accidental and spectacular view.

He frowned. He was thirty. Not seventeen. Leering at a houseguest, no matter how punch-in-the-gut gorgeous, was not acceptable or respectful.

He couldn't exactly remember the last time he'd had sex. And that meant it had been way too long. He'd been busy, had other things on his mind. But since Summer had walked in, it had been the *only* thing on his mind.

She handed over the knife and then bobbled her wine glass in her haste to get out of his way.

Carter caught his mother's smug smile out of the corner of his eye and frowned harder. He knew nothing would make her happier than to see him stupid in love. But a fling with a writer that he'd never see again? That didn't qualify.

He concentrated on salvaging what was left of the carrot while Summer peppered his mother with questions about the farm's humble beginnings. He moved on, expertly dicing pepper, onion, and radish.

"You're good with a knife," Summer observed. He hadn't rattled her too badly, he decided.

Carter snuck a piece of pepper off the mound and popped it into his mouth.

"Is that kitchen or Army expertise?" she pressed.

His brother's greeting from the front door saved Carter the trouble of answering.

Beckett strolled into the kitchen carrying a six-pack, his wingtips echoing on the hardwood.

"Didn't we say dinner was casual?" Carter eyed Beckett's pinstriped trousers and unwrinkled button down. Only his brother would wear a starched, white shirt to a spaghetti dinner. The only nod to casual was that Beckett had removed his tie and opened his top button.

Carter and his youngest brother, Jackson, shared a suspicion that Beckett slept in a suit.

"Give me a break," Beckett grumbled. "Mediation ran long. Didn't I order my spaghetti with no beard hair?"

"Boys!" Phoebe said in mock exasperation. "Not in front of our company."

Carter saw the exact second that Beckett registered Summer's appeal. There was a widening of his eyes, and he smoothly shifted into baby-kissing mode.

"You must be Summer," he said, taking her hand in both of his.

"And you must be Phoebe's favorite son," Summer quipped.

"You're obviously very observant," he grinned down at her.

"Writers generally are," Carter muttered, glowering at Beckett behind Summer's back. His brother was still staring and still holding her hand. He put the knife down on the cutting board a little louder than necessary.

"What's in the six-pack?"

Beckett finally let go of Summer's hand and brought the pack around the island. "A variety of BP's finest."

Carter met him at the fridge and opened the doors.

"Why didn't you tell me she looked like that?" Beckett hissed, throwing an elbow in Carter's gut.

"Don't even think about it," he muttered, checking Beckett with his shoulder.

"Are you calling dibs?"

"She's a woman, not the last piece of fucking pie. And yes, I'm calling dibs if it keeps your hands off her."

"Did someone say pie?" Summer asked hopefully from across the island.

"If you two are done with your conference over there, I need someone to cut up the garlic bread." There was amusement in Phoebe's voice.

"I can do it," Summer offered.

"No!" Carter insisted, a little too sharply. "I got it."

He pulled a bag of spinach out of the fridge and gave Beckett one last shove before moving back to the island.

"Where is it?" Beckett called from the depths of the refrigerator.

"Where's what?" Summer wanted to know.

"Boys and their beer," Phoebe sighed and topped off their wine glasses. "My sons are obsessed with home brewing."

Beckett triumphantly pulled an unlabeled bottle from the vegetable crisper. "You think you can hide this pretty little CP Blonde from me." He grabbed another bottle from the six-pack he brought. Opening them, he slid one down the granite to Carter.

Taking a deep swig of his bottle, Beckett sighed. "It's almost as good as my IPA that you're drinking."

"Almost as good as? I think you meant to say 'blows my IPA out of the water.'"

"Clearly your beard has ruined your taste buds."

Phoebe winked at Summer. "They can go all night like this if we don't distract them."

"CP and BP? Carter Pierce and Beckett Pierce?"

Carter nodded. "We have an ongoing competition."

"Can I try one?" Summer asked.

Did anyone ever say no to those baby blues?

Carter slid his bottle across the island to her. "This is one of Beckett's. An India pale ale. It's not too bad."

Summer picked up the bottle, and Carter watched her lips wrap around the mouth.

Shit.

Realizing his mistake, he turned his attention to assembling the salad.

Phoebe, her kitchen prep done, settled in to tell Summer how she had earned a degree in sustainable food and farming and met the boys' father while researching her master's thesis.

"John Pierce took one look at me and tried to run for the hills, but he never stood a chance."

"You knew what you wanted," Summer said.

"He had these soulful, gray eyes and unruly hair and was frowning more often than not. I fell head over heels. The work he was doing here didn't hurt either. This used to be 200 acres of broken down fields and ramshackle buildings rotting on their foundations."

Carter moved around the kitchen, grabbing a basket for the garlic bread, and started to slice. "Mom and Dad took what had been a century-old dairy farm and turned it into Pierce Acres."

"What kind of animals do you raise here?"

"We don't raise most of them in the traditional farm sense," Phoebe said. "We've got free-range chickens for eggs and horses for the riding program. But everyone else is a pet or a rescue."

"Mr. Vegetarian here lets his bleeding heart make the decisions," Beckett said, snagging a piece of steaming bread.

Carter shot Summer a glance and saw her mentally filing information away. He didn't like it. Every conversation with her would be focused on dragging private details out of him. He took another swig of beer.

"I still say spaghetti without meatballs is sacrilege," Beckett sighed.

"You'll get over it." Carter tossed him another piece of bread.

A knock at the side door caught their attention. The three Pierces shouted a welcome, and the door swung open.

"Joey, how many times do I have to tell you that you don't have to knock?" Carter reminded her.

~

THE WOMAN who let the screen door slam behind her had the height and strut of a runway model. "Unlike you gentlemen, I wasn't raised in a barn. Besides, I don't want to give any of you the idea you can burst into my house any time you want," she said in a voice as husky as a jazz singer.

She strolled in, navy riding breeches and tall boots accentuating legs that went on for days. Her long sleeve polo was untucked, and her chestnut hair was pulled back in a low, sleek ponytail. Summer felt like she was looking at a Ralph Lauren Polo ad come to life.

"You wouldn't have let them in the house, either, if you were their mother," Phoebe joked from the stove.

"You just come from the barn?" Carter asked, seemingly oblivious to the fact that a beautiful woman had just entered his house.

"Yeah. I stayed after the lessons to check on Gonzo. He was favoring his front leg today, and I wanted to make sure it wasn't anything serious. He's fine. Just being a baby."

Joey worked her way through the greetings. A kiss on the cheek for Carter and Beckett and a tight hug for Phoebe.

"Joey, this is Summer. She's writing the article on the farm. Joey is our on-site horse whisperer," Carter said.

Summer offered her hand and they shook.

Joey's brown eyes coolly measured. "Hi."

"It's nice to meet you," Summer said, hoping a friendly smile would disarm her.

Joey dropped her hand and shifted her attention to Phoebe. "Thanks for having me to dinner."

Not a warm and fuzzy kind of girl. Summer could respect that.

"Anytime, sweetheart. You're always welcome to help me even out the testosterone," Phoebe chuckled, her glasses steaming from the contents of the pot.

Joey dumped a worn tote on the counter and Beckett dove for it. "Please tell me you brought dessert. Apple crisp?" he asked hopefully.

"Peanut butter pie," she corrected.

"Are those crumbled up peanut butter cups on top?"

"Of course."

"When are you going to give up spending all your time

with horses so you can marry me and make me desserts every day?" Beckett sighed.

Joey rolled her eyes to the ceiling. "Keep dreaming, Mr. Mayor. I have no desire to be first lady of Blue Moon."

"You're the mayor?" Summer asked, eyebrows raised. That was an interesting tidbit. Beckett had to be a year or two younger than Carter's thirty years.

"Mayor and an attorney. You couldn't tell from the bullshit that spills out of his mouth?" Carter smirked.

"Carter Pierce, you watch your damn mouth," Phoebe warned, brandishing salad tongs.

"Yes, ma'am," Carter answered contritely.

Beckett flipped him the bird and quickly ran his hand through his thick, dark hair when Phoebe set her sights on him.

"Put that finger away before I break it, Beckett," she ordered.

"Yes, ma'am." He turned back to Summer. "I am the mayor, two years into my term."

"It was either Beckett here," Joey jerked a thumb in his direction. "Or Crazy Fitz from the bookstore. And Fitz wanted to make it mandatory that all residents had to build fallout shelters." She leaned in and snagged a cucumber out of the salad.

"For the love of—if you all are going to keep picking, we might as well eat," Phoebe sighed.

Dinner was an entertaining and informative peek into family life. The Pierces—and Joey—bickered and laughed their way through dessert. It was an easy dynamic, one bred from years of knowing every detail of each other's lives.

Summer sat back and did what she did best, observed the action. Her family dinners hadn't had the casual familiarity the Pierces exhibited for years, and it was refreshing to watch the friendliness, the easiness.

She tried to pay attention to everyone, but her gaze always returned to Carter. After his shower, he had changed into clean jeans and a long-sleeved tee that hugged every inch of muscle. He had a scar that split his eyebrow and traveled up, carving a path into his forehead. He looked like a warrior. Where Beckett was smooth and polite, Carter was rough around the edges.

There was something there that intrigued her. Something miles beyond his attractive looks and her desire to tell his story.

She liked looking at him, liked listening to the rumble of his voice. And, for now, she would leave it at that. She was here to write his story, the story of farm and family. Not throw herself at him.

After cleanup—in which they all participated—Phoebe brought out photo albums. "I thought you'd like to see where it all started," she said, sliding onto the bench next to Summer.

The photos were faded with age, but Summer could see the hopeful beginnings of a life on the land.

John Pierce was a tall, striking figure. A doting husband and father, Phoebe explained, he had a quiet, patient way with the land and the animals that made everything thrive.

"You boys look so much like your father," Phoebe sighed, cupping a hand to Carter and Beckett's cheeks as they leaned over her shoulders to see the album. "He'd be so proud of you."

Carter kissed her palm. "No more wine for you. It makes you sappy," he teased.

In defiance, Joey topped off Phoebe's glass.

"Oh look, here all three of you are," Phoebe said pointing

to a picture of three little boys with jet-black hair and varying degrees of bruises and grass stains. "And here's one of you and Jax, Joey."

Joey didn't look, but Summer did. A mini Carter-looking boy was holding the lead of a pony that a small, grinning girl rode.

"I forgot how good he was with horses," Phoebe said, tapping a finger over the picture.

Joey shoved her chair back and abruptly got to her feet. "Thanks for dinner, everyone. I've got an early morning." And with that, she stalked from the room. They heard the screen door slam shut a few seconds later.

Phoebe sighed.

"It's been eight years," Beckett said. "At some point, shouldn't it stop hurting?"

"Some things aren't healed by time," Carter said, taking a long draw from his beer and laying a hand on his mother's shoulder.

Phoebe squeezed his hand. "Sorry about that, Summer. Jax and Joey were high school sweethearts, and it ends the way so many of those stories do."

"With a broken heart?" Summer supplied.

"He left town in the middle of the night. No explanation. Just 'I'm going to California.' We didn't see him again until Christmas the following year. Joey still hasn't seen him."

"Mom, I don't think Summer needs all this background," Carter contended.

"And Joey would *hate* us sitting around all 'poor Joey,'" Beckett added.

Phoebe closed the photo album. "Well at least you know not to ask Joey anything about the third Pierce brother. Now, if numbers one and two can help carry my things to the car, I'm going home to put on pajamas with an elastic waistband."

4

$\mathcal{C}$arter gave Summer points for dragging herself out of bed at the un-Manhattan hour of 6 a.m. And even more for wandering into the kitchen fresh faced and smiling.

"Good morning." Her voice still had the huskiness of sleep, but her eyes were bright.

"Morning," he said, pulling a second mug out of the cabinet. "Coffee?"

"All that you have and more," she said wiggling her fingers toward the mug.

He filled it and handed it over. "Cream's in the fridge. Sugar's on the counter."

She shook her head. "I work for a fashion magazine. If you're going to drink your calories, it's booze, not cream and sugar."

That silvery blonde hair was pulled back in a perky ponytail. She was wearing a touch of makeup, designer jeans, and brand-new hiking boots. Too pretty for a workday on the farm.

"How long have you had those boots?"

"I just got them. Do you like them?"

Carter shook his head. "You're going to be on your feet all day in brand-new shoes."

She waved his words away. "If I can spend thirteen hours in stilettos, I can walk around in these."

He arched an eyebrow at her. "Don't say I didn't warn you."

"Are you always so adversarial in the mornings?" she asked, frowning at him over her mug.

Only when he spent half the night tossing and turning, trying to force thoughts of a certain baby doll blonde down the hall out of his mind.

"How do you like your eggs?" he asked, ignoring her comment.

~

OVER PERFECTLY SCRAMBLED eggs and toast that she burned a little, Summer plotted how best to ease Carter into the interview process. Direct personal questions seemed to put his back up, and that didn't help anyone.

She washed down her handful of pills with water and took her dishes to the sink. And then, because they were there, she washed them quickly and put them on the drying rack.

She needed Carter open, and that meant he had to trust her.

"So, let's talk about the article for a minute before the grand farm tour. Obviously this isn't going to be some exploitive tell-all. I don't know if you've ever read *Indulgence*—"

"Do I look like I read *Indulgence*?"

Summer did a head-to-toe scan of him. Scarred work boots, another Henley today with a huge hole in the forearm, and those piercing gray eyes.

"No," she decided. "However, in addition to the usual fashion-led content, we always include a bigger picture feature. Something about improving the world we live in. Last month's issue was on an American couple working with refugees in Europe."

"And you think running a family farm ranks up there with offering shelter to refugees?"

"I do." She nodded earnestly. "What you do here matters. And you're going to help me tell the story."

"Fine. I'm just not very comfortable with strangers poking around my life looking for meaning behind every little thing."

"Well, then you'll just have to get to know me so I'm not a stranger."

"Funny," he said dryly.

They decided on the tour first followed by an afternoon of actual work.

"If there's anything work-wise that you can't handle, you tell me." Carter demanded, grabbing bottles of water out of the fridge. "Don't try to prove yourself. You could get hurt or destroy crops or burn down the farm."

Summer grimaced. "Your confidence in me is inspiring."

They left the safety of the kitchen via the side door and entered the unknown of farm life. Carter was leading the way to the garage across the driveway when something brown and hairy nibbled at Summer's jeans.

She yelped and grabbed for Carter. Clinging to the waistband of his jeans, she peeked around his back.

"Oh my God! What is that? It tried to bite me!"

Carter dragged Summer out from behind his back and anchored her to his side. He was trying not to laugh. "You've never seen a goat before?"

"They're not exactly wandering around the streets of Manhattan!" She was embarrassed and startled. Plus, the thing had yellow eyes. What animal had yellow eyes?

Carter leaned down to offer the goat a friendly scratch on the head. "This is Clementine," he said as the yellow-eyed monster rubbed her head against him affectionately. "Clementine, meet Summer."

"Nice to meet you, Clementine," Summer said tentatively. "Why'd you eat a hole in my jeans?" She felt it with her finger. High enough on the hip that the blue lace of her underwear was now visible. Her investment in the denim from the right designer that hugged all the right places now seemed like a rather large waste.

"That's how she says hello." Carter held up his ripped sleeve. "This was 'Hello and why haven't you fed me yet?'"

"So she's not trying to rip off limbs?"

Carter laughed. "No. She's just attention-seeking. The only person she'd try to rip limbs off is Jax. They share a mutual hatred of each other."

Clementine made a bleating noise and became marginally cuter. Summer tentatively reached out her hand and let Clementine nuzzle it. "I guess she's not so bad, minus the pants-eating."

Carter eyed her jeans. "Sorry about that."

"It's all part of the experience. I have another pair with me."

Summer pulled her phone out of her back pocket. "I guess this is a good way to start documenting my first day here. Come here," she said, tugging Carter down.

"You're not seriously taking a selfie with a goat."

"I'm taking a selfie with you and a goat," she corrected. "It's for the blog. I can see you judging me, Carter. Smile."

He glanced at the screen and heard the click. "I've never taken a selfie before."

"Your first one? I'll text it to you," she promised. "Are all of your animals so... free range?" She stowed her phone back in her pocket and glanced over her shoulder to check for new biting threats advancing on them.

Carter's eyes twinkled. "Free range doesn't mean no fences. Clem escaped, which means either there's an open gate somewhere or someone left a bucket too close to the fence and she jumped it."

"There you are!" A young man, more boy than man, jogged across the driveway. "Shit. Sorry, Carter. She got past me again."

"No problem, she just came to introduce herself," Carter said, giving the beast another ear scratch. He made the introductions and Summer learned that Colby worked part-time on the farm and part-time in town at an HVAC place.

"It was nice meeting you," Colby said. "I'm gonna get Clementine back to her home before she can wreak any more havoc."

"Make sure you move the bucket away from the fence," Carter called after him.

He led the way to the Jeep and they headed down the dusty lane toward the main road. "I'll show you the horses first since that's a big part of our operation here. Joey runs most of that side with some help from Colby and the others."

He turned onto the main road and headed south. Fields of what Summer assumed was corn flanked the road on both sides.

"Is this all Pierce land?"

"Yeah," he nodded, turning the Jeep onto what looked like a paved driveway. "And these are the stables."

They rounded a bend, and the corn opened up to riding rings and a large metal and stone building. Beyond the barn were green, green pastures. Summer counted more than a dozen horses grazing.

"Wow."

"Come on," Carter said, unbuckling his seatbelt. "I'll show you around."

They went inside first, where he gave her the tour of the indoor riding ring with its sawdust floor and high timber ceiling. Next came a tack room so spotless and organized a surgeon would have given it the nod of approval. There was an office that looked barely used and a closet full of supplies and snacks where Carter grabbed an apple. And then came the stalls, twenty of them in all.

"This is amazing," she breathed.

Carter led the way down to the last stall. A spotted gray mare stomped anxiously. "This is Lolly. We just got her a week ago from a neglect situation, and she's still a little shy. Here." He handed Summer the apple.

"What do you want me to do with this?"

"Give it to Lolly."

"Do I just put it in her feed thing?" She pointed at the bucket mounted on the door.

He grinned. "No. You hold it out like this." He gripped her wrist and slowly extended her arm toward the horse. "Go slow. Don't scare her."

His heat seeped through the thin layer of her shirt, and Summer paused to memorize the moment. Dusty sunlight streamed through windows to lie in pools on the straw-covered floor. The unmistakable scents of straw and leather and sawdust mingled in the air. Carter's strong fingers held her wrist just over her racing pulse.

Lolly took a tentative step to her and then another.

Her soft nose brushed the apple and Summer's hand.

"Is she going to bite me?" Summer whispered. Lolly dropped her head, snuffling at something on the ground.

"She's playing hard to get. Just hold your hand flat," Carter said in her ear. His warm breath tickled her neck.

Summer uncurled her fingers, balancing the apple on her palm. "Come on, pretty girl."

Lolly lifted her head and tossed it.

"It's okay. I won't hurt you," Summer whispered.

The horse whickered softly as if to ask permission before taking the daintiest bite.

"She's eating it!" Summer said with wonder.

Carter squeezed her wrist. "Nice job. She doesn't take food from just anyone."

"Will she stop once she gets to the bottom, or will I lose fingers?"

"Usually she stops," Carter teased.

When Lolly finished her snack, Carter suggested they look for Joey. They found her in the ring astride a horse so tall Summer couldn't figure out how she got on it.

The horse didn't seem inclined to behave. It danced sideways, head tossing and tail swishing. Joey's face was a mask of determination. She adjusted the reins and dug her heels into its chestnut flanks. The horse's head bobbed, and Summer was sure it would disobey the order. But then it leapt forward. Summer caught Joey's look of triumph as she and the horse moved as one, galloping around the ring, glossy tails streaming behind them.

She snapped several pictures with her phone and crossed her fingers that one of them would turn out to be good enough for the blog.

After a few laps, Joey slowed the horse and came to a stop inside the fence in front of them.

"Progress," Carter said as Joey slid to the ground.

She thumped the horse in the chest. Her beautiful face was impassive again, but her eyes still sparkled.

"Yeah, he's doing well. Some more work, and I think he'll

be a good show horse for some of the more advanced students."

"Let me know if you want me to take him out this week to see how he does for another rider," Carter offered.

Joey nodded briskly. "Sure. You two here for a ride?"

Summer's eyes widened. "Oh, no. Carter's just giving me the tour."

"Have you ever been on a horse before?" Joey's lips curved.

She grew up in New York. She couldn't just hop on a horse instead of the subway or a taxi. "No, I've never ridden before."

Joey and Carter exchanged a look.

"Oh, no." She shook her head vehemently. "I'm writing an article, I don't need to—"

"If you're scared, you don't have to do it," Carter said sweetly.

"Yeah, not everyone can handle riding." Joey's voice was laced with what Summer recognized to be mock sympathy.

She knew when she was being played. "Fine," she sighed. "But do you have one smaller than him?"

Carter laid a hand on her shoulder. "I think we can find someone more your speed."

Ten minutes later, she was wearing a helmet and sitting astride a pretty little mare named Charcoal. Summer's knees were glued to the horse's sides, her knuckles white on the reins.

"Loosen up on the reins," Joey called from the end of the lead rope she was holding.

Summer let some reins out but kept her grip tight.

"Okay, we're gonna walk now," Joey said.

"Wait! What if she runs? What if I fall off?"

"Keep your heels down, grip with your knees, and let your hips rock when she moves."

"I don't know what that means," Summer called out, trying to keep the panic out of her tone.

"You will in a second," Joey said and signaled Charcoal forward.

Summer clutched at the horn of the saddle as she was lurched into motion.

"Keep your back straight," Joey ordered. Charcoal moved slowly, making a wide circle around her.

"Get a grip," Summer whispered to herself. She released the horn and sat lower in the saddle. Her knees were locked on the mare's sides so hard her thighs trembled. She straightened her spine and tried to look confident.

"Better," Joey told her as Charcoal ambled past the fence.

Summer forced her heels down and felt her hips start to move with the horse. Charcoal's ears twitched as if congratulating her.

"You got it now!" Carter grinned from his perch on the fence.

Summer couldn't stop the grin from spreading across her face if she wanted to. "Can we go a little faster?" she called out to Joey.

"Next pace is a trot. It's harder to sit than a walk. Sit deep in the saddle and give her a squeeze with your legs," Joey instructed.

Summer did as she was told and was delighted when the mare pranced into a trot. She was jostled about for the first few steps before regaining her seat. She followed Joey's instructions to refine her form and felt braver and more confident with every circle.

"Okay, now let's try stopping," Joey called. "Take the reins and pull back very gently."

Summer did as she was told and was delighted when

Charcoal came to a neat stop in front of Carter. He slid down from the fence into the ring.

"Take your right foot out of the stirrup and swing your leg over," he told her.

"Okay, but how do I get down—"

He plucked her off Charcoal's back like a child and set her on the ground.

"I did it! I rode a horse! My mother is never going to believe this," she said, turning to face him. She lost her train of thought. He was inches away. She was trapped between him and the horse. Charcoal shifted and hip-checked Summer into Carter. Her palms splayed across his chest, and she tilted her head back, the weight of the riding helmet made the strap dig into her chin.

"Nice job," Carter said with a half smile that did nothing to soften the intensity of his gaze. He tugged the end of her ponytail.

"What the hell are you two doing over there?" Joey's voice had Summer trying to push both man and horse back to get some breathing room.

Carter took the reins from her. "Come collect your horse before she tramples Summer," he told Joey.

～

AFTER THE HORSES, Carter drove Summer around the farm to show her the rest of the property. Fields, barns, the pond and creek. He knew she was dying to ask questions, but she seemed willing to take it all in without muddling the experience with unnecessary conversation.

He pulled up in front of the house. "Let's break for lunch, and then we'll tackle some work in the afternoon. Okay?"

"Sounds good. Can I ask you some questions while we eat?"

And just like that, his reprieve was over.

"Sure," he sighed.

Summer patted his arm. "It won't be so bad. I promise."

They exited the Jeep and were heading toward the house when a squeal caught their attention. Two pigs clamored against the gate against the driveway.

"Well, since you already rode a horse today, you might as well meet the pigs," Carter said, taking Summer's hand in his. He led her to the gate and unlatched it.

Sensing her hesitation, Carter went in first. "Come on before they get it in their head to take a field trip. The little one's fast. She's hard to catch."

Summer stepped inside and jumped back when the pair nosed up to her.

"Meet Dixie and Hamlet." Carter crouched down, and both pigs greeted him, their curly tails wagging.

"They're like dogs," Summer murmured.

"They're actually smarter than most dogs." He thumped Hamlet on his flank. He bent down and picked up a blue rubber ball. "Here, throw this."

"They do not fetch! Do they?"

"Throw it and find out," he said, arching an eyebrow.

Summer snatched the ball out of his hand and showed it to Dixie. She heaved it toward the far end of the field "Go get it, piggy. Go get the ball!"

Dixie took off with a squeal of delight, Hamlet hot on her heels.

"There's no way she's going to..."

"Pick up the ball and bring it back?" Carter smirked, as Dixie dropped the ball at Summer's feet.

"How did you teach them to do that?" She picked up the

ball and threw it again. This time Hamlet—who had a good fifty pounds on the delicate Dixie—got to it first and pranced back with Dixie jockeying for position. He wasn't as inclined to give up the ball as his sister had and waddled off to hide his treasure in a shady corner.

Dixie nudged Summer with her wet nose.

"She wants you to pet her," Carter said.

"Well, if you insist," Summer said, kneeling down. Dixie wiggled with pleasure as Summer stroked her hands down the pig's side.

Carter's phone rang in his pocket. It was his mother's ring tone.

"Morning, Mom," he said, walking a few paces away.

"How's everything going?" Phoebe asked.

"By everything, you mean Summer, right?"

"You're a smart boy. No wonder you're my favorite. Now tell your mother what she wants to know."

"I'm not overworking her. She's playing with Dixie and Ham right now. Joey got her up on a horse this morning, too."

"Good. I just wanted to make sure you weren't working her into the ground."

"There will be some actual farm labor in her future, but I promise not to do any permanent damage."

His mother sighed. "Well, that's all I can ask. This article could be a very good thing, you know. A little attention for the farm wouldn't hurt."

"I know, Mom." He turned and spotted Summer on her knees petting both pigs at once. She laughed as Hamlet tried to shove Dixie out of the way. The light spring breeze teased Summer's ponytail. Pretty as a picture.

"Listen, I gotta go, Mom. We're going to have lunch before we tackle any real work. I'll tell her you said hi."

~

OVER LEFTOVER SPAGHETTI, Summer's inquisition began.

"Do you mind if I record this?" she asked, waving her phone.

Carter shrugged. Of course he minded. He minded this entire thing. A lot. "It's fine."

"It helps me stay focused on the conversation instead of trying to take notes. Plus I can eat," she said, hitting record. "So let's talk about why you went organic."

He was relieved by the softball question. "We decided to make the switch a few years ago. Science and agriculture are constantly changing, and one of those variables is pesticides. Which ones are 'safe,' which ones have been reclassified. We can't predict the long-term effects of some of these chemicals. Throw in the unknown of genetically modified plants, and it's too big of a gamble to make. We're all firm believers that the closer you can keep things to nature, the better."

"Makes sense. Did you have any backlash from the rest of the farming community here?"

Carter laughed. "I'll show you around Blue Moon, and you'll see what I mean when I say we don't do backlash here."

"I'm intrigued." Summer took a bite of spaghetti and continued. "How do you believe growing and eating organic plays into the bigger picture of health?"

He expertly twirled pasta onto his fork. "Health isn't just one big decision. It's hundreds of smaller ones that add up to a way of living. Take what we're eating right now. It's a fast, easy lunch in the middle of the day. Some people would grab a frozen meal or go through a drive-thru. But how fast was it to reheat the spaghetti sauce made from homegrown vegetables and herbs and whole grain pasta? And which choice is better for you?"

"Do you think that organic produce and a plant-based diet can play a role in healing?" She was just toying with the pasta on her plate now, watching him closely.

She was fishing for something. He just wasn't sure what. "I'm no doctor. But I do think between the sun and the fresh air, being that close to nature is a smart place to start. What you fuel your body with during any kind of recovery is going to play a role in how successful you are," he continued. "You can't fight an injury or a disease as efficiently on fast food and soda as you can with plants and healthy grains and water."

She changed the topic to the horse program, and Carter counted his lucky stars. He didn't like talking about healing. It skirted territory that he had no intention of sharing with a stranger. Besides, he had spent a good year talking it to death with his family when he returned home. Dredging it all up again didn't help.

5

The lettuce field stretched out in front of her. Rows and rows of romaine stood at attention like perfect soldiers.

There were four of them against the legion of leafy greens.

Beckett, in jeans, a t-shirt, and boots nearly as worn as Carter's, sighed. "I'll start over there." He gestured at the far row.

Colby took the middle, leaving Carter and Summer alone at the edge.

"This is a row crop knife," Carter said, holding up an orange-handled blade. "You grab the plant a few inches off the ground with one hand and cut with the other." He leaned over, grasped the stalk, and swiped down with the blade. He freed the lettuce head from the earth and tossed it into a wooden crate on the ground. "Don't hold too far down on the plant or you'll be cutting your hand. Got it?"

Summer nodded. "Grab, slice, toss. Got it."

"It's hard work," he warned.

She nodded again. If Carter was waiting for her to flake out, he could just keep waiting. She could spend an afternoon in the dirt, and the story would be better for it. Besides, the monotonous work would help her brain sift through their lunch conversation. She knew there was so much Carter hadn't said, and she had a feeling that that's where the real story was. She would get him there. Trust grew slowly. She knew that for a fact. She had a week here to get him to open up.

"I'll start here and work my way in," she said, pointing at the outside row.

He handed her a blade. "I'll start over there and work my way to you. If you get tired, let me know."

She wouldn't. In her career as a writer and then editor, Summer had interviewed sources through a translator, followed a team of scientists into a bat cave, and once sat down with a troubled model/actress for an interview in the limo on her way to rehab. Plus, she had already been on the back of a horse today.

Harvesting lettuce, she could handle.

Beckett and Colby were already moving like machines up their rows.

She shoved up the sleeves of her shirt and bent from the waist.

Grab. Slice. Toss. Grab. Slice. Toss.

The first few tries were sloppy, and she had to take a second and sometimes third pass with the knife. But as her crate slowly filled, she hit a rhythm.

Grab. Slice. Toss.

There was something satisfying about having her hands in the earth, about seeing her progress when she looked back at the empty stalks. Another few heads, and she straightened to take a drink.

Her back sent a swift and undeniable complaint of discomfort. Her feet were echoing the sentiment.

She felt eyes on her. Carter, of course. Checking on either her progress or physical well-being. Pretending not to notice, Summer took a quick swig of water and bent over again. The complaint from her back got instantaneously louder, but she sliced through the next head of romaine with authority.

Grab. Slice Toss.

Once her crate was full, Summer struggled to pick it up.

"Summer, leave it," Carter called. He was already stepping over the rows separating them. He hefted the crate and carried it to the truck bed where he grabbed an empty.

She used the opportunity to jab her fingers into her throbbing lower back. "Thanks," she said, pasting a smile on her face.

"Doing okay?" Carter asked, tugging her ponytail.

"Sure," she answered with more enthusiasm than she felt.

He raised an eyebrow before heading back to his row.

To save her back, Summer crouched down. She couldn't swing the knife as efficiently, but at least her back wasn't taking the brunt of the effort.

Grab. Slice. Toss.

~

Summer hated the farm. The dirt. The stupid lettuce.

But most of all she hated the smirks Carter and Beckett were throwing her way. Colby was at least polite enough to look at her with pity when he picked up her crate.

She had tried standing, crouching, and kneeling. The only thing left was to lie down in the dirt and crawl through the field. She was seriously considering that option when she ran into a pair of work boots. Strong arms lifted her up despite the protest in her lower back.

Carter held her by the shoulders until she found her footing, which took longer than it should have once she realized he was shirtless. Ripped did not do justice to the chest and torso she was staring at. Broad shoulders and an expansive chest tapered down into a six-pack that would make most of the male underwear models Summer knew cry. His jeans rode low on his hips, revealing those exquisite twin creases that directed her eyes lower still. There were scars, too. On his shoulder and his chest.

Her hand raised to touch them before she stopped it.

Summer's cheeks flushed, and she brought her wayward hand to her hair. "Why are we stopping?" She willed herself to look only at his face and tried not to sound so out of breath.

"We're done."

She looked around. What had been a green field hours before was now empty. She'd been so absorbed in the labor, focusing only on the next head of romaine, that she hadn't realized how much had been accomplished.

Beckett and Colby were loading the last of the crates into the back of the pick-up.

"We're done," she repeated.

Carter relieved her of her knife and work gloves. He pressed a fresh water bottle into her hands. "Drink."

Gratefully, she obeyed.

The cool water slid down her dry throat like a deluge after a drought.

To think that he did this every damn day of his life. She stole a glance at him. Dirt and sweat streaked across his forehead and did absolutely nothing to make him less attractive. His work gloves were tucked in the back pocket of his jeans. The slight sheen of sweat that coated his chest and back made her lick her lips before she realized what she was doing.

It was clear that nothing about the work had left his body weeping the way hers was.

He waved Beckett off as the pickup pulled away heading in the direction of the little barn.

Carter flipped over an empty crate and dropped it on the ground behind her. "Sit."

"Why?" Summer asked, even though her entire body begged her to obey.

Carter merely advanced on her until the backs of her calves met the crate, and she sank down.

"I'm fine," Summer muttered.

He crouched down to her level, and his broad shoulders shrugged. "I didn't say you weren't."

Annoyed, she picked at the lace of her boot. "I'm just not used to this." She crossed her arms over her chest. "Yet." His lips quirked at her stubborn promise.

"You did a good job today. Not everyone can spend three hours harvesting lettuce."

"It was harder than I thought it would be," she admitted. *It was harder than it should have been,* she corrected herself, and that made her mad.

"Anything worthwhile is." He tugged at the leg of her jeans. In addition to the dirt-caked knees there was another hole now, this one near the ankle.

"I missed a head and got my jeans," she confessed.

Carter's long fingers probed the hole looking for a wound. The line between his eyes was back.

"It's fine," Summer sighed. "I just got denim. No flesh."

"No blood, no foul. You ready to go?"

"Where are we going?"

"Don't you get tired of asking questions?"

"No," she said primly. "Where are we going?"

"Home." He tugged her to her feet.

"Are we done for the day?" Summer tried to sound

47

nonchalant, but there was nothing she wanted more in the universe than to be done.

"We're done, but we're going out to dinner. Can you be ready by six?" He kept his hand on her lower back as they walked toward the Jeep. It still felt nice. Steadying. It gave her something else to think about besides the grating pain radiating from her back.

"What time is it now?"

He smirked. "Four."

"That's two hours from now. Are you being a smart ass?"

"Not entirely," Carter grinned. "Who knows how long it takes you city girls to wash the farm off you?" He picked a leaf out of her hair.

~

THEY HAD BEEN HOME for twenty minutes, and Carter had yet to hear the shower upstairs. She was probably unconscious in her room. Lettuce harvesting was one of those shit jobs that no one wanted to do because it was so back breaking. He felt a little tug of guilt. If his mother found out that he let Summer spend three hours cutting lettuce, he could kiss his ass goodbye.

She had worked without complaint and had done well. He kept waiting for her to admit exhaustion and defeat, but she soldiered on. He should have made her stop. The labor had hollowed her out. The work was hard, but it shouldn't have hit her as hard as it did. This wasn't just someone used to sitting at a desk all day. The exhaustion in those beautiful blues of hers came from something else.

Guilt had him tossing a sock full of rice in the microwave. While it heated, Carter poured a glass of iced tea and dug out a bottle of over-the-counter pain relievers.

He would just check on her and make sure she was okay, he thought as he took the stairs.

Her door was open, and he found her facedown on the bed. Her boots were on the floor just inside the door and he saw a crop of red blisters on both feet.

"You okay?"

The quilt muffled her reply. He took it as an invitation to come in.

"Is it your back?"

"Mm-hmm." Summer turned her head to the side. "Every time I move it feels... horrible. I don't think I like lettuce anymore. It's evil. Why can't it grow taller so we don't have to hunch over all day?"

Carter smiled. He poured out two pills. "Here. Take these, and then we'll see what we can do." He dropped the pills into her palm and handed her the iced tea.

She eyed the tablets. "I don't like to take drugs."

"They're over-the-counter. Take them."

Summer raised up high enough to swallow the pills and collapsed back down on a groan. "Carter, I swear I'm not a wimp. I go to the gym, I work long hours, I take vitamins."

"Honey, no one said you were a wimp."

"You didn't have to. I could see it in your judgmental face."

"I don't have a judgmental face," he said, slightly offended.

"You frown a lot. Like you're mad."

"I prefer to call it being intense. Can I take a look at your back? Maybe I can help."

"I don't care if you rip my spine out and try to insert a new one," Summer sighed into the pillow. "Anything has to be better than this."

She was probably in spasm. Carter eased onto the bed and tried not to think about other activities that would end with them both in the same bed. His fingers slid her shirt up to the bra strap. Rough fingers against the silk of her skin. He watched in fascination as goose bumps appeared.

"I'm going to rub your back, okay? It should help the muscles relax."

"Okay." Her reply sounded slightly breathless, but he couldn't tell if it was nerves or the fact that she was suffocating herself with bedding.

Carter gently worked his thumbs into the exposed flesh of her lower back. After a few minutes of twisting his arms this way and that, it was clear the angle wasn't working. He tried to think of a polite way to keep some distance between them, but in the end there was only one answer.

"Summer, are you okay if I uh—" He wasn't about to say, 'straddle you.'

"Whatever you have to do. Please."

He swung a leg over her to straddle her legs. Carter felt her stiffen under him and tried to force himself to think of anything else but what he was doing.

His thumbs traced down her spine to the very top of her jeans. He applied the slightest bit of pressure, and the moan that came out of her mouth had him hard in half a second.

He took a steadying breath and continued to probe the muscles. "Does it hurt here?" Now he was the one who sounded like he was halfway through a marathon.

"It's a little lower." Her tone was shy.

Carter dipped his thumbs into the waistband of her jeans and found the lace that he knew was the color of spring skies thanks to Clementine. He pressed firmly with both thumbs, his fingers fanning out over the gentle curves of her hips and waist.

She was thin. Almost too thin. Delicate bones wrapped in satin skin. Tight muscles demanding his attention.

Her breathy sigh had his cock straining against his zipper.

He circled his thumbs lazily, trying not to apply too much pressure or rest his weight on her. He felt the knots and probed gently, searching for the release. Every time Summer moved or moaned under him, another drop of sweat would appear on his forehead. It was a cruel joke. He had spent the afternoon unintentionally torturing her, and now she was returning the favor.

"How's that?" He fought the gruffness of his tone with the gentleness of his hands.

"Much better. Thank you," Summer murmured.

Reluctantly, Carter pulled his hands out of the waistband of her jeans and picked up the warm sock. "I'm going to put this on your back for a few minutes. The heat should help the muscles relax."

"What is it?"

"It's a fancy farm heating pad. A tube sock filled with rice. You microwave it and it holds the heat."

"I need one of these at home," she sighed.

Carter shifted off her, trying to ignore the throbbing the movement caused for him. He ran his hand down her leg and pulled her foot up for a better look. Blisters from the new boots.

"Stay here." He was grateful that she had her face buried and didn't see him leave the room with a hard-on. He headed down the hallway to his bathroom where he collected a box of waterproof bandages and some antibiotic gel.

She was still facedown when he returned. Sinking down on the bed next to her, he ran a hand down her leg and pulled it back toward him.

"What are you doing?"

"Your feet are a mess," he said, gliding gel over a blister and fastening a bandage in place.

"Are you going to say 'I told you so'?" she asked mournfully.

"I'm not my mother." He covered another blister and then reached for her other foot. "If she were here you would have heard it about six times already."

"But you're thinking it, aren't you?"

"I'm thinking that you're in unnecessary pain because you're stubborn."

"That sounds about the same as 'I told you so,'" she mumbled. Carter smiled.

Summer's phone rang from the nightstand. "Can you see who that is, please? I'm not ready to use my body yet."

He picked up her phone. "Caller ID says The Wolf."

"Crap."

"Not a fan of the Wolf?"

"No, he's just another one who would say 'I told you so.'"

Carter hit Ignore and returned her phone to the nightstand. "Boyfriend?" He congratulated himself on not choking on the word. The fantasies he was having right now were not appropriate if she belonged to someone else.

Summer snorted. "Niko? No. We're just friends. His type is more model than human being."

Carter started on her other foot. "What's your type?"

She laughed. "I don't think I've dated anyone long enough to determine if I have a type. Smart. Someone who can carry on a conversation without mentioning how many ad campaigns they landed last year or how many hours they spend with a trainer in a week. Generous. Someone who does things for others without weighing what kind of return he'll get out of it."

"It sounds like you spend time with some interesting people."

"It does, doesn't it? But it's not all bad. For every five

underfed runway models and smarmy agents, you run into someone truly exceptional. A brilliant designer, a politician making a difference, a woman who auctioned off her entire art collection to fund disease research. What kind of people do you spend time with here?"

Carter wrapped the last bandage around her toe and lowered her leg. "Blue Moon is a microcosm of weird. It started as this tiny farming community, and then 1969 happened."

"Woodstock?"

"The story goes that two dozen or so hippies got lost on their way home and ended up here. They liked it and made it their new home."

"How prevalent was that culture here?" Summer asked, switching into interview mode even with a pillow in her face.

"There is no 'was.' Their influence was contagious. They settled down, got married, started families, opened businesses. You'll see tonight when we go into town." He patted her leg. "Listen, I'm going to go shower, and then I'll come back and we'll see if we can get you up and on your feet."

"Thank you, Carter."

6

———————

Summer took a hot, steamy shower, spending most of it thinking about shirtless Carter and back rub Carter. By the time the water went cold, she felt mostly human again.

She straightened her hair into a sleek bob that made her feel put together. Her cheeks were still a little too pale, so she added a healthy brush of blush for color. She changed into her only pair of non-distressed jeans and a crisp white button-down. Driving moccasins covered most of the bandages.

She turned her back on the bed that was calling her name and gave her reflection one last check before heading downstairs.

She found Carter sorting mail in the kitchen. He had changed into clean jeans and a black lightweight sweater. She handed over the rice sock. "Thanks for... everything."

Sterling eyes scanned her head to toe before returning to her face. "You sure you're up for dinner?"

"As long as there's no manual labor after dinner." Oh, God. "There isn't, is there?"

Carter's lips quirked. "I think we're done for the day." He

glanced at the watch on his left wrist. "And since you're ready early, we can make a stop before dinner."

Summer's aching body was grateful when Carter guided her to the large pick-up truck in the garage instead of the Jeep. She settled back in her leather seat and sighed. Dinner was sounding better and better. And when they got back, she'd do some work on the blog and then pass out in bed.

Carter turned right out of the driveway and headed south. In five minutes, the fields gave way to Blue Moon Bend. Tradition was evident in the tidy brick two-stories with wrap-around porches. Other influences could be seen in the unusual color choices for the Victorian trim on otherwise stately manors.

Summer blinked at a canary yellow three-story with purple scallop trim. The house number was carved in a peace sign.

As they drove further into the heart of town, homes gave way to smart storefronts. Carter turned down a block and then up a side street where he pulled into a small parking lot. It was the first floor of a three-story brick building. The window displays highlighted footwear of the cowboy persuasion.

Blue Moon Boots.

"What are we doing here?"

"Getting you a pair of boots that won't destroy your feet," Carter said, unfastening his seatbelt and getting out of the truck.

Summer met him on the sidewalk. "Cowboy boots?"

"They're comfortable and heavy duty. A pair of these will last you years longer than those hikers. Plus you can ride in them."

He held the door for her and instead of the typical bell that announced visitors, a digital yee-haw sounded from a speaker above the door.

"Carter Pierce!" A woman with blonde hair wrapped in a long, thick braid greeted them. "I know you're not coming back to find a replacement for your boots already."

"Hey, Willa." Carter laid a hand on Summer's shoulder. "This is Summer. We're looking for a pair of boots that will get her by for a week on the farm."

Willa made her way out from behind the desk. She was wearing an ankle-length skirt and a dozen silver bangles on her wrist.

"Welcome, Summer." She reached out both hands to her, sending the bangles jingling. "Any friend of the Pierce family is a friend of mine. I'm sure we can find the perfect match." She paused, her lavender eyes glazing over. "Something strong and sturdy that will protect you but with a little give." Willa flitted off, leaving Summer frowning after her.

She shot Carter a sidelong look. "Is she talking about boots or men?"

"You never know with Willa. Her mom was the town psychic for a few decades until she retired and moved to Boca. Willa claims that she 'sees' things, too."

The clever displays of boots and barbed wire and wooden crates drew Summer deeper into the store. She had taken a few design courses over the past two years and could tell that a lot of thought as well as a natural knack had played a hand in the creative visuals.

Willa returned in a cloud of sandalwood with a white box in her hand. "These should do," she said. The front door yee-haw sounded as a couple in their fifties entered the store. He was balding and wearing a Grateful Dead tee. The woman was wearing a conservative navy pantsuit and had her rich brown hair pinned back in a sleek bun.

"Rainbow! Gordon! I'll be right with you," Willa called to

her visitors. "Carter, do you mind helping Summer with these while I take care of Rainbow and Gordon?"

"Sure." Carter took the box from Willa and shot a suspicious glance at the visitors.

"What? What is it?" Summer whispered.

"The Berkowiczes," Carter said, guiding her to a chair.

"Rainbow Berkowicz? You're just screwing with me now, aren't you?" She sat and slipped off her shoes.

"She's the president of the bank next door. Gordon's her husband. He runs the seasonal garden shop just outside of town." Carter flipped the lid off the box and pulled out a cowboy boot in a rich chocolate tone. Thin turquoise stitches wove a pattern around the supple material.

Summer snatched the other boot out of the box. "These are incredible! Why are you glaring at the Berkowiczes?"

Carter yanked the boot out of her grip and grabbed her foot. "I'm not glaring. I'm trying to figure out their game. You need socks." He glanced around and grabbed a pair off a rotating display.

"Here, put these on." He ripped off the tag and handed them over, continuing to frown at Willa and her visitors at the front of the store.

The knee socks were the same blue as the stitching on the boots with candy pink hearts. They were kind of adorable. Summer pulled them on over her bandaged feet. "Why are they looking at us and whispering? Is it because we're looking at them and whispering?"

"No. They're plotting," Carter said, grabbing her foot and easing it into a boot. He shot another glance at the trio.

Summer grabbed him by the chin and turned his head to her. His beard tickled her palms. "Is this something you can explain to me without glaring at them?"

Carter reached for her other leg, and Summer tried to

ignore the delicious tingle that shot up from her toes at his touch.

"Sorry," he muttered. "I've just never been in their sights before. I heard rumors, but I never thought it would happen to me."

"Carter, you're starting to scare me."

"Don't look at them!" he barked. He stuffed her foot into the other boot.

"Are they casting some kind of spell on you?"

He shook his head. "Worse. They're matchmaking."

"Who—?" Summer looked down at Carter, kneeling before her, his hands holding her calves. "Oh."

"Shit," Carter muttered, abruptly standing up.

Summer rose with him. "What do a bank president, a boot seller, and a garden center guy have to do with matchmaking?"

"They're part of the Beautification Committee," he said as if that explained it all.

Summer waited. "And?"

Carter swiped a hand over his face. "And it's basically a cover for a not-so-secret society of busybodies. And those three are some of the busiest. Their favorite thing to do is pick out poor singles and pair them up. They claim it makes the town a better place to live if everyone is 'in love.'" Carter threw up the air quotes, and Summer bit her lip trying not to laugh.

"Exactly how many couples have they tortured into love?" she asked.

"I don't know. Something like twenty or so." He turned so that he stood between her and their prying eyes.

"And they all fall in love?"

"They claim they have a one-hundred percent success rate. Damn it. Fred and Phil just got married last month, so they're probably looking for their next happily ever after."

"Maybe they're talking about someone else?" They peeked

at the front of the store, and Willa, Rainbow, and Gordon all turned away. Gordon started whistling. "Or not."

"Let's just get out of here. How do the boots feel?"

Summer looked down at her feet. "Actually they feel amazing. They're a perfect fit."

"Of course they are," Carter grumbled.

She turned sideways and looked in the long mirror. "They look good, too."

"Great. Awesome. Let's go."

Carter grabbed the empty boot box and threw her moccasins inside. He grabbed her bag off the chair and dragged her to the front of the store.

"I can't believe you're so flustered," Summer laughed.

"Flustered? I'm not flustered." Carter took offense.

"Well, it was nice seeing you, Willa," Rainbow said in a voice that was a little too loud.

"Yeah, great to see you. You too, Carter and Summer," Gordon waved as they hustled out the door.

"How did he know my name?" Summer whispered, waving after him.

Carter dumped the box on the counter. He tossed a credit card on the counter. "We'll take them."

"There's also a pair of socks," Summer told Willa as she grabbed for her purse. "You can't buy me these," she said to Carter.

"I can buy boots for an acquaintance. Because that is what we are. Acquaintances."

Willa smiled sweetly as she rang up the sale. "It looks like you found your 'solemate.' Which socks did you decide on?"

"The turquoise ones with the, uhh, little umm..." Carter stalled.

"The ones with the cute pink hearts on them? Aren't you

sweet?" She swiped Carter's credit card. "And are you staying in town while you're here, Summer?"

"Uh, no. I'm staying on the farm."

"With Carter? How lovely! I have a feeling you're going to have a wonderful time." Willa winked.

~

CARTER MANAGED to calm himself down by the time they turned onto Main Street. And Summer relaxed enough to enjoy a look at the town square, a pretty green space with a gazebo and picnic tables.

"One Love Park," Summer read aloud from the park's sign. She raised an eyebrow.

"Honey," Carter shook his head. "We're just getting started."

He pulled into an empty parking space in front of Peace of Pizza.

"Peace of Pizza and One Love Park? Promise me we're going to take a walk after dinner," Summer said, her gaze glued to the hodge-podge downtown.

"Your feet are covered in blisters, and you want to take a walk?"

"I think I've proven that I'm willing to suffer for article research," Summer sniffed.

Carter shook his head in resignation. "If you save room for dessert, we'll walk down to Karma Kustard for gelato after dinner."

Summer slid out of the truck. "One-thousand words isn't going to scratch the surface on this," she whispered to herself.

Peace of Pizza was all that she hoped it would be. They were seated in a cozy booth in the corner under a large poster of Jimi Hendrix. A lava lamp on the table bubbled lazy, orange blobs.

Summer glanced around them. "Why did they put us back here away from everyone else?"

They had walked past several tables full of diners, including a gentleman Carter had addressed as "Big Ben." But it was just the two of them in the cozy little corner.

The waitress delivered a pair of ice waters and a candle just as the lights in the restaurant dimmed.

"Goddamn Beautification Committee," Carter muttered under his breath. Summer bit her lip.

"Want to hear the vegetarian specials, Carter?" The waitress asked pulling a pen out of her apron that was dusty with flour.

"Sure, Maizie. What have you got?"

She rattled off a surprisingly large number of meat-free specials. "And Summer, if you're a meatatarian, we've got a bunch of other options," she said with a wink.

Summer blinked. Did everyone in town know her name? "Um, thanks, Maizie."

"Can you handle a cheese pizza and a garden salad?" Carter asked her.

"Perfect."

They handed over the menus to Maizie and tried to ignore the ambiance. Summer's cell phone alarm signaled, breaking the awkward silence, and she dug her pills out of her bag.

"Thought you didn't like taking drugs?" Carter asked, eyeing the tablets and capsules in her hand.

"They're mostly vitamins. Everyone's got to stay health conscious these days," she said, washing the handful down with a big gulp of water.

Carter stared pointedly at Big Ben, who was scarfing his

way through a Stromboli with a side of gravy fries three tables away. "Not all of us," he whispered.

Summer laughed. "So I'm curious about the vegetarian thing. Why did you give up meat? Was it a health choice?"

"Back to the interview already? I thought I could buy you off with a pair of shoes."

"Nice try, Mr. Pierce."

"Guess we'll have to try the dress and gold bar store next."

"Back to why you became vegetarian." Summer wouldn't let him push her off center.

"It happened after I came back. I was home for a few months when Joey brings these two pigs to me. They fell off the back of a truck on the highway headed for who knows where. I had empty pastures."

"So you rescued them."

He shrugged. "I had the doc come out and look them over. We were standing there talking, and they just started running around the paddock. Dancing, playing. I swear I saw Dixie smile. I never touched bacon again. It wasn't a conscious choice. It just happened."

Summer propped her chin on her hand. "God, Carter. How is it that you're not married yet?"

Carter's eyes widened over his glass. "What?"

"Seriously. You are stunningly gorgeous," Summer said, laying a hand over his. "You have impeccable taste when it comes to home decor, and the Dixie story just exploded my heart. How are you not married with a dozen babies by now?"

He raised a dark eyebrow and his eyes searched hers. "Are you asking for the article?" He turned her palm up but continued to hold it toying with her fingers.

"Just me," Summer said, tilting her head. "For now," she qualified.

"I wasn't in a great place when I came home. Relationships were low on my list of priorities."

"Now?"

"Now, I'm in a better place. But the farm is the love of my life right now. You?"

"Why aren't I married?"

He tapped her ring finger, sending a warm shiver through her.

"I don't have much time for relationships right now."

"You ever plan on making the time?" Carter's thumb skimmed the skin of her palm.

"Someday. You?"

He gave a one-shoulder shrug. "Someday." He was staring at her, holding her in his steely gaze.

Summer sighed and withdrew her hand. *What was she doing?* He was the subject of an article—a smart, sexy, hot one, at that—not a potential date.

"Comin' at ya, Pierce."

A woman with silvery dreadlocks slid a steaming pizza onto the table. Summer leaned back against the booth. "Tray's hot. Watch out."

"Thanks, Bobby."

She looked pointedly at Summer until Carter caught her drift. "Bobby, this is Summer. She's writing an article about the farm."

"Nice to meet you, Summer," Bobby said, offering a strong hand.

"It's great to meet you, Bobby. This smells amazing."

"That's the fresh herbs in the sauce from some hippie's organic farm." She clapped Carter on the shoulder. "Speaking of, don't be late with Thursday's delivery. We're already running low."

"If you need something early, let me know. I can have Beckett bring it out."

"Appreciate that," Bobby nodded. She turned her attention back to Summer. "A writer, huh?"

"Editor actually," Summer said, sliding a slice onto her plate.

"Too bad. Your mom would be over the moon if this was a date," she winked at Carter. "How long are you in town, Summer?"

"A week."

Bobby harrumphed. "A week is plenty of time for romance. Speaking of, it's nice to see your mom out and about with her new beau. I ran into them at the winery in Coopersville last weekend when I was visiting my sister. Anyway, I'll grab your salads."

Summer caught the fierce look that Bobby missed on Carter's face. "So, I take it that was news to you?"

"Goddamn Blue Moon busybodies." Carter frowned fiercely. He yanked his phone out of his jeans and fired off a text.

Summer dropped a slice onto his plate. She had a feeling the Pierce family's peace and quiet was in for a shake-up.

$\mathcal{S}$ummer woke disoriented in the dark to the sounds of a scuffle.

It took her a moment to remember where she was. Carter's house. Blue Moon Bend. After dinner the night before, she had posted a blog and started organizing her interview notes for the article before exhaustion forced her into bed at the pathetic hour of 9 p.m. No wonder she was confused.

Another thud from downstairs sounded. That was most definitely the sound of a body hitting the floor.

She yanked on a cardigan over her tank top and boxers and scurried down the stairs. Her trembling fingers found the light switch just inside the front door. She flipped it on and flooded the foyer with light.

Carter, wearing only pajama pants, was rolling around on the floor grappling with another man.

"Goddammit, you know who I am, Carter! Stop hitting me, asshole," the stranger cursed.

"I know it's you. That's why I'm hitting you," Carter grunted, releasing him from the chokehold.

They sat up, and beyond the twin bloody noses and blooming bruises, Summer saw the family resemblance.

"Jackson," she gasped.

Both men swiveled to face her. Carter dragged his brother to his feet.

"This Summer?" Jackson asked, swiping at the blood on his face.

"How the hell does everyone in this damn place know who I am?" Summer groaned. She stomped past the brothers to the kitchen.

They followed her back and watched her start the coffee pot. She tossed a box of tissues at Jackson, who shoved one up his nose to stem the bleeding and passed the box to Carter who did the same. "What is wrong with you two?"

"He broke into my house. He could have been a crazed maniac trying to kill you," Carter started.

"You knew who he was when you punched him in the face," she accused, dumping some ice cubes into a resealable bag. She threw it at Jackson, who put it on his eye.

"I wasn't one-hundred percent certain."

"I said 'It's me, Jackson. Stop punching me in the face,'" his brother interrupted.

"Any maniac could have done some basic research and used that line."

"Let's get back to the main questions here, Jackson," Summer said, snatching coffee mugs out of the cabinet. "What are you doing sneaking into your brother's house at 5:30 in the morning, and how the hell do you and everyone else in this ridiculous town know who I am?"

"Well, you're all over the Blue Moon Gossip group, and your blog came up in my Google alert for the farm."

"Hang on." Summer pinched her nose between her finger and thumb and turned her back on Carter so she wouldn't be distracted by his spectacular pecs. "What's the Blue Moon Gossip group?"

"It's a Facebook group for the town. See?" Jackson pulled it up on his phone and slid it across the island to her.

Summer scrolled through the photos and posts.

Spotted: Carter and Summer satisfying their sweet tooth with gelato and a romantic walk around town.

Spotted: Carter Pierce and Summer Lentz looking cozy at Peace of Pizza. Could this be the end of bachelorhood for the oldest Pierce brother?

Spotted: Carter Pierce treats his special lady friend, Summer, to a pair of vegan cowboy boots. Has he finally found his "solemate?"

Spotted: Carter Pierce opening his home to editor and blogger Summer Lentz. Could love be in the air on Pierce Acres?

The last post included a link to her blog, which explained the sudden jump in site traffic over the last two days.

"This is like Blue Moon's answer to Page Six," Summer groaned. "I need to sit down."

Carter shuffled her to a barstool. His long fingers pulled her cardigan together, and he worked his way down the buttons. Summer blushed, realizing her tank strap had slipped off her shoulder and was hanging precariously low.

He returned to the coffeemaker and started pouring mugs.

"While Summer wraps her head around becoming a Blue Moon celebrity, let's get back to what the hell are you doing breaking into my house?"

"First of all, you never lock your door, so it doesn't count as breaking in. Secondly, when you hear why I'm here, you'll be pissed you wasted so much time trying to pound my face in."

The bickering continued while Summer scrolled through the Facebook group. "Hey, can I join this group?"

"Sorry. You have to be a Blue Moon resident, past or present," Jackson explained.

The front door opened.

"Why the fuck am I getting a pre-dawn summons from Jax?" Beckett's voice thundered down the hall.

"Oh, yeah. I called Beckett," Jackson grinned.

"What the hell is going on here?" Beckett stomped into the kitchen. He was wearing gym shorts, a hooded sweatshirt, and neon running shoes.

"Quit whining. You were up already." Jackson said, getting up to offer his brother a one armed hug.

"I was on my way to the gym." Beckett slapped Jackson on the back. "What the hell are you doing here, Hollywood? I miss a fight?" He asked looking at the fresh bruises.

"Not much of one. LA's softened him up too much. He was all 'No, please, don't hurt my pretty face,'" Carter mimicked in a girly whine.

"Oh for the love of God, will someone let Jackson tell us why he's here?" Summer shouted.

"Thank you, Summer," Jackson said. "Now, let's go."

"Where?"

"Mom's. I went there first to catch some sleep before surprising your asses with my presence. But she wasn't alone."

Carter's gaze darted to Summer.

"What do you mean she wasn't alone?" Beckett demanded. "Is Aunt Rose staying with her?"

Carter smacked him. "No dumbass. Would Jackson come over here babbling about an overnight guest if it was Aunt Rose?"

"It was a man," Jackson interjected.

"Uncle Melvin?" Beckett asked hopefully.

"Sleeping in Mom's bedroom? No. It wasn't Uncle Melvin. His car was in the garage, not parked in the driveway or on the street. She's definitely hiding him."

"Is this the same guy you texted me about? The one Bobby saw her with at the winery?"

"I have no idea," Carter shrugged.

"It better be," Beckett frowned. "Well, let's go." He dug his car keys out of his pocket.

They piled into Beckett's SUV, Jackson in the passenger seat and Summer and Carter in the back.

"Why would she keep something like this from us?" Jackson muttered from the front seat.

Summer didn't have the heart to point out that the three reasons were hurtling toward Phoebe Pierce in an SUV as dawn broke.

~

THEY WASTED no time letting themselves into Phoebe's tidy townhouse. The front door opened to the kitchen and dining area on one side of the stairs and a living room to the left.

A chorus of "Moms" brought Phoebe downstairs in an ice blue fleece robe. "Boys. You're old enough to make your own breakfast," she laughed nervously. "Jackson! What are you doing here? What are any of you doing here at six in the morning?"

"I might ask you the same thing, Mom," Jackson said, crossing his arms.

"Don't you have something you want to tell us?" Beckett demanded.

"Is there someone you'd like to introduce us to?" Carter tried more gently.

"I don't know what you three are talking about. And Carter, where is your shirt? Why did you drag Summer over here in her bare feet?"

"Whose car is in your garage, Mom?"

The man almost made his escape in the midst of the chaos. If Summer hadn't caught a glimpse of pajama pants and a bathrobe shimmying down the front porch roof, he would have been home free.

She clapped a hand to her mouth to silence her gasp, and Phoebe tried to wave her off, but Carter chose that moment to turn around.

"What the—"

The brothers charged out the door and down the porch stairs where they yanked the man off the porch roof into the shrubs below.

"Oh, dear," Phoebe sighed and poured a little wine into a coffee mug.

They returned in a tangle of limbs and swearing with a middle-aged man in their midst.

"Now listen, boys. I think there's been a misunderstanding. I was just checking the shingles—"

"Save it, Franklin," Phoebe groaned.

"Franklin?" Beckett took a look at the intruder's face. "Shit." He released the man's arm.

"Good to see you, Beckett. Hey, what time is the Chamber meeting this week?" Franklin asked.

"You know this guy?" Jackson demanded.

"It's Franklin. He owns the Italian place. He buys produce from us," Carter said, dropping the other arm.

"Well, boys, your mother and I—"

"I need to sit down," Beckett announced and flopped down on the ottoman in the living room.

Jackson went to the fridge and pulled out a container of roast beef.

"Jackson Scott! That's my lunch for today," Phoebe yelled.

"I'm eating my feelings, Mom!"

Summer reached around Carter and offered her hand to Franklin. "I don't think we've met yet. I'm Summer."

"It's nice to meet you, Summer. The editor, right? Phoebe is really excited about the article. And I've heard a lot about you since you got into town. Sounds like love is in the air everywhere," he winked.

Carter groaned.

"Oh my God. Summer, you're not going to write about this, are you?" Beckett demanded, shoving his hands into his hair making it spring out between his fingers.

"I don't think this will really fit well into the piece," Summer said diplomatically. No one would believe her anyway.

Carter moved Summer out of his way and headed to the coffeemaker. "I'm going to need more caffeine for this." He jabbed the buttons on the machine until it sputtered to life. He lined up five mugs on the island before grudgingly grabbing a sixth.

"So, Mom. Where do you want to start?" he asked conversationally.

"How about how long has this been going on without you feeling the need to tell your own sons about it?" Beckett grumbled from the living room.

Phoebe sighed. "Well, if you're all here, we might as well do this over breakfast. Jax, honey, I'm happy to see you, but if you don't put the roast beef down now, I'm going to beat you with a spoon," she threatened.

Jax reluctantly shoved the container back in the refrigerator. "Fine, then I want eggs," he said, pushing a carton of Pierce Eggs into her hands.

"And pancakes," Beckett called.

"I make great pancakes," Franklin announced, hurrying into the kitchen to join Phoebe at the stove. "Carter can you hand me the griddle? It's in the cupboard on your left."

"He knows where the griddle is," Jax hissed at Beckett.

"He was climbing out of Mom's bedroom window," Beckett muttered through the throw pillow he was holding over his face. "He knows where a lot more than the griddle is."

Carter pushed a mug of coffee into Summer's hands. "Thank you for not laughing out loud," he whispered in her ear.

"Are you mad?"

"I'm... open to hearing their side of the story," he decided.

"Will they be okay?" Summer nodded toward his brothers. Jax had joined Beckett in the living room and was unwrapping a dozen mini candy bars he found in a dish on the coffee table.

"They'll be fine. In a decade or so."

8

With the scowl still in place, Beckett dropped everyone off at the farmhouse and sped off to take care of his mayoral duties for the day.

"You've got to hand it to Franklin," Jackson yawned. "He does make a mean batch of pancakes."

"Are you going to be okay with your mom dating?" Summer asked him as they trooped back the hall to the kitchen.

Jackson shrugged. "No one should go through life alone. They obviously care about each other. I just wish they would have told us about it before we had to haul him off a roof."

"It's a waste of time wishing that family would have made different decisions," Carter said quietly. He wasn't looking at Jackson when he said it, but the implication was clear.

"We've all made mistakes, Carter," Jackson said evenly.

"I know," that steely gaze leveled at his brother. "And it's up to us to fix them. So make sure you do."

There was a brisk knock at the side door before it opened. Joey marched in carrying a stack of papers. "Please tell me there's coffee," she yawned.

Jackson started for her, and Joey froze in recognition. The papers in her hand tumbled to the floor in a slow motion whoosh. He didn't stop until he was on her, hands threading into her hair, pulling her face in. His mouth met hers like it was locking in on a purpose for being.

Eyes wide, Summer wondered if all Pierce men kissed that way.

Joey pulled back looking dazed.

"Hey, Jojo," Jackson breathed.

Summer saw the fire in Joey's eyes and braced for it, her fingers digging into Carter's arm, but Jackson never saw it coming. He only had eyes for Joey and missed the wind up. Her palm connected with his face with a resounding slap, knocking him back a pace.

Her boots echoed on the hardwood as she marched out the door. The screen door slammed behind her, papers forgotten on the floor.

"Should have seen that coming," Carter grinned.

"God, I love that woman," Jackson whispered holding his cheek.

~

CARTER WRIGGLED his frame under the trailer hitch and pulled the cover off the wires. The taillights were shorting out, and he didn't want to give Donovan Cardona, Blue Moon's sheriff and his high school buddy, a reason to pull him over and razz him.

It was nice and quiet here on the floor of the barn. He debated hiding out here all day.

He had put Summer and Jax to work divvying up the shares for their community supported agriculture program tomorrow. It was their biggest year yet. They had sold out in record time, and thankfully the early spring had been kind to their harvest of lettuce, radishes, broccoli, and squash.

His brother was back, and Carter didn't know what it meant. Jax had come home for holidays occasionally over the years, but this visit felt different. Everything felt different.

He had a woman staying in his house that he couldn't stop thinking about, one who questioned his every move. He had a group of well-meaning Mooners out to get him and force him into settling down. His mother was dating. He didn't even want to think about what Jax's return meant for Joey.

Thank God Beckett was still the same obnoxious smartass. Some things would never change.

Carter disconnected a wire and cleaned up the contact.

Only a few days ago, he would have been doing this with the certainty of solitude. No one asking him a thousand questions. No one to keep from injuring herself. He could just grab a sandwich for lunch and eat on the go. No one sleeping in the guest room wearing those little cotton shorts and tank top so thin he could see her—

His hand slipped and his knuckles grazed a bolt, drawing blood. "Son of a bitch!" Just the thought of Summer turned him into a ham-fisted moron.

He crawled out from under the trailer and was wrapping his hand with a mostly clean rag when he heard the yelling.

He was out the door in a flash and was halfway to the house when he spotted what was causing the commotion.

Clementine had Jax by the jeans, and at the rate she was going, there wouldn't be much left. Summer was standing on the other side of the fence with the pigs, watching through her fingers in horror as the goat devoured his pants.

"Get off me," Jax bellowed, trying to drag the denim from Clementine's teeth. "Jesus, are you on fucking steroids?"

He spun around, once and then twice, but the goat held on.

Jax gave one more tug and it was too much for the fabric. The back pocket and a good portion of his underwear were ripped clean.

Clementine trotted away with her prize. "Goddamn it! Those were Hanros," he said, clutching at his shredded underwear.

Summer's horror turned to giggles. Jax turned to glare at her.

"I'm sorry, Jackson!" She clapped a hand over her mouth. "I don't mean to laugh at you."

Jax pushed past Carter muttering how much he hated that "stupid fucking goat."

"Welcome home, Hollywood," Carter called after him.

Jax mustered as much dignity as he could with his bare ass hanging out and raised his middle finger high as he stomped up the porch steps. "Fuck you, Carter."

～

WITH THE CSA shares sorted and Carter nowhere in sight, Summer decided she would head into town. She had jeans to buy, and after pizza last night, she wanted to get a better feel for Blue Moon.

She changed out of her work clothes and was leaving a note for Carter in the kitchen when Jax came in through the side door.

"Don't you clean up nice?"

"I don't always have vegetable dirt smeared all over me," she laughed. "I'm heading into town. I need more jeans."

"Clem get you, too?"

"First day here. They were True Religion." She grimaced.

"Damn goat. She's got good taste. Mind if I tag along with you? I've got some shopping of my own to do."

"Sure."

"Just let me get changed. I'll meet you out front."

Five minutes later, Jax was sliding the passenger seat in Summer's rental all the way back. Those long Pierce legs required a lot of room.

"So where's the best place to buy goat-proof jeans?" Summer asked, guiding the car down the driveway.

"There's McCafferty's on the square. They've got some heavier-duty options," Jax said, running a hand through his short, choppy hair.

He was a little leaner than his brothers. Jax topped out an inch or two over six feet, but the profile, the walk, the eyes, they were all Pierce. He had a vibe that was uniquely his, though. Where Carter was the peaceful warrior and Beckett the cautious, by-the-book politician, Jax threw off the air of enigmatic artist.

Joey must have been head over heels for him in high school, Summer thought.

McCafferty's Farm Supply took up all three floors of the skinny white clapboard building at the end of the square. From the outside it looked just as tidy as the rest of the buildings flanking the green, but on the inside, it was crammed full of chaos from top to bottom.

There didn't appear to be any rhyme or reason to the organization. Gas-powered generators sat next to a rounder of coveralls and extension cords. Horse bridles hung from pegboard behind a stacked display of wax logs. Cowboy hats and flowered straw hats were clumped together on top of every flat surface.

"Oh, my."

Jax laid a hand on her shoulder. "Most of the clothes are upstairs, and if we're careful we can avoid—"

One of those flowered hats floated toward them.

"Jackson Pierce, as I live and breathe!"

The hat, and the short, round woman under it emerged from the sales floor. She was wearing thick glasses and a denim shirt embroidered with the McCafferty logo.

"Miz McCafferty!" The enthusiasm in Jax's voice didn't quite reach his eyes.

"I haven't seen you in what is it now? Eight years? You lit out of town right before graduation after that horrible accident. My, you've grown," she said, eyeing him appreciatively. "You Pierce boys sure give us ladies lots to look at in Blue Moon." She perched her elbows on the register counter. "I hear you're a big-time movie maker now."

"I just write 'em, Miz McCafferty. Someone else makes 'em."

"Now, who's being modest?" she chuckled. "Notice I'm not asking what Joey thinks of you coming home. I'm no busybody. No siree. I keep my nose in my own business. Although, I'm sure you've been getting peppered with questions since you came home..." She waited for him to fill in the blank.

"This morning."

"Right, this morning." She smiled, knowing she had hit fresh gossip. "Now what can I help you find?"

Jax shoved Summer toward the stairs. "We're just here for some jeans."

"Oh, hi there, Summer!" Mrs. McCafferty called. "I didn't recognize you there with the wrong Pierce brother. If there's anything you two need, just let me know." She was already reaching for her cell phone as Jax shoved Summer up the stairs in front of him.

"And you willingly came back to this?" Summer wondered, climbing to the second floor.

"You know how sometimes with time and distance you can romanticize things?"

"Yeah?"

"I think with time and distance, I forgot all about Miz McCafferty."

"She'd be heartbroken to hear you say that."

"Jeans are over here," Jax said pointing to the back corner.

They were piled on the floor, stacked on shelves, and hung from clothing rods. It was a mountain of denim.

"How do you find anything?" Summer asked.

"Just start digging."

It took her ten minutes to find two pairs of jeans in her size plus a pair of comfy-looking cargo pants. On the bright side, all three together were still significantly cheaper than the pair sampled by Clementine.

"We can try everything on in there," Jax, holding an armful of clothing, pointed to two stalls cordoned off with sagging rope and tarp that acted as fitting room curtains. "I'll take this one," Jax said, gesturing to the room with the curtain that sagged to mid-chest.

Summer gratefully pulled the tarp closed on the room with slightly taller coverage and was delighted to find that all three pairs of pants fit perfectly. The jeans had reinforced stitching and seats and would look great with her boots. The cargos were as comfortable as sweatpants and looked much nicer on her butt.

She exited the room, pleased with her finds and was greeted by a shirtless Jax digging through a messy pile of t-shirts.

Wow. Those Pierce genes were experts in crafting perfection.

"Find what you need?" Jax asked, oblivious to her gawking.

"I think so."

"You might want to consider a couple of three dollar t-shirts," he said, tossing her a cherry red V-neck.

Back into the fitting room she went. She heard Jax's phone ring next door.

"What's up?"

"Yeah, she's with me."

"What are we doing? We're getting naked."

Summer heard his quick laugh. "*Relax*. We're enhancing our farm wardrobes at McCafferty's."

Jax was quiet for a minute. "How about we bring home dinner? Will that make you less of a dick? You call it in. We'll pick it up."

Okay. Later." He hung up. "I'm breaking a brotherly code here, but Carter was not happy about the idea of you getting naked with me," he called over the tarp.

Summer was glad he couldn't see the blush creep across her face. "He's probably protective of all his houseguests."

Jax laughed. "You keep telling yourself that, Summer."

By the time they left, Summer had amassed a collection of pants, shorts, t-shirts, and a baseball hat all for less than the pair of destroyed jeans. Flushed with success, she gleefully tossed the haul in the trunk of her car.

"Wow, you can't buy a t-shirt for thirty dollars in Manhattan, let alone three."

"L.A., too. The underwear Clem satanically destroyed cost me seventy-five." He threw his bag in the trunk and closed the lid. "What else do you want to see while we're here?"

Summer looked down the street. "What's OJ by Julia?" she asked, spotting a colorful chalkboard sign in front of a neon green shop a few buildings down.

"Organic juice shop. Ever have a wheatgrass shot with an apple ginger juice chaser?" Jax asked.

"Can't say that I have," Summer laughed.

"Well, let's give it a whirl."

OJ by Julia was just as colorful on the inside as the out. Deep purple cushioned benches slid up against lime green wainscoting and flanked black tables. Stainless steel industrial lighting fixtures highlighted coolers of mason jars filled with colorful juices. There was a bar with high-backed stools, and the menu was written in a charming script on blackboard in neon chalk.

A lavender head popped up from behind the counter.

"Well, well, well. Jackson Pierce. Of all the juice joints in all the world, you had to walk into mine."

"Julia," Jax grinned. "Look at you all entrepreneurial."

She scooted out from behind the counter, leading with a very pregnant belly. "And pregnant as all hell," she said, hugging him as best she could.

"You were pregnant at Dad's funeral, weren't you? This still the same one?" Jax teased.

"That was my first. We're on our third now."

"Holy shit, Jules."

"I know, I know. But Rob and I wanted to get them all out of the way before we're too old to play or tackle them when they're awful." She tossed her light purple curls out of her face. "Now what can I do for you two?"

"My friend Summer here has never had wheatgrass." Jax said pulling out one of the stools for her.

"Well, Summer, you're in for a treat. First wheatgrass is on the house," Julia winked.

"I'm anxious to try liquid grass." Summer sat, as Julia cut spears of green grass from a potted flat on the counter.

"Summer's here doing an article on the farm," Jax said, taking the seat next to her.

"I know," Julia winked. "But I find it incredibly rude when strangers skip over the whole introduction part even though they already know who you are and where you got your cowboy boots."

"Not to mention creepy," Summer added.

"You get used to it eventually," Julia said running the blades of grass through a hand-cranked juicer. Juice the color of spring clover trickled into the shot glass.

She wiped her hands on her apron and put a glass in front of each of them.

"Cheers," Jax said, raising his glass.

"Cheers." Summer echoed, clinked hers to his. She briefly wondered whether she should hold her nose but decided to just go for it. She downed it quickly like medicine.

"It's sweet," she said in surprise.

"What did you expect?" Julia teased.

"I think something that tasted a little more like dirt. Are there health benefits?"

"Oh, lord," Jax chuckled. "Prepare to be educated by Dr. Juice."

"The benefits of drinking clean, fresh juice are numerous," Julia began.

Twenty minutes later, Jax helped Summer lug her eight jars of juice to the car. "Between the clothes and the juice, this qualifies as a shopping spree in Blue Moon. You and your purchases will be all over Facebook."

"And you will too, by association."

They swung by Righteous Subs, a tiny sandwich shop squeezed between the bank and Karma Kustard, to pick up dinner before heading home.

"I had fun today. Thanks for being my shopping buddy," Summer said. It sure beat harvesting lettuce.

"No problem. It's nice to ease back into life here."

"Is it rude if I ask about the accident Mrs. McCafferty was talking about? I promise, you can tell me to shut up, and I'll only be moderately offended."

Jax eyed her over his sunglasses. "I can see Blue Moon is already rubbing off on you."

"Very funny."

"Joey and I used to date, as I'm sure you're aware," Jax said. "Right before graduation we were in a car accident. I was driving."

He said the words casually, but the way his fingers gripped his leg was anything but casual. She let it drop.

"So. Why did you come back?"

He sighed and propped an elbow on the door. "Your picture."

"What picture?"

"The picture on your blog of Joey."

"But I just posted it yesterday."

"I told you I have a Google alert set up for the farm. I've been thinking about coming back for a while. And when I clicked that link and saw her, I knew it was time."

"Just like that?"

"Booked a red-eye, and here I am."

"And you're back for good?"

"If she'll have me."

"You think there's a chance."

"Oh, I know there's a chance."

"She hit you pretty hard. You might have a concussion and be delusional."

"Funny girl. That just means she still has feelings for me," he winked.

Summer found his confidence endearing. And maybe a little naïve.

"What about all your stuff in L.A.? Your house, your seventy-five dollar underwear collection, your job?"

He shrugged again. "It'll keep."

She let that drop, too.

"So you write movies?" she asked, changing the subject.

They talked writing and process until Summer turned toward the farm.

"Do you mind if we make one more stop? There's one last thing on my shopping list."

9

*E*rnest Washington's used car lot occupied an acre on the outskirts of town. EW's VWs specialized in restoring vintage Volkswagen buses. There were five of them gleaming bright in a rainbow of color against the road.

"Please tell me you're getting that one," she said, pointing to a purple camper model as she got out of the car.

"I could have made good use of a van with a bed in the back in high school," Jax waxed nostalgically. He led the way toward the office/garage.

A man in neatly pressed khakis intercepted them. His wispy white beard came to his chest, and the hair on top of his head was tamed by a blue bandana.

"I thought I saw a Pierce meandering about out here," he said, clapping Jax on the back.

"Good to see you, Ern," Jax said. "This is my friend Summer."

Ernest took her offered hand and kissed her knuckles. "A veritable pleasure, Summer. What brings you two to my humble entrepreneurial endeavor?"

"I'm in the market for some wheels," Jax told him.

"Planning to replant some transplanted roots, I hear," Ernest said, wiggling his bushy brows.

"That's the plan. What have you got for me?"

Ernest surveyed the lot. "Well, we've got your buses there, your Dubs there, a couple of sedans over yonder. But I'm thinking a man such as yourself needs a little more power under the hood."

"I knew you'd have something squirreled away," Jax nodded. "Tell me more."

"How does a 1969 350 small block with black on black sound?"

"Like you're about to make me the happiest man on the planet."

Ernest chuckled. "Let me introduce you to your new bride." He keyed in a code on one of the garage bays and the door rose silently.

Jax let out a low wolf whistle. "Hello, beautiful."

The black car squatted under a lift. Beefy tires and sleek, shiny lines gave it an aggressive look that even Summer found appealing.

"Summer, do you know what this is?"

"It appears to be a car of some sort."

"You'll have to excuse her, Ern. Summer's from Manhattan. This car, Summer, is a 1969 Chevy Nova."

Ernest tossed him the keys. "Might as well escort her out on a date. See if it's true love."

"Come on, Summer. Let's see what she can do."

She did a lot, in Summer's estimation. The Nova's deep purr was capable of shifting into a full on roar and gluing her shoulder blades to the pristine vinyl of the passenger seat.

After a five-minute thrill ride, Summer's heart was in her throat, and Jax was sold. He and Ernest haggled—more out of habit than necessity—for briefest of moments before settling on a price and shaking on it.

"I'll treat her right," Jax promised.

"You be sure to do so," Ernest said, pocketing the check. "Summer, it was a delight."

$\sim$

CARTER WAS ATTEMPTING to enjoy a few moments of peace and quiet with a beer and some Beethoven when they returned. He nearly laughed when he watched his brother cart in eight jars of Julia's wares. "I see Summer met Julia," he said.

"We're having a tasting," Jax said, heaving the jars onto the counter. "Break out the shot glasses."

Summer came in behind him, lugging what looked like a dozen shopping bags. Her face was flushed and happy. It hit him like a fist to the gut how much he liked seeing her in his house. As much as he enjoyed his solitude, his peace, there was something to be said for a beautiful woman happy to see him.

"Looks like shopping was successful," he said, taking the bags from her and putting them down.

"I don't know what came over me, Carter. I just went for one or two pairs of jeans and look what happened!"

"Summer got to meet Mrs. McCarthy," Jax said, pulling plates out of the cabinet.

Carter dumped the subs out of the bag while he listened to Summer chatter about their afternoon. A wax paper bag came tumbling out of the sub bag. Inside he found two heart shaped cookies.

The BC strikes again.

He held them up, and Jax laughed. "I take you didn't order those?"

Carter glared at him. "No. I did not order pink and blue heart cookies for dinner."

His brother fished a set of car keys out of his pocket. "After you're done crumbling cookies, check out the new wheels."

"You took Summer car shopping?"

Jax shrugged. "She took me juice shopping."

"Jax spent way more than I did," Summer said, defending herself. "Go meet his new lady, and I'll get dinner ready."

Since there was no actual cooking to be done, Carter figured it was safe to leave Summer alone in the kitchen.

The car was impressive, the test drive Jax allowed him was even more so.

It didn't surprise him that his brother went vintage. Even in high school when everyone else thought newer was better, Jax and Joey bonded over their love of American muscle.

What did give him pause was the fact that buying a car appeared to be a real sign that his brother was serious about staying put. He wondered what that meant.

When they returned, Summer had neatly arranged the subs on plates and filled shot glasses of juice at each place setting on the island. She couldn't cook to save her life, but her presentation was appealing.

"How was the ride?" she asked, all blue eyes and full lips.

"She moves," he answered.

"Why do men refer to cars as women?" she asked, frowning.

"There's only one other thing that gets a man's blood up like the rumble of an engine," Jax said.

"And that's a beautiful woman," Carter added.

She laughed, and he couldn't stop himself from putting his hands on her shoulders. "So what are we sampling here?" he asked.

"Julia was so passionate about what she does and the health benefits of it, I picked up the ones she recommended."

Being OJs by Julia's main supplier of organic produce and herbs, Carter had tried most of the juices before. He knew which ones were palatable, delicious even, and which ones were to be avoided at all costs.

"Food or juice first?" he asked, taking the stool next to her.

Jax picked up a glass and sniffed it with suspicion. "Let's juice first and wash it down with food just in case they taste like they smell."

Summer swigged back a shot of the Citrus Berry Brew. "That one was really good," she said, licking her lips.

Jax went for the Ginger Sunrise and drew in a breath through his teeth. "That one has a bit of a kick."

Carter hid his smile as they both reached for the Jolly Green. He grabbed a shot of the Beet Root Reboot. "Cheers."

"Cheers," they answered.

Summer clinked his glass and drank hers down. The reaction was instantaneous. She clapped both hands over her mouth to keep the juice from coming back out. Jax wasn't as dignified. He raced to the sink, spit out the offending juice, and drank straight from the faucet.

"What the fuck was that?" he gargled.

Summer gagged. "It tastes like... feet. Disgusting, horrible feet."

Jax groaned in the sink.

Carter roared with laughter.

"You knew!" Summer stared at him accusingly.

"As soon as I'm sure I won't puke, I'm gonna kick your ass," Jax grumbled.

Summer took matters into her own hands and filled Carter's empty glass with Jolly Green. "Drink up. We're in this together."

Carter eyed her up and then sprinted around the island.

"Come back here, you coward," Summer yelled, running down the hall after him while wielding the glass.

She saw him dart into the dining room and chased after him, not realizing it was a trap.

Carter jumped out and snagged her around the waist. Summer shrieked and bobbled the glass. He snatched it out of her hand and pushed her up against the wall. "I think you want another shot of this, don't you?" he teased.

He used his body to hold her in place and playfully brought the glass to her lips. Summer clamped her mouth shut and shook her head from side to side.

"Come on, baby, open up."

She turned her head to the side. "Not as tough as Jax? Can't handle a little juice?" she asked.

"You manipulative little—" he grinned.

"Be careful how you finish that sentence, Carter." Her eyes had gone deeper than the Atlantic. "I was just making an observation. Obviously, given the current evidence, I can't help but assume that your brother is more of a man than you are." She shrugged delicately.

"My brother is puking in the sink."

"No, I'm not," Jax yelled from the kitchen.

"Sounds like he survived it. Are you afraid you won't?" She was cocky now, and it was a fucking turn-on.

Carter held up the glass. "What do I get, sweet Summer, if I drink your poison?"

"What do you want?" Her smile was slow and dangerous.

That smart mouth on his. That lithe body wrapped around him. Those sea goddess eyes opening in his bed in the morning. That's what he wanted.

He leaned in an inch closer, and those plush lips parted for him.

"You can owe me one," he said, stopping a breath before her mouth.

He raised the glass, dipped a finger in it, and painted it over her open lips. Her tongue darted out to taste his finger, and he downed the contents of the glass. The touch of her tongue to his skin overrode the sensation of liquid garbage sliding down his throat.

"You owe me."

"Try and collect," she said saucily.

"Manipulative," he said, pinching her as she walked past him.

"Calculated," she tossed over her shoulder and sauntered back to the kitchen.

Jax was out of the sink and swigging soy sauce straight from the bottle. "I can't get rid of the taste," he groaned.

"Gimme that," Carter said, snatching the bottle from him and pouring some into his own mouth.

∼

CARTER RETREATED to the great room after dinner. It had been a productive day. Orders delivered, grass mowed, crops mulched with the clippings. Jax was showing off his car to Beckett, and peace once again reigned in the house.

He picked up a book and turned on some music, classical piano so as not to disturb Summer who was still working in the kitchen. She had changed, yet again, this time into cotton pants and a little tank under a soft sweater. Her hair was carelessly piled on top of her head. He liked her this way best.

Comfortable, unguarded.

He liked watching her work, enjoyed the way she alternated between squinting at her screen and smiling at it.

Lord knew what was going through her mind. Unfortunately, it was *her* that kept running through *his* mind.

She worked all day by his side, and then every night, she sat at the kitchen island until yawns of exhaustion forced her upstairs to bed. He doubted she got enough sleep. By evening, she was pale with shadows under her eyes, but still she soldiered on.

He'd looked up her blog the night before and was pleasantly surprised.

She wrote with a simple directness that made him feel like she was having a friendly conversation. There were behind-the-scenes posts from photo shoots or magazine events, but most of her posts trended toward health and lifestyle topics.

She shared interesting research and short snippets of the biographies of interesting people she met. He couldn't quite connect the woman who diligently slaved for the higher-ups and advertisers of a magazine featuring skinny, pouting models to the one who wrote so passionately about the New York make-up artist to the stars who was supporting her parents and siblings in her home country of Namibia.

Others seemed to appreciate Summer's blog, too. Each post had dozens of comments and hundreds of "shares." Whatever those were.

He skimmed her last post on the farm on his tablet, frowning at a picture of himself before scrolling lower. There were more comments here. Ones that nearly made him blush.

"Hey." Summer came in from the kitchen carrying her laptop. "Can I show you something?"

Carter hit the power button of his tablet to hide the screen. "Uh, sure."

She sat cross-legged next to him on the couch. "Okay. So I noticed you didn't have a graphic or logo for the farm and I thought maybe you could use one. Do some branding and merchandising."

He blinked. "Merchandising?"

"You know like reusable totes or t-shirts for the riding school. That kind of thing. Plus it's something we could run with the article."

Carter nodded. It sounded like a smart idea.

"Anyway, here's what I came up with." She passed him her laptop.

On the screen was a vibrant red apple with an arrow through it. The words Pierce Acres rounded under the apple.

"That arrow?" He frowned and cocked his head. It looked familiar.

"It's based on the weather vane on top of the little barn. On the surface, the apple is because your mom told me the orchard is a big producer. Everyone loves Pierce apples. But it also represents natural, organic produce." She bit her lip. "What do you think?"

Carter peered at the screen and back at Summer. "This is really good. You did this?"

She grinned and nodded. "Do you really like it?"

"Yeah, I do. It looks like us. Thank you," he said, laying a warm hand on her knee. "What's an artist like you charge for this?"

Summer laughed. "Got any ice cream in the house?"

10

<hr/>

*J*t was delivery day for Carter in town, and rather than set tongues wagging by accompanying him, Summer wrangled a lunch invitation out of Beckett. It was the perfect opportunity for her to get a little more background for the story.

Carter dropped her off in front of a rambling Victorian. Unlike the home next door with its midnight blue siding and Pepto-Bismol pink front door, Beckett's was a stately gray with white trim.

"His office is on the side," Carter called from the driver seat, pointing at the far end of the porch. "Be back in an hour."

Summer waved him off and opened the wrought iron gate to the walkway. The Pierce men were certainly eclectic with their taste in homes, she mused.

She followed the flagstone path to the front porch and wandered around the side. The sign on the fanciful glass door politely asked her to *Please Come In*. Summer stepped inside and found herself in a cheerful sunroom off the back of the house.

The girl behind the large mahogany desk was wearing a

leather collar with metal spikes. Her black hair was combed into two neat pigtails. She smiled through her black-as-midnight lipstick. "Are you Summer?" she whispered.

"I am," Summer replied in a hushed tone.

"I'm Ellery, Beckett's paralegal. I'd like to say that he'll be with you shortly, but he's in there with the Buchanans." She gestured to the closed door behind her. "Their mediations usually run a little long. You can have a seat. Can I get you something to drink?"

"I'm fine, thanks," Summer said, taking a seat on the sun-faded sofa facing Ellery's desk.

Within a few minutes, the paneled door behind her opened, and Beckett emerged, wincing at the raised voices behind him. The sleeves of his button down were rolled up, and his tie was loosened. He looked like he was sweating.

"Summer, I'll be just a few minutes more," he said, reaching for the glass of ice water that Ellery handed him.

"It's no problem," Summer assured him. "Take your time."

He drank like a man in the desert, straightened his shoulders, and marched back into the room.

Within seconds, the shouting dropped to a low roar, and in less than five minutes, it stopped completely.

The door opened again, and this time a smiling couple in their fifties walked out. He was tall and lanky with eyes that crinkled when he smiled. She was a round little thing who modeled her wardrobe after Stevie Nicks.

"Thanks again, sweetie," she called over her shoulder. "We'll see you next week."

Ellery waved them off and, the second they were gone, poured two fingers of scotch into a rocks glass. "Here," she handed it to Summer. "He's going to need this."

Summer took the glass and knocked on the open door.

Beckett was seated at a long library table, head in his hands. "I'm not here," he said without moving his hands.

Summer set the glass in front of him. "How about now?"

A gray eye peeked through fingers. "They don't tell you about these things when you're in law school."

Summer took the seat opposite him. It was a good room. Shelves lined with bound books rose to the ceiling with its original chandelier. A bow window overlooking the backyard let in the midday light.

"Rough day?" she asked.

Beckett picked up the glass and sipped. "I'd tell you that it's attorney-client privilege, but they aren't clients. I've never actually *done* anything for them."

"See, now you have to tell me," Summer insisted.

"The Buchanans came to me once right after I started the practice to help with their divorce settlement. Apparently I mediated so well that they changed their minds and decided to stay married. Now they think I'm some kind of marriage counselor. Every time there's an argument about the in-laws or the butter dish, they make an appointment. This time it was what cable package they should get." He scrubbed his hands over his face.

"It sounds like you play an indispensable role in their marriage," Summer said, trying not to laugh.

Beckett downed the contents of the glass. "Sorry for dumping all that on you. Please don't—"

"Write about any of this?" she finished.

"Sorry. Again. It's the lawyer in me."

"Understood. Well, the writer in me is curious. Why a lawyer?"

Beckett shrugged, a spitting image of Carter's habit. "You grow up with two brothers and Phoebe Pierce, and you learn to love arguing."

"And you stayed close to home?"

"Carter was off to the Army as soon as he graduated high school, and when Jax lit out of town a few years later, it was just my parents and me. Dad needed help on the farm, and Blue Moon was always home. Later, when Dad got sick, Mom and I took on everything we could with the farm, and the town stepped up. For the six months leading up to Dad's death, there were an extra half-dozen hands every single day. And they were all there because in some way, shape, or form John Pierce had done the same for them."

"You were still in law school and running the farm?"

"It wasn't pretty," he grinned.

Summer shook her head. "I just can't wrap my head around that kind of community. It's amazing."

"It really is. Even after his death, when Mom and I were having serious thoughts about selling, they were there for us. Sometimes from sun up to sun down. It was a smaller operation then. Carter has really scaled it up since he came home."

"And now you're mayor."

Beckett nodded. "After everything this town did for me and my family, I owed them. Still do."

Ellery came in with a tray of boxed lunches and waters. "I picked up lunch for you two from Over Caffeinated. Mind if I head out now?" she asked Beckett.

"Thanks, Ellery. Did you—"

"I left a message for Mr. Goodloe about coming in to sign the papers.

"Great, how about—"

"I re-drafted the settlement agreement for the Hadwens and put it on your desk."

"And were you able to—"

"Yes. And they said no problem with rescheduling for next Thursday."

"You're the best." Beckett said it with real affection. "Appreciate the help today."

Ellery beamed. "Happy to! See you tomorrow. Nice meeting you, Summer," she called.

"Great to meet you, Ellery."

"She's something, isn't she?" Beckett said shaking his head.

"Is she psychic like Willa?" Summer couldn't help but ask.

Beckett laughed. "No. She's just very good at her job and knows me better than I know myself. So," he said, peeking into the boxes of food. "Do you want the Greek salad or the chicken pesto tortellini?"

"Excuse us for interrupting." A man who looked like a grumpy Santa bustled into the conference room followed by a woman in heavy-duty khakis and a polo. "But we've got an important situation that needs your attention, Mr. Mayor."

"Bruce. I've told you a thousand times, please call me Beckett."

Bruce was already shaking his head. "Your office deserves respect, and that's what you get from Bruce Oakleigh," he said, drilling a finger into his own chest. "But not everyone has respect. No siree. What kind of a message does it send our youth if the town council allows Beverly here to add one of those flailing armed inflatable freaks in front of her building. Where is your respect for tradition, Beverly? Your father didn't run that HVAC business with a *blow-up doll* in the parking lot." He waved his arms in the air. He was wheezing slightly after his tirade.

Beverly rolled her eyes. She yanked an inhaler out of the pocket of Bruce's cargo pants and handed it to him. "Beckett, can you please just tell Bruce it's fine for me to display a ten-foot *air dancer* in the parking lot for our week-long maintenance package sale so I can get back to my job and you can get back to your lunch?"

"A week?" Bruce's snowy eyebrows rose. "Well, why didn't you say so? I thought you were making it a permanent, tawdry fixture. Mr. Mayor, please strike my comments from the record," he said, offering Beckett a little bow.

"Consider them stricken," Beckett said, his tone serious.

"Want to go grab a smoothie, Bruce?" Beverly offered.

"That would be lovely," he said, letting her lead the way.

∾

THEY WERE INTERRUPTED two more times before Carter returned to pick Summer up, but she felt like she had gotten a good, clear picture of the middle Pierce brother. Beckett was the picture of loyalty and stability. Family was his center, and that family extended to the residents of Blue Moon Bend.

Evidence of this was framed on the walls and shelves of his office. There were pictures of his brothers, his parents, and his townspeople. Babies, firemen, newspaper clippings from town meetings. Beckett's heart belonged to Blue Moon.

"How did it go?" Carter asked as she climbed into the truck.

"I really like your brother," she said, missing the frown that marred Carter's face.

11

Over the fluid notes of Chris Botti's trumpet and the punchy words of the latest spy novel, Carter heard Summer muttering from the kitchen island.

She had set up her laptop after dinner and gone to work like a general directing troops. She wanted to get a solid outline of the article done, she said. But her phone hadn't stopped ringing since she sat down.

From the great room, he had heard every conversation. First there was the model's agent who wasn't happy with the placement of an ad. Then came the higher-up who needed something proofed *immediately* because the post on moisturizers was *life and death*. Now she was on the phone with her friend she called the Wolf. And in between calls, he heard her furiously answering emails and muttering about blog trolls.

It was stressing him out.

"I don't know why they didn't give you a copy of the article either, Nikolai," Carter heard her sigh. "Of course you need to know what you're shooting."

He gave up trying to read and headed into the kitchen. Summer was sitting with her hand on her forehead.

"Look, I'll email you a draft of the article as soon as I send Katherine her moisturizer thing."

She rolled her eyes while she listened.

"Mm hmm. Mm hmm. Yeah. Okay, bye."

She hung up and covered her face with her hands. "I adore him, but when he goes all temperamental artist on me, I want to murder him."

He could tell that she was beyond frustrated. "What's going on?" he asked, sliding on to the stool next to her.

"It's nothing. A lot of nothing. I'm just falling behind on work while I'm here and—" The ringtone of her phone cut her off again. "Hang on," she said, answering the call.

"Miguel, thanks for getting back to me. Yeah, Carl somehow got his hands on a few extra pages of proofs and isn't happy that his ad is so close to the piece on a minimalist wardrobe…"

She refreshed her email while she listened.

"He feels that we're telling consumers not to consume his line… Well, we need to move it. His ad rep should have known better… I realize that. This can be avoided in the future if we can get the reps to pay more attention in the layout meetings… I know. It's a losing battle."

Summer rubbed the spot between her eyebrows. "Okay. Thanks, Miguel. I appreciate it."

She put her phone on the counter and stretched her arms overhead.

"This must all seem so stupid to you," she said, rolling her head on her shoulders. "You fought for your life and country, and here I am stressing out over ad placement and moisturizer."

"It's all relative," Carter shrugged.

She shot him a disbelieving look. "No. It's not. I know that none of this is life and death, but I can't seem to not get sucked into the stress of a false sense of urgency."

"When everything is important—"

"Nothing is important," she finished for him.

"Exactly. Are you done with the moisturizers?"

"Yes. Well, sort of. I should take another pass at it to make sure it's clean. But I haven't even tackled the outline yet, and I need to get rid of the spam comments on my blog."

Carter looked at his watch. "You have five minutes to do whatever absolutely has to get done and change."

"Carter, I really don't have time for games. I've got a lot of things to take care of."

"And none of those things are remotely life and death. You're missing out on what's important. Five minutes."

She looked good and pissed, which in Carter's opinion was better than stressed and drowning. "What happens in five minutes?"

"We're going out. You need jeans and your boots. And a sweatshirt if you have one."

"I don't have a sweatshirt. Are we doing more work?"

"Stop asking questions. You have five minutes."

Her dramatic sigh ended in a growl. And when she began frantically typing, Carter knew he had her.

He left her to her panic and went upstairs to change. It was the perfect night for it, and damned if he was going to sit there and watch Summer stress herself out over things that didn't matter.

He'd show her how he learned to slow down, get perspective.

He passed her on the stairs. "Two minutes," he reminded her.

She grumbled and stomped into her room.

In the coat closet by the front door, he pulled out a plaid flannel jacket.

Summer hurried down the stairs, her boots clattering on the wood.

Her cheeks were flushed and she was frowning.

"Here," he helped her into the coat. "Ready?"

"I don't know! You won't tell me what we're doing!" Exasperation laced her tone.

Why was it so sexy and sweet when women wore men's clothing? he wondered as he smoothed out the material on her shoulders.

Carter tugged the end of her ponytail. "We're going for a ride."

~

"I THOUGHT YOU MEANT IN A VEHICLE," Summer grumbled when they pulled into the stables.

"The best place to see a sunset is from the back of a horse."

"I'm pretty sure it's from a beach with a Cosmo in your hand."

"You'll see." Carter took her by the hand and led her into the stables.

"Isn't it going to be dark soon? What if we get lost? I'm not ready for this."

He stopped in front of her and she ran into his back. Carter turned and took her by the shoulders. "Do you trust me?"

She looked up at him with those ocean deep eyes wide and scared.

"Summer," he pulled her in a step closer. "I'm not going to let anything happen to you, okay?"

Inexplicably, tears welled in her eyes.

"There are some things you can't be protected from," she said quietly.

He pulled her in to his chest, his chin resting on the top of her head. "I need you to trust me on this. I will keep you safe." Damn if she didn't fit perfectly in his arms.

He felt the hot breath of her sigh through his shirt and held her a little closer.

"I'm sorry, Carter. I'm not usually such a baby," she said pulling back to look up at him. "I'm just overwhelmed."

"Stop apologizing for being human. Besides, it's probably just the juice talking."

She gave a little laugh against his chest.

It was killing him, holding her like this. He just wanted a taste, wanted to know if she'd respond to him the way he imagined she would. But he couldn't. She wasn't a toy. She was a woman here to do a job. He settled for brushing his lips against her furrowed brow.

He heard the quiet intake of breath, watched her part her lips. Saw her eyes zero in on his mouth. An invitation. An anticipation.

But if he kissed her now, he wouldn't stop. And that wasn't what he brought her here to do.

"Wait here. I'll saddle the horses."

～

THEY WERE the sexiest words ever uttered to Summer in her twenty-six years of living. *Wait here. I'll saddle the horses.* She had almost kissed him, twice now. She had wanted to, desperately. But he had backed off.

And now she was on the back of the dainty Charcoal, plodding into the dusky evening behind Carter on his big bay, Romeo.

She was an emotional disaster tonight. Trying to do too many things to the point where everything felt like an emergency. And Carter's simple declaration. *I'll keep you safe.*

He couldn't. Not from what really threatened her. No one could. But somehow the words still loosened something in her chest.

Carter turned in the saddle to look at her. Without speaking, he pointed to the right where three deer strolled through the meadow. She shifted to get a better look. "They're so small," she whispered, not wanting to startle them. Charcoal's ears twitched at her voice.

Carter nodded. "A mom with twins."

In the dimming light she could just make out the spots. Fawns. She had never actually seen fawns in real life, just in cute email forwards.

She followed Carter past the white fence that divided pasture from crops and wound around a copse of trees. The leafy branches stretched and reached toward the full, orange moon hovering just beyond. The sky was layered with colors that had never touched the Manhattan skyline.

Crickets and fireflies sang and danced in the dusky light.

She followed Carter over a low, rolling hill. He stopped, and Charcoal drew up next to Romeo. The creek bubbled below them, reflecting the colors of the sky as the sun began to set across the fields and woods.

"Wow," Summer whispered.

Carter smiled. "Yeah."

Charcoal shifted under her, and Summer realized she had actually ridden here. On a horse. Without falling off and getting trampled. She was sitting on a horse watching an incredible sunset with a man who gave her butterflies. In the city, she would have been working late most likely. Maybe heading out to a reception or a cocktail party. Or holed up in her apartment poring over blog stats.

This was better. This was perfect.

She reached over and touched Carter's hand. He opened it, and she interlaced her fingers with his. And together they watched the sun sink as the moon rose.

12

———

 $\mathcal{S}$ ummer had collected eggs—and gotten flopped by a chicken—boxed 250 shares of spring vegetables, and ridden shotgun on the fertilizer run for the acres and acres of corn. Her manicure was shot, and she was in bed by ten every night. Except the other night when Carter had taken her out for ice cream.

He hadn't even let her change. They went into town and stood in line for the ice cream truck. She had been startled to note that most of the other patrons were in various states of undress, too, giving the line waiting experience the festiveness of a slumber party.

And yet, somehow, there was something stirring inside her. A contentment, a sense of security, that made absolutely no sense to her. She was excited to wake up every morning. She couldn't wait to get downstairs and see Carter. To walk the land with him, to watch him move through his world.

"I don't know, Niko," Summer sighed into the phone. "I feel like I'm missing the puzzle piece on this article. I can't articulate the appeal of this place."

"Maybe there is no appeal," he yawned.

"Very funny. Although how anyone can live without fresh bagel and coffee delivery is beyond me," she said, crouching down to examine a weed. "Sorry for waking you. I just had a break and forgot what it's like to be human and sleep past six."

"No, it's fine. I have an early shoot at the museum. Romero's in town for his exhibit's opening, and I have the pleasure of doing the meet and greet and a couple publicity shots. Where are you by the way?"

Summer stood up and looked around. Rolling hills, a hulking silhouette of the huge stone barn, and a tree line whispering with the warm breeze. "I'm in the middle of a soybean field."

"Sounds horrible."

"It's really kind of beautiful. You're going to love shooting out here."

"Are you drunk on raw goat's milk?"

"Very funny, smart ass."

Nikolai yawned again in her ear. "How are you feeling otherwise? Are you taking it easy or being an idiot and pushing yourself too hard?"

"I feel... good." She really did. She was exhausted every night, but it was a satisfying fatigue that came from using her body. "There might be something to be said about not sitting at a desk ten hours a day."

"Just make sure you're not overdoing it."

"Yeah, yeah."

"I miss your face," he told her. "Don't fall for a farmer and forget to come home, okay?"

She thought of the other night. Of holding Carter's hand in the moonlight. "I'll do my best."

Summer tucked her phone back into her jeans and finished her crop inspection before heading toward the little barn. Her job on this warm and bright Saturday—because apparently farmers didn't take the weekend off—was to help Phoebe distribute the first shares of produce to their subscribers.

All 250 of them.

Phoebe had beaten her to the barn and was already double-checking the alphabetical list of subscribers against the contents of their crates.

"Good morning," Summer called to her. "How's Franklin?"

Phoebe pinked up and smiled. "Oh, he's just wonderful. Thanks for asking. How are my boys doing with it all?"

"I think they'll be okay," Summer said evasively. They would be eventually. "Carter doesn't seem to have any issues with him."

"Carter doesn't have any issues with anyone," Phoebe said, checking off another box. "It's the other two I'm worried about."

"They'll come around. They love you."

"And I love them. Even when they act like fools. So I hear our Joey slapped the crap out of Jax."

"She didn't seem to appreciate his greeting," Summer said, sliding the big barn door open to let in the sunshine.

"Those two are meant for each other," Phoebe said, shaking her head. "They just don't know it yet."

"Maybe the Beautification Committee will work their magic," Summer suggested.

"I hear they have someone else in their sights," Phoebe winked.

"Can't you set them straight? I mean, they have to understand that I'm only here for a few days. And in a professional capacity. I can't just date the people I write about." Summer crossed her arms in exasperation. "Why didn't they pick someone from town?"

"Because my son doesn't look at the girls in town like he

looks at you," Phoebe said, smiling at her clipboard. "If I were you, I wouldn't fight the Beautification Committee. They usually know what they're doing. Nice boots, by the way."

Summer glanced down at her feet. She was happy to put them on every day, and when she looked at them, she thought of Carter. And her heart did a little flip flop every time those gray eyes met hers.

"Here comes our first customer," Phoebe nodded toward the pickup that pulled up to the barn. "Let the games begin."

~

IT WAS EXHAUSTING WORK, but Summer enjoyed it. People filtered in and out all day. Some in beat-up pickups, others in leather-seated SUVs. All, however, knew the Pierce family.

Blue Moon was an extension of that family, Summer saw, as Phoebe and then Jax greeted friends and doled out boxes of leafy greens and fresh produce. The residents were abuzz with the return of Jackson Pierce. The welcome was much warmer than the one Joey had given him.

Summer caught more than a few "innocent" questions about where Joey was and if she was happy to have him back. With a lifetime of experience avoiding personal questions, Jax skillfully evaded even the most persistent visitors.

They were into their last hour of pick-up when a Mrs. Elvira Eustace popped by in her Prius.

"It's a shame about Carson, isn't it?" she whispered conspiratorially to Phoebe.

"What trouble has he gotten himself into now?" Phoebe asked, rearranging the last few crates.

"He broke his leg yesterday being a damn fool," Elvira sighed, studying a radish. "He was trying to clean the gutter on his front porch, and off that ladder he fell. Right into the hydrangeas."

"That stubborn-headed farmer. He's what? Eighty years old?"

"Eighty-one last February," Elvira corrected, smoothing down her salt and pepper curls. "Eighty-one and still climbing around on ladders. I guess that's what happens when your kids grow up and move away."

"Who's going to help him out on the farm?" Phoebe frowned.

"He's got a son and a nephew flying in next week. He was planning to harvest this weekend. I'm afraid he's going to try to get it done himself with that big ol' cast."

Phoebe turned to Summer. "Summer, do me a favor and track down Carter, will you?"

Summer hurried off in search of the man who had been conspicuously absent from the day.

She found him taking soil samples of the cornfield.

"Are you hiding out here?"

"Yes."

"I didn't see Willa or the Berkowiczes today."

"There's others," he paused and took a swig from his water bottle. "So what's up? Are you done already?"

"No, we still have half an hour for pick-ups. But your mom wants you. She's talking to Elvira about someone named Carson."

"I heard he broke his leg."

"How did you hear out here in the middle of a field?"

"I joined that stupid fucking Facebook group."

Summer snickered. "Come on. You can walk back with me."

"And set off the town rumor mill? By the way, since I took you for ice cream the other night, they're predicting a

November wedding. You'd better walk ten paces in front of me and pretend you don't know me."

They returned to the barn, and it took Carter a good five minutes to work his way through the greetings before he made it to his mother. "This is why I don't do pick-up day," he muttered to Summer.

"There's my favorite son," Phoebe grinned, tucking her arm through Carter's. "What are you doing tomorrow?"

13

Blue Moon residents mobilized as fast as, if not faster than, the National Guard. They converged on Carson's property in droves Sunday morning.

Those with strong backs and a working knowledge of farming equipment broke off with the Pierce brothers to tackle the winter wheat harvest. The rest descended on the house. Carson, who was indeed 81 and adorable in a John Deere hat and suspenders, was put in a seat of honor under the great oak in his front yard and waited on hand and foot while his house was cleaned top to bottom.

Summer washed windows and weeded the flowerbeds. She even helped Joey finish cleaning the gutters that Carson had started.

A pack of teenagers mowed the vast expanse of lawn while broken fence posts and loose shingles were replaced. Freezer meals aplenty arrived and were safely tucked away in the kitchen and the basement chest freezer.

Elvira stopped by with eight gallons of lemonade and six pairs of sweatpants with one leg cut off at the knee to accommodate Carson's cast.

Rainbow Berkowicz popped in to lend a hand with his bill paying for the month while her husband Gordon cheerfully edged the flowerbeds and watered plants. Children chased the barn cats around the front yard and played on the tire swing that had seen more than one generation in its time.

By evening, everyone was tired, dirty, and happy. And Carson was speechless.

Franklin left his restaurant early and showed up on the farm with an SUV full of Italian catering, paper plates, and plastic utensils. A gentleman named Julius drove up in a ying-yang painted delivery van and dropped off a keg, several cases of soda, and even a few boxes of wine "for the ladies."

A full-blown, town-wide picnic was being set up on the lawn when Carter and the rest of the harvesting crew ambled out of the barn to give Carson an update.

"You're all set," Carter said, clapping the farmer on the shoulder. "It's all in the bins, and we'll come out and check the moisture levels."

Summer watched Carson's throat work as he blinked back tears. "I thank ya. I just can't thank everyone enough."

He was immediately surrounded by women of all ages fussing over him. Someone brought out a guitar and someone else a harmonica, and in no time, there was music.

Summer found Beckett sitting on the tailgate of a truck eating a plate full of pasta.

"That's Franklin's baked ziti you're inhaling there," she warned him.

"Damn it." Beckett paused. He frowned at his plate, shrugged, and went back to devouring it. "Maybe he's not totally a horrible human being."

Phoebe, having the hearing of a mother of three boys, snuck up next to him and kissed him on the cheek. "That's my favorite son."

Summer wandered further across the lawn to the edge of the shadows where grass met field. Here she could watch the happenings. Her throat was tight and her heart full.

Community.

That is what she had been missing. With the article and possibly even beyond the words she had been searching for.

There were no strangers here. Only neighbors helping neighbors and having a damn good time doing it.

On impulse, she pulled out her phone and dialed.

Her mother answered cheerfully. "Hello?"

"Hi, Mom."

Annette Lentz's voice brightened. "Summer! I didn't have my reading glasses on. I couldn't see who was calling."

"How's Alaska?"

"Breathtaking," she sighed. "Your father had me up at six this morning to catch a sunrise flight with the bush pilot he's interviewing."

"How is Dad?" Summer asked, already feeling the slick mix of guilt and anger churn in her stomach.

"Oh, you know your father," she said lamely.

Summer certainly did.

"Now, where are you? I see on your blog that you're on a farm somewhere?"

At least one of her parents was interested enough to follow what she was doing. "I'm on an assignment for the magazine. It's a piece on an organic family farm upstate."

"That farmer doesn't look like any of the ones I grew up around," her mom teased. Annette had grown up in a small Pennsylvania farming community north of Philadelphia.

"He isn't like anything I imagined," Summer confessed.

Her mother must have detected something in her tone. "Are you seeing anyone?"

"I don't really have time, Mom. Work has been so busy."

"Work, work, work. You're so much like your father."

The words were both balm and burn.

"Well, you eventually wore him down and got him to take a good look at you," Summer reminded her. "Maybe someday someone will wear me down, too." Her parents, both career-oriented professionals, hadn't met and married until their mid-thirties.

"Darling, as long as you're happy. That's all I want. I don't care what it looks like. Just be happy."

Summer smiled. "I will do my very best."

"Good girl. Now, do you want to talk to your father?"

Summer's stomach plunged. She wanted to say no. She wanted to end the call on a high note. She was tired of trying. Tired of disappointing.

"Oh, he must have just ducked out. Phil!" Annette yelled for her husband.

"Don't bother him, Mom," Summer insisted. She imagined her father had left the room the second he heard Annette offer him up for a conversation. Maybe he was tired of the disappointment, too.

"Well, I'd better go," Summer said with forced brightness.

"Thanks for calling, sweetie. Talk soon."

Summer hung up and stuffed the phone into her back pocket.

"Now you're the one hiding." The voice behind her, so familiar in such a short time, sent a warm tingle up her spine.

Summer turned to Carter, his face shadowed in the waning evening light.

"Hi," she said quietly.

"Did you get anything to eat?" he asked.

"I'm not really hungry," Summer admitted.

Carter nodded, studying her. "Your parents?"

"Eavesdrop much?"

"I live in Blue Moon. They teach a class on it in junior high."

"It was my mom. I was just checking in with her."

"And that made you sad?"

It was unsettling to have someone see her. *Really* see her. In the city, she could walk down the street sobbing and not be bothered by a soul. But here with Carter she wasn't just another stranger.

"My relationship with them is... strained." She chose her words carefully.

"Let's take a walk." Carter slung his arm over her shoulders and led her further away from the house.

She let him. For just a few minutes, she wanted to pretend to have someone to lean on. Someone she could trust. She wondered if Carter felt that way about all of Blue Moon.

"You're all very lucky to have each other. I never knew it could be like this. Back home, we don't trust anyone. Not our neighbors, not our co-workers, and certainly not strangers on the street. Sometimes not even family. We kind of operate like everyone else could be out to get us."

"It's not healthy, seeing everyone as a potential threat," he ventured.

Summer nodded. "You know, I've never met my next door neighbor. And the only conversation I've had with the lady across the hall is when she accused me of stealing her cat."

"Did you?"

Summer smiled. "No. Her ex-husband did. But look what you have. A whole town turned out today to help a man who didn't even ask for it. And now it's a party with music, and food, and a campfire." She gestured toward a clump of Mooners who were dancing and swaying and giggling under a cloud of blue smoke.

Carter sniffed the air. "Honey, that's not a campfire."

"Oh."

"What about your family? Do you have siblings?" he asked.

She shook her head. "Only child."

"What are your parents like?"

"They're RV-ing in Alaska right now."

"That's what they're *doing*. That's not what they're *like*."

Summer weighed her words. "They're retired. My mom was a social worker, and my dad was a journalist turned journalism professor. We used to be really close, my dad and I. He'd read the Sunday paper to me like it was a bedtime story. He was old-school journalism, you know? Independent, unbiased, advertisers and politics be damned."

"What happened?" Carter kept their pace slow and even as they followed the edge of the field.

"I was supposed to follow in his footsteps. Be the *New York Times'* second-generation Lentz."

"But you didn't want that?"

She shook her head. "So much had changed in journalism by then. It was one of the reasons my father left the paper and started teaching. Where he saw a decline in print, I saw an opportunity for growth on the digital side. Newspapers weren't quick to change, so I set my sights on magazines. They were faster to adapt to the demand for digital resources."

She closed her eyes, remembering the conversation. The argument. The hurt.

"I expected some resistance from him. You can't expect a newsman to just forget about the newsprint that's been in his blood for twenty-five years. But he dug in so deep, and I didn't expect it. He was very disappointed when I shifted my focus in college and even more so when I took the job at *Indulgence*."

Disappointed was a kind word.

When she changed her major her junior year, he cut off

her college funding after a spectacular Thanksgiving dinner argument. Phil Lentz was used to getting his way. Used to having his little girl agree with his well-formed and well-communicated opinions.

But didn't she deserve to stand on her own two feet?

"How are things now?" Carter skimmed his hand down her arm.

"Chilly," she said, with a grim smile. "A little better now that we don't see each other twice a month for Sunday dinner anymore. Less disappointment to be felt by all."

"He's disappointed in you and your choices, but does your father know that he disappointed you?"

Leave it to Carter to get to the heart of the matter.

She shook her head. "No. When he refused to listen to my reasons for going into magazine work, I refused to keep defending my decision. We don't talk much now." She looked up and out over the gentle shadows of hills and fields.

She leaned into Carter, wanting to feel that solid presence.

Summer smiled sadly. "I bet your mom wouldn't let something like that happen."

Carter's laugh was soft. "No, Phoebe Pierce would not stand for estrangement. She'd show up at your door every day for as long as it would take for you to let her in again."

"She's a wonderful person."

"We are very lucky to have her. Lucky to have had our dad, too. Together, they were something. I think that's why none of us have gotten close to marriage yet. They set the bar pretty damn high, and none of us want to settle for anything less."

"I love how close you all are," Summer said, envy in her tone. "Sometimes in a city of millions I feel like I'm all alone. Maybe more often than not." She looked down at her feet.

Why was she spilling all this?

"Summer, you're never alone," Carter's grip on her tightened. "You're an honorary Mooner. We don't let anyone be alone. This group of well-meaning weirdos got me through a lot."

"Like what?" She liked the way she felt with his arm around her. Liked the way her name sounded on his lips.

"Like when I came home with bullet holes and anxiety so bad I still felt like I was in the field."

They stopped walking and Summer turned to face him. "I'm so sorry, Carter."

"PTSD, they said it was. But I got through it, thanks to these people," he jerked a thumb behind them. "Beckett would get in the ring with me when I felt like I couldn't fight back the shadows alone. Fighting someone felt better to me than fighting something. Those first few weeks back were a nightmare. One or both of us was constantly sporting a black eye." He shook his head at the memory.

"I had help on the farm, help with the house. Mom made me lunch every day and stayed until I was better. Jax called every damn day for six weeks straight. And Joey got me on horseback. The closer I got to animals, to nature, to real people the more pieces of my soul I got back."

Summer laid a hand on his arm. "What was it like? The PTSD."

He looked out into the darkness. "Like everything was a threat. Like there was no hope or happiness. Just a constant state of alert. And I was angry. It took a long time to feel anything but anger or fear. But through that, I learned that we're stronger together."

Carter put his hands on her waist and pulled her in.

"How do you feel now?" she breathed, her heart hammering in her ears.

He threaded his fingers through her hair, settling his thumbs under her chin. "Let's find out."

This time there was no wavering. No second-guessing.

The sweet, gentle pressure of his lips on hers had Summer bringing her hands to his chest where her fingers gripped his shirt. He smelled like sunshine and grain. He tasted like nothing she had ever sampled before.

Carter teased her mouth open, and Summer sighed into the kiss as it deepened. The sweetness slowly began to melt into something more intense. One of his hands dove into her hair and fisted there. Her breath caught in her throat.

"God, I love your hair," he whispered against her mouth. "And your eyes. When you look at me, it just guts me."

She shivered against him and he pulled her in tighter. He took ownership of her mouth under the spring moon. Her heart stuttered and tumbled as the kiss turned gentle again.

His hands streaked up her sides, down her back holding her to him. His warmth penetrated the chill of the evening. She wanted more. So much more.

"Will you take me home?" she whispered. "Please."

"Yes."

14

*C*arter was careful to touch only her hand on the way home. He was worried if he touched her that he'd pull over and ruin what should be something special. She deserved romance, stars and candles, and soft words, not the backseat of a Jeep.

He didn't want to scare her with the ferocity of his need. His blood was pumping in hot, hard thrums. And still, he only stroked her thumb with his.

He eased up to the front of the house, fearful that his heart would explode before he got his hands on her. Summer unfastened her seatbelt and leaned across to kiss him. It was all the invitation the beast inside needed.

Their mouths met in a tangle, and the whimper from the back of her throat had him cruising his hands over her curves. She perched on the console, working him from his jeans while her mouth devoured his.

Her slim hands circled his shaft and pumped. Once. Twice. He felt the wetness seep out and knew he was in trouble.

"Christ, Summer," he hissed.

He pulled her hand free and returned his focus to her mouth. So much sweetness and need. It tempted him, tortured him.

When her hand skimmed down his body again, he dragged her across the console.

Trying to get out, he found he was still wearing his seatbelt. And he'd left the Jeep running. After yanking off the belt and turning the key, Carter pulled her out the door. Summer wrapped those long, long legs around his waist, and he leaned her against the fender of the Jeep.

"I can't get enough of your mouth," he murmured. He pressed his lips to hers as his hands cruised over her body. The slim hips, the flat stomach, her soft, round breasts. Her fingers threaded into his hair and gripped as he crushed his mouth to hers.

Carter carried her to the porch. The front door was unlocked, but it seemed so far away.

She unwrapped her legs and slid down his body. When her boots hit the porch, she dropped to her knees and with no warning took him into her mouth.

It happened so fast he had no time to brace himself. Those soft lips wrapped around him, taking the head of his shaft into the back of her throat. She moaned, and the vibration nearly sent him over the edge.

"Summer, wait—"

But she didn't listen. That hot mouth slicked over him again and again, drawing him deeper into heaven. He was too close.

Carter grabbed her hair and yanked her up. "Not yet, baby." He needed her lips off his dick so he could touch every inch of her, discover all her secrets. He wanted to taste her, stroke her, worship her.

He dragged her to the porch swing, unbuttoning, unzipping as they went. He shoved her down on the swing and dropped to his knees. Her boots were first. He tossed one and then the other over his shoulder. Next came the jeans. He worked them down her hips, careful to leave her underwear in place.

He had plans for that lace.

Carter freed one leg from her jeans and spread her thighs. In the moonlight, the plum scrap was the only barrier between him and what he desired most of all. He pressed a kiss to it and groaned when Summer's legs wrapped around his shoulders, drawing him in.

"Look at me." His voice was jagged as gravel.

Summer's gaze, wide and glassy, met his. He tugged her underwear to the side and slid two fingers into her tight center.

She closed her eyes on a gasp, arching against him.

"Open your eyes, Summer." He wanted to watch her as he ravaged her. Wanted to know the thoughts behind her eyes were only of him, his hands and the pleasure they brought.

Her lashes fluttered open, and he withdrew slowly before driving back inside. She was so tight around his fingers. It made him grit his teeth to imagine what it would feel like to take her.

He pulled out of her, brought his fingers to his mouth, and tasted. She whimpered and strained against him, needing more.

Carter slid his hands under her perfect ass and lifted her to his mouth. His tongue followed the sweet, slick folds to her sensitive bud. He flicked it gently and heard her sob. His mouth moved lower until he found her center. With a deft thrust of his tongue, he tasted heaven.

Her thighs quivered. He tasted and licked, thrusting just enough to make Summer cry for more.

She was so close already. He needed to take her over the edge. "I need you to come, baby." He sheathed his fingers in her again as deep as they could go and stroked her with his tongue. She writhed against him.

"Carter!" There was panic there, but he held tight and continued his merciless pillage.

He felt the flutter around his fingers and groaned as she let go. Her moans made him ache to be inside her. His cock demanded he end this sweet torture. But not here.

Summer trembled as the orgasm blazed through her system. He watched her as it broke inside and wished he could capture and hold this moment forever.

"Carter?" she whispered, his name on her lips was a sigh.

He gently withdrew his fingers and gathered Summer to him, lifting her in his arms.

"Where are we going?"

"Upstairs," he said, his mouth playing over her lips as he wrestled the front door open. "Take off your shirt, baby."

Her fingers fumbled with the hem before yanking it over her head.

"Bra," he ordered.

Summer released the front clasp and the matching lace fell away. Carter lifted her higher until his mouth found her breast. His lips locked on a sensitive peak, and he began to suck. Long, deep pulls that made his cock painfully harder. She gasped in pleasure. Wrapping her arms around him, she held him to her breast.

He started up the stairs, blind to everything but Summer's taste, Summer's scent.

His shaft was nestled between her legs, those wet folds teasing him with dark promise. He groaned as every step stroked him closer to orgasm.

Finally they stumbled through his bedroom door. He

released her breast long enough to dump her on the bed and strip out of his boots and jeans. Summer's slim hands worked his shirt up and over his head. Only his briefs were left, and he was already halfway out of them.

He settled her back against the pillows to feed again. He latched onto her breast again to suckle. As he devoured her, Summer found his shaft again. She began to stroke him.

He wasn't going to last long. Not with the grip she had on him. And not with the noises she made. Soft little whimpers that went straight to his throbbing dick.

He needed to be inside her, surrounded by her, part of her.

Shifting, he positioned himself at her center, his shaft begging to be buried in her. "Baby, are you ready?"

"God, yes!" Her hands fisted the sheet. "Please, Carter."

He said a prayer of thanks and slid into her inch by sweet inch until he was completely sheathed in her wet heat.

She was everything he'd been missing.

Summer drew her knees up, and he clenched his jaw at the sensation the movement caused. His instinct was to plow into her over and over again, filling her with his seed. He was going to humiliate himself if he didn't get a grip.

"Oh my God!" The panic in her voice cut through the haze of lust. "Carter, we forgot a condom. I'm not on birth control."

Shit.

"Fuck."

In his thirty years, he had never been so caught up that he forgot protection. Not even at sixteen when he had talked Ally Lynch into taking off her clothes in her daddy's barn.

"Stop moving baby, or there won't be time for a condom," he grimaced. He had condoms, didn't he? If there was a God in heaven, there was a box somewhere. Under the sink in the cabinet maybe?

Carter clenched every muscle in his body and slowly

pulled out. Fighting every instinct he had to slam back into her, he ran for the bathroom. He gutted the cabinet, dumping cleaning supplies and bathroom miscellany onto the floor before he found the box in the back corner.

"Thank you," he whispered. He grabbed two and hurried back to the bedroom. Summer was on her knees on the bed.

"Hurry, Carter." Her voice was a breathless plea.

His cock jerked as he climbed back onto the bed.

He ripped one of the foil packets open and rolled it onto his shaft as quickly as his shaking hands would allow. The second it was on, Summer was dragging him over her. He didn't give her any time to prepare. He entered her with a violent thrust, filling her. There was no stopping him this time. He pulled out and slammed back into her.

Her muscles clenched him. A slick, velvet vice.

Her breasts trembled with the force of every thrust. Hands gripping him, pulling him down against her. Hard nipples teased his chest. The pace he set was furious.

She was made to take him, he thought as Summer let him ride her into oblivion.

Her nails dug into his back. That little hint of pain only pushed him harder.

He felt her quicken around him. The beginning of her orgasm was all it took to send him over the edge.

His balls tightened, and he emptied into her with a force he had never known as she shattered around him.

Summer brought her hands to his face, and they watched each other as they came together.

15

Carter recognized that, though it had been a while since he'd last had sex, it had never been like this. And he would never be the same again.

He rolled off Summer and, gathering her close, pulled her into his side. He couldn't get close enough. Not without feeling her from the inside. Her soft silvery blonde hair cascaded over his shoulder and chest like a blanket. "Are you okay? Did I hurt you?"

Summer nuzzled in to his neck and sighed contentedly. "I feel like I exploded into a million pieces. Like a starburst."

Carter stroked her back. "I'm sorry about the condom. I'm not usually in such a hurry," he murmured.

He felt her smile against his neck. "I should have told you earlier I wasn't on the pill. I wasn't exactly thinking clearly either. It was amazing, Carter. You're amazing."

He kissed the top of her head. "Are you sure you're all right? I wasn't very in control there."

She pressed a kiss to his throat. "It was perfect. I've never felt that way before. So craved, so desperate." Her fingers trailed across his chest and stalled. "Is this where you were shot?" she whispered, fingers gently skimming scars. One on his shoulder, one over his ribs.

Carter grasped her fingers and brought them to his lips. "Yeah."

She shifted over him and dropped a gentle kiss to each scar.

"What about this?" she asked, tracing a finger over the scar that split his eyebrow.

"That's from Beckett shoving me out of the hayloft when we were kids. Landed on a pitchfork."

"Oh, my God."

"It's okay. I got him back by accidentally slicing his leg open with electric hedge trimmers."

"Your poor mother. It's a wonder any of you survived."

"Farm-raised kids are tough."

"Are you saying city kids aren't?" Eyes still closed, she pinched him.

"I would never insinuate such a thing," he teased.

"Good because I would have to hail a cab and run your fine ass over," she yawned. And on that threat, his sweet Summer fell asleep.

Carter let his thoughts drift. He had told her more than he intended to about his experiences. The PTSD and recovery weren't secrets, but he wasn't usually so open about them. After having dragged his still-grieving family with him through a rocky recovery, it was nice to let the past stay the past.

Wounded didn't have to mean broken.

He had moved forward, grateful for the support of his family and community. It had been a battle, just as much as the ones he fought with his men. But, as in war, he learned that there was strength in numbers.

After a few empty flings when he came home, Carter had made the conscious decision to give up on the meaningless and focus on meaning. He redoubled his efforts on the farm and gave Phoebe the confidence in him to move into her own place. It was a gift to them both. A new start, a new hope for the future.

And now his family was back together—for as long as Jax deemed fit—the farm was humming along, and he had Summer wrapped around him. This was no fling. This was the beginning of something special. If she wanted it to be. He wanted what his parents had shared. A partnership, a friendship, and something so much more. He could see having it with her.

Carter drifted with the memories of his parents until the scene in his head changed to one of gray and dirt. Of huts and cold.

He clutched his M16 and held up his left hand in a fist. The men behind him halted.

"It's clear," came the dispassionate voice of his second in command in his ear.

He signaled his men forward, advancing toward the adobe walls of the complex looming in front of them in the darkness.

"Hold," Hawkeye's voice warned him.

Carter and his men flattened themselves onto the ground. "Got eyes on two guards on top of the wall."

"Take the shot," Carter ordered, his breath puffing out in a silvery cloud.

Even with the silencer, his well-trained ears caught the sound of bullets striking their targets.

"Clear," Hawkeye said calmly. Just another day in Afghanistan.

Carter's team silently pressed forward to the walls. They secured two ropes to the top and scaled the wall in silence.

Carter was the last up and the first to move forward. Scanning the courtyard below, he spotted another guard. He signaled to the man on his right, Hector "Ninja" Ramirez. Ninja moved down the wooden stairs like a wraith. Sticking to the shadows, the guard never saw him coming. He collapsed into the darkness of death.

With the courtyard clear, Carter moved his team forward toward the small mud building on the right. According to their intel, the target was still inside, and his gut agreed.

He signaled to the two men on his left. They broke formation and moved to the door of the other building. They would take both buildings simultaneously.

He felt the adrenaline surge through his system, knew his men felt the same. It was always the same no matter how many doors they breached, no matter how many buildings they cleared. There was always danger.

Carter gave the signal, and both doors were smashed down within the span of a heartbeat. He was over the threshold, gun up and ready, before the wood had hit the ground. A quick sweep of the dim room, and he was moving to the back room. "Front clear," he announced and heard Paul give the same report from next door.

The flimsy door was locked, but a well-placed boot had it bouncing off its hinges.

"Weapons down," he shouted in Pashto. He sensed Ninja on his side. Laser sights focused on the foreheads of the two men in robes clutching semi-automatic pistols. Their beards were long and unkempt. "Put your weapons down, now," he said, switching to Uzbek.

He heard the cry, a terrified wail, and shifted his sights to the corner. A little girl, no more than six or seven cowered on the floor.

"Get the girl," Carter ordered Ninja.

The shot that rang out had Carter's heart stopping as the little girl's wails ceased instantaneously. The only sound that remained was the horrible, wheezing laughter.

$\sim$

CARTER'S BODY jerked hard in his sleep, jolting Summer awake.

"No!" It was a shout of despair, of anger, of horror.

She grabbed him by the shoulders. "Carter, wake up! Carter!"

"No." This time it was a whisper of pain.

"Carter!" she shouted his name. Straddling him, she shook him. "Please wake up."

He was drenched with sweat, every muscle in his body vibrated. In the moonlight, she saw his eyes flit open. There were tears in them.

"Summer?"

She held him to her chest. "You scared the life out of me." She pressed her lips to the top of his head. "Are you okay?"

She felt the roughness of his beard against the skin of her chest. His mouth scorched a trail over her breasts. And when his mouth closed over her nipple, she felt his cock stir to life under her.

"Tell me what to do," she shuddered as adrenaline turned to need.

He answered her with his mouth, drawing deeply in pulls that she felt to her very core. His erection swelled against her, parting her already slick folds, probing. Summer moaned. How could she want him so desperately, so fiercely?

She caught a glimpse of the foil packet on the nightstand

and reached for it. Her breast released from his mouth with a smacking sound.

"Hang on." She soothed him with her voice, with her hands. Ripping open the packet she shifted to guide the condom over the broad head already wet with need. Her fingers trembled as she rolled it down his thick shaft.

Carter groaned as she gripped his length.

She climbed back up and leaning forward positioned his crown at her entrance. Summer leaned forward to grip the headboard and let her hips sink down onto him, taking him into her until she was stretched tight. Full, whole, she gasped.

She lifted her hips and slammed down onto him. A cry tore from her throat as she began to ride. Her breast brushed his face as she moved over him, and he reared up to take her soft, ripe flesh into his mouth.

Summer's knuckles whitened on the headboard. There were too many sensations warring for her attention. His mouth at her breast, the impossible fullness of taking him into her. He stretched her so tight, she felt every inch of him as he moved in and out of her.

What was building between them was bigger than them both. This wasn't just sex. This was a meeting of souls.

She felt thousands of delicate muscles fluttering around him as she sank down his throbbing shaft again and again. His hands found their way to her hips, and he slammed her down on him.

"Carter." His name tore through her. His mouth released her breast, and as she cried out, she found the other aching with need for his attention. It was too much. As he drew her nipple into his mouth, Summer came in an uncontrolled explosion. Carter grunted against her breast, his hips flexing as her orgasm ripped his out of him. He flexed into her again and again he spilled his hot seed into her until there was nothing left.

Shaking, she collapsed on him.

"Thank you," he whispered against the velvet skin of her shoulder. "Thank you."

16

---

*C*arter woke before the alarm as the sun crested the horizon. It was a new day. One begun with a sleeping Summer in his arms.

He remembered. The dream, the... after.

Usually when a nightmare gripped him before dawn, he would wake shaky, his head aching. It would be a bad day, maybe two. But this morning began warm and bright for him. And he owed it to the woman clinging to his chest.

She had been his shelter, his protection last night. She drove out the dark memories and brought him to the light of a new day.

Another sign. He wouldn't forget that.

He pressed a kiss to the top of her head and ran his fingertips from her shoulder to her hip and back again. Her skin was the silkiest of cashmeres.

She stirred, snuggling closer. "Carter," she murmured against his chest. He occupied her dreams, and that had the last tightness in his chest loosening.

He rolled, gently shifting her to her back.

A frown marred her pretty face as she slowly fought her

way to awake. Her eyes fluttered open, and he grinned at the confusion he saw.

Recognition, remembrance, had her sitting bolt upright, her eyes darting around the room.

"Oh thank God! It wasn't a dream," she said, flopping back down on the pillows. She turned to him. "I was afraid I had sex dreams about you all last night and I'd have to play it cool all day long."

Carter laughed, a booming sound that bounced off the rafters in the ceiling.

"Speaking of dreams," she was back to frowning again. "What was that last night?"

Carter leaned over and kissed her on the mouth. "Nothing to worry about. Just some old demons trying to get out."

She cupped her hands to his face, her expression serious. "Is everything okay?"

"Everything is very, very good. I promise." Carter brought her hand to his mouth and kissed her palm. "Are you hungry?"

"Starving."

They dressed and went downstairs where they found Summer's t-shirt and bra on the stairs.

"How about you start breakfast while I hide the evidence?" she suggested.

"Teamwork," Carter nodded.

When she returned to the kitchen, she found him prepping omelets and frying potatoes.

"We should probably talk about this," Summer said, perching on the island and watching him move between cutting board and stove.

"What part of 'this' should we start with?" Carter asked, moving between her legs and kissing her.

She purred as his lips found hers and sighed with regret as

she put a hand on his chest to push him back. "Expectations. It's important to talk about expectations," she said breathlessly.

Carter grinned. "I expect the rest of your time here to be a lot like last night."

"That would be good," Summer nodded. "Very good."

She bit her lip. "What about after this week?"

He was going to lay it all out. No sense in hiding it. "I'm not willing to let you leave here without knowing when I'm going to see you again."

She flushed and smiled down at her hands. "I'll be back in a month with Niko for the photo shoot."

"I need to see you before then."

"Maybe we could meet halfway?" she suggested. "Spend the night together somewhere?"

"I like that," he nodded.

"So..." She trailed off.

"While I'm seeing you I won't be seeing anyone else," he said, squeezing her hips. "I expect the same from you."

"Definitely a deal breaker," she agreed. "So does this mean we're in a relationship?" She didn't sound as casual as she tried to look.

"Let's call it the very early exploratory stage," Carter said with a grin.

"And as such, we should probably keep it private. At least as private as possible," Summer suggested.

Carter thought of his mother, his brothers, of the Beautification Committee. "Definitely."

"Also, I want to keep this," she said gesturing between them, "separate from the article. Mixing business with pleasure might be more common on this side of journalism, but I've never done it before, and I'd prefer if the office didn't find out I used this trip as a sexcation with my new boyfriend."

"Boyfriend. I kind of like the sound of that," Carter said, leaning in for another taste.

"You're going to burn the eggs," she whispered.

"Fuck the eggs," his mouth was zeroing in on hers when the front door flew open. They jumped apart. Carter moved around the island to see what the commotion was.

Jax stomped back to the kitchen, his arms full. He was still wearing pajama pants. "I'm moving in. If I have to listen to Mom and Franklin through the wall—"

Carter smacked him with the spatula. "I'm going to stop you right there before I throw up or kill you."

Jax looked at Summer on the counter and back at Carter, his eyes narrowed. "Christ. Everyone but me is having sex."

Carter watched the blush flood Summer's cheeks as her hands flew to her hair, seeking the evidence that gave them away. She did have sex hair, he thought with a grin. Well-earned sex hair.

"What do you mean—" Summer started innocently. Until Jax dumped one of her boots and her jeans on the island.

"Found these on the porch."

Carter tossed Summer the spatula and dragged Jax out the side door.

"What the hell are you doing here, Jax?" he asked when they were outside.

"I told you, I can't stand listening to Mom and—"

Carter cut him off. "I mean in Blue Moon. What the hell are you doing in Blue Moon?"

His brother shoved his hands in the pockets of his plaid pants. "It's a long story."

"Are you in trouble?"

"What? No!" Indignation flared.

"You packed up and left in the middle of the night days after scaring the shit out of all of us. Joey was still in the hospital. You stayed away for all these years, and now you're just back?"

"I was eighteen. And an idiot. And I don't know how to apologize for that. There had to be more to the world than farming and Blue Moon."

"You wanted more. You found it," Carter said, crossing his arms. "Fancy house, beautiful women, four movies. Mr. Hollywood."

"And now that I've seen it and done it, I want this back. I can still write. I can write from anywhere. But I want to be here."

"What does that mean for Joey?"

"I want her back, too. Maybe more than all the rest of it."

"You broke her heart when you left. If you fuck that up again, Beckett and I are going to hunt you down and break your face."

"Fair enough," Jax nodded. "I'm not fucking it up again."

"Really? Because your whole 'Hey Joey, I'm back' thing didn't work out so well."

"She kissed me back before she hauled off and slapped me. It was worth it," Jax grinned. "So speaking of women. What's happening here?" He jerked his chin toward the house.

"With Summer?" Carter kept his tone neutral.

"Oh, don't even try that shit with me." Jax punched him in the shoulder. "I see the way your hairy face lights up whenever she's around."

Carter scuffed his big toe across the floorboards of the porch and smiled. "She's... something."

"It's good to see you happy."

"Well, I was until my little brother announced he was moving in."

"I'll work for room and board if that works for you. I think Mom needs her space."

"Don't start that again."

"You think you and Summer can contain your activities to the bedroom?"

"I'm not promising anything."

"Listen. There's something else I want to talk to you and Beckett about. Have time tonight?"

"Tonight? Yeah. Poker after? It's been a while."

"That would be good."

"I'll put out the word. In the meantime, you can take your pick between weeding the beans or figuring out why the tractor's stalling out."

"Dibs on the tractor. Just keep that demon hell spawn away from me."

"You mean sweet little Clementine?"

"I hate that fucking goat."

They went back inside, and Carter rescued the omelets from Summer's ministrations.

Jax was helping himself to coffee when the knock at the side door sounded. Joey ambled in, holding a travel coffee mug.

Carter shook his head. A week ago, he could have had breakfast buck-naked in the kitchen and enjoyed his solitude. Now he had a houseguest with benefits, a roommate, and Joey.

"Morning, Joey," Summer greeted her. Joey took one look at Summer and her gaze darted to Carter. She smirked.

Everyone's sex radar seemed to be working just fine today. He'd better avoid his mother. And anyone from town.

"Want some breakfast, Jojo?" Jax offered. "Carter's cooking."

Summer held her breath, and Carter braced for the retort.

But the war didn't come. "No, thank you," she said politely. "But I'll take some coffee."

She didn't make eye contact with Jax, but she did let him take the mug from her without braining him with it. Carter considered it progress. He winked at Summer. "Want to help me weed today, pretty girl?"

"Sure!" Those blue eyes sparkled at him, and he had to resist the urge to kiss her. He was going to take a hit on this one. A hard one. But it wasn't worth thinking about now.

Joey rolled her eyes at them.

Jax tightened the lid on her mug and handed it back. "Two sugars, right?"

She nodded briskly. "Thanks."

"We're playing poker tonight," Jax said, pressing his luck. "You in? It's been a while since I let you take my money."

Joey frowned and took a step back as if she was trying to avoid being cornered. "Summer and I are going out tonight."

"You are?" Carter and Jax asked in unison.

"Um, yes." Summer cast a furtive glance in Joey's direction. "We are."

❧

CARTER TEXTED Beckett about poker and put him in charge of contacting the usual suspects. He caught up with Jax that afternoon on the front porch after a very entertaining shower with Summer, during which they promised that no one else besides Jax and Joey would catch on to them.

Jax had brought a nice six-pack of brown ale with him from L.A., and since it was in his refrigerator, Carter had helped himself to one.

"Who's in for tonight?" Jax asked.

"The three of us plus Cardona and Fitz. Beckett's on his way over now so you can talk to us about this mystery thing you want to discuss."

"Okay. A sixth would be better," he said.

"Keep dreaming. There's no way Joey is sitting in on a game with your ass."

"I hate to suggest it," Jax said, "but I'm going to anyway since it will piss Beckett off and make Mom happy."

"Franklin?" Carter asked.

"Yeah."

"I'll see if he can come. Maybe he'll bring some lasagna or something."

"Good call. What do you think the girls are going to do tonight?" Jax asked, shooting a glance behind them at the house.

"Talk about us."

"That's what I was afraid of. Do you think Summer will put in a good word for me?"

"I think you could have the Dalai Lama and a children's choir put in a good word for you, but it wouldn't help your case with Joey," Carter said.

He put in the call to his mother, who relayed the message to Franklin.

"He's in, and he's bringing individual portions of ravioli with garlic bread," Carter said, hanging up.

"I'm starting to like this guy," Jax said.

Beckett arrived, lugging a case of beer. "What's that?" he asked, nodding at Carter's bottle.

"Little brother's brown ale."

"Nice."

"Help yourself," Jax called after him.

Beckett returned to the porch with his own bottle. "We have a sixth? You talk Joey into it?"

Jax grinned at Carter. "No, we figured we'd keep it testosterone only tonight."

"Meaning, Joey turned him down," Carter supplied.

"Naturally," Beckett nodded. "So who is it?"

"Well, you know how good that ziti was at Carson's?"

"You've got to be fucking kidding me! Franklin? Come on! I'd expect my brothers to at least support me here. And why is it *Franklin*, anyway? Why not Frank?"

"I don't know, *Beck*," Carter sneered.

"And why the hell do you look like you got some?" Beckett grumbled.

"How do I look like I got some?" Carter asked in exasperation.

"You have that smug look on your face, at least from what I can see of it. Summer?"

"I'm not talking about this. And leave my beard and Summer out of it."

"One of these days I'm going to sneak in here while you're sleeping and shave it off."

"Not while Summer's in his bed," Jax snickered.

"So it *was* Summer." Beckett was like a dog with a bone or a goat with Jax's pants.

Damn it. Carter and Summer weren't doing well with the whole secret thing.

"I'd appreciate it if you kept your stupid mouth shut about it. We're trying to keep this quiet while we figure things out," Carter said.

"I should have put money on it," Beckett muttered.

"I was going to," Jax said, taking his phone out. "But the odds weren't worth it."

"Don't even tell me this is on Facebook," Carter barked.

"Just messing with you," Jax said, slapping him on the back.

"Sometimes I hate you guys," Carter grumbled.

"Feeling's mutual," Beckett said.

Joey interrupted their bickering in her gleaming '67 pick-up.

She hopped out in curve-hugging jeans and a deep V-neck. Her hair, normally pulled back from her face, hung down her back in soft, loose waves.

"Close your mouth," Carter muttered to Jax, who was gaping at her like a fish.

"Play it a little cool at least," Beckett ordered.

"Summer ready yet?" She asked, crossing her arms and leaning against a beefy fender.

"I'm here! I'm coming!" Summer hustled out of the open front door. She was wearing some kind of tiny patterned shorts paired with her ankle-breaking sandals that showed off her legs. A body-hugging boat neck sweater didn't show any flesh but also didn't leave much to the imagination. Her blonde hair had a little curl to it and those full lips of hers were covered in a slick coat of gloss.

She paused in front of Carter, unsure what to do with an audience. "I'll see you later?" she asked a little breathlessly.

Carter gripped her by the shirt and yanked her in to him. Even in heels, she barely came to his shoulder. He saw the surprise, the quick burst of excitement, just before his mouth claimed hers.

"Oh, for Pete's sake—"

"Would you two knock it off?"

"For the love of—get a damn room!"

Carter pulled back, smiling when she followed. "Have a good time. Be safe."

Dazed, she would have stepped right off the porch if he hadn't caught her by the shoulders.

"Bye, Carter," she whispered.

"Bye, beautiful."

They drove off with Joey's truck leaving a plume of dust in

its wake. Carter watched them go. When he turned back to his brothers, they were both grinning like idiots.

"What?"

"Be safe, my little love muffin," Jax said in a voice a few octaves deeper than his own.

"I'll miss you, my handsome sex biscuit," Beckett said with a girlish giggle.

"Hey, asshole, that's your girl out there, too. They're gonna get a lot of attention together," Carter said, rubbing it in.

Jax frowned. "Maybe we should cancel the game?" he suggested.

Beckett slapped him in the back of the head. "Can you two stop thinking with your dicks for five whole seconds?"

"Why aren't you thinking with yours?" Jax asked. "You break it?"

"I've sworn off women for the rest of the year," Beckett sighed, taking a seat in one of the rocking chairs.

"What happened to what's her name? Judith? Judy?" Carter asked.

"Trudy. It was all fun and games until she starts telling everyone who'd listen to her that she's going to be first lady of Blue Moon. Like that's even a thing. Then she starts telling me how I'd make a great congressman."

"Like that's even a thing," Jax joked.

"She had her eyes on the prize. Only the prize wasn't me."

"How'd she take it?" Carter asked.

"Let's just say Cardona knows not to let her lurk near my place. She was a mean one." He shivered with the memory.

"Not all women can look adoringly at us like Summer looks at this guy," Jax said, batting his eyelashes.

"You guys are assholes," Carter sighed.

"It's in the DNA. We just learned it from our big bro. Didn't we, Jax?"

"I thought this was supposed to be bust on Beckett night?" Carter grumbled.

"There's plenty to go around," Beckett grinned. "So what the hell am I doing here early besides bringing beer?"

"Hollywood has something he'd like to discuss," Carter said, taking the chair next to Beckett. "You have the porch," he said with a sweeping gesture.

"Yeah, now don't fuck it up," Beckett warned him.

Jax leaned against the railing. "I've been thinking about coming home for a while. Since you two came out to visit last year."

"That was a good trip," Carter said, remembering.

"What was that beer you brewed? The coffee stout?" Beckett asked, taking a drag from the bottle. "That was a good one."

"That's why I'm back. I want to start a brewery. Here. With you."

"A brewery?" Carter repeated.

"More like a brew pub, I guess. We could do food, too. Farm to table stuff. People love that shit. We've already got the farm. We just need the table."

"Where exactly would this magical brewery be?" Beckett wondered.

"In the stone barn. It's just sitting there begging to be used. We could set up brewing equipment on the first level." He paced while he painted the picture. "We could turn part of the fields around it into parking. Those top two floors are big enough that we could host events. Weddings and parties and stuff."

"Sounds like you've thought a lot about this," Carter said.

"The idea is all well and good. But there's a hundred other things that have to be looked at," Beckett reminded him.

"There's permits, construction, suppliers, equipment, start-up capital, ownership." He ticked them off on his fingers.

"We'd own it outright. The three of us together. I've got capital. I've got more than enough cash."

Carter tipped his beer at Jax. "We could grow some of the hops here," he mused.

"Yes, we could." His brother grinned.

"This is something we're going to have to think about, talk about," Beckett said. "I need some time to wrap my head around all this."

"It's a big decision."

"And there's the question of how do we know you're not going to bail again?" Beckett asked.

Jax leveled his gaze at him. "I'm sticking."

"Then we'll talk about it," Carter decided.

17

"Since when did you start wearing lipstick?" Sheriff Donovan Cardona asked as he dumped two bags of chips on the island.

Carter swiped a hand over his mouth and swore. He'd spent the last thirty minutes with Summer's lip gloss smeared all over his mouth and neither of his brothers thought to mention it. Beckett and Jax snickered.

"Thanks. Thanks a lot, dicks." Carter grabbed a paper towel and started scrubbing.

"It's a nice color on you," Fitz offered.

Bill "Fitz" Fitzsimmons was closer to Franklin's age than the rest of them. Bald on top, he had an impressive braided rattail that hung down the back of his Save the Whales t-shirt. He owned and operated Bill's Books, a used bookstore that trended toward conspiracy titles. He had also smoked more than his fair share of pot back in the day.

Donovan had a theory that, in its earlier days, Bill's Books sold more weed than books. But after a short jail stay courtesy of Uncle Sam and the IRS, Fitz claimed to have righted his ways... mostly.

Donovan cracked open a soda.

"You on call tonight?" Carter asked his friend.

"Yeah, 'til midnight."

"I should have pocketed all of your money by then," Beckett said, tearing open one of the bags of chips.

"You wish," Donovan said, slapping the chips out of his hand and sending them flying.

"Hey! Keep it clean in here," Carter warned them.

"Yeah, he's got a live-in lover to impress now," Beckett said.

"You talking about Summer or Jax?" Donovan asked blandly.

Carter sighed. So much for secrets.

The doorbell rang and everyone yelled, "Come in."

Franklin, in a loud Hawaiian shirt and khakis, bustled in carrying six to-go boxes that smelled gloriously of garlic.

"I hope everyone is hungry," he said sliding the containers on the granite.

"Thanks for coming, Franklin," Carter said.

"Thanks for inviting me. It's been years since I've had a poker night."

"Running a restaurant probably doesn't leave a lot of spare time in your day," Beckett said, looking pointedly at Jax.

"Well, neither did raising three daughters. But I'd do both all over again if I could."

"That's good to hear," Jax said, shooting Beckett a sneer.

Beckett stalked into the great room.

Carter made the introductions, which in Blue Moon were purely perfunctory since everyone already knew everyone else by sight if not by name.

"You want a beer, Franklin?" Jax offered.

"I wouldn't say no."

Jax grabbed one out of the fridge and handed it over.

"Fitz, these aren't the special brownies like last time, are they?" Donovan demanded, frowning at the aluminum tray on the island.

"I told you a million times, man. I got the labels confused. It won't happen again." Fitz waited until Donovan took a brownie with him into the great room before picking up the tray and checking the bottom. He gave Carter a relieved thumbs up.

"Table's in there, gentlemen. Let's get some food and lose some money," Carter announced.

∼

JOEY PULLED into the gravel lot of Shorty's Sports Bar. "Is here okay?" she asked, shutting off the engine.

"Sure," Summer shrugged. With its stone and wood exterior, it reminded her of the Vermont ski lodge that her parents had taken her to one winter.

Joey hadn't been particularly talkative on the drive over, so Summer followed suit. She could deal with silence sometimes easier than she could a Chatty Cathy.

They took seats at the bar where the bartender greeted them both by name.

"Summer, this is Ed Avila."

"Nice to meet you, Summer. You can call me Shorty."

"Ed's the runt of the family," Joey explained.

Summer estimated his height to be at least six-feet four-inches. "My brothers are six-five and six-six," he explained. "What can I get you ladies to drink?"

Summer revised her martini order to a glass of wine when Joey ordered a beer.

"Aren't you going to ask me why we're here?" Joey said after Ed delivered their drinks.

"I figured you'd tell me in your own good time," Summer said, taking a sip of her house red.

"I guess it was a better option than me spending the evening alone and you spending it with a houseful of men whining about beards and chips."

"I'll drink to that," Summer nodded.

"You really like him, don't you?"

"Carter? I really do. What's not to like?"

"I'm just saying, you'd better really like him. He deserves good things, and if you're not one of them, you'd better move along."

"Point made. You two are close," Summer said. It was a statement of fact, not a question.

Joey shrugged. "Beckett, too. We grew up together."

"And what about Jax?"

Joey's eyes narrowed.

"Now before you go and shoot eye daggers at me, what's a ladies' night out if we aren't talking about emotionally scarring relationships?"

"I should have played poker instead," Joey grumbled.

"Very funny. Okay, let's skip over He Who Shall Not Be Named. What about you? What do you do outside of horses?"

"There's not much room for anything besides horses. Carter and I were just talking. It's time to hire on some part-time help in the stables. Operation's big enough now that it warrants the extra hands."

"What you do—what you all do—here is pretty impressive," Summer said.

"What about you? Do you spend all your time prancing around in heels in the office?"

Summer rolled her eyes. "I am deeply offended. I don't prance. I saunter. And yes. I work, and that's about it. Not enough time to do anything else."

"So what exactly does an associate editor for *Indulgence* do?" Joey asked, reaching behind the bar and snagging two food menus. "I Googled you, by the way."

It was Summer's turn to shrug. "I write, I edit, I proofread, I work with photographers, models, advertisers."

"Your blog," Joey said. "It's a lot different than the stuff you write for the magazine."

"You did do your research."

"The stuff you write in the magazine is like shiny and fluffy. Annoying. But I didn't hate the blog."

"Thanks?"

Joey shrugged. "Sorry."

"It's okay. It sort of sounded like a compliment. Moving on. How about families? Is that a safe topic?"

"As long as you're not asking me when I'm going to start one?"

"Do people still do that? Where I'm from, people think it's an accident if you have kids before forty."

"Different worlds."

"So, families?"

"My parents live an hour from here. They wanted to stay close to my sister and her kids."

"Are you close with them?"

She shrugged again. "I wouldn't call them up if I needed a place to stay, but we do the holiday thing, the birthday thing."

Summer waited.

"My dad doesn't understand why I work for Carter," Joey said, taking a deep drink of her draft.

"Because?"

"Because of Jackson." Joey didn't quite choke on his name, but it didn't flow out either. "Dad isn't his biggest fan. He'd rather I go run someone else's operation."

"But you stayed."

"The Pierces are more family to me than my own. Carter's a fair boss, and I call the shots when it comes to the horses. Plus, Blue Moon is home. Crazy, weird, bizarre home."

"Do you ever wish you would have gone somewhere else?"

"I went away to college. Centenary for their equine program. It was a solid program, good school. But Blue Moon was always home." She shook her head. "And I'm not going to be chased out of my home by ghosts of relationships past. You?"

"Only child. My parents are..." How could she describe them? Distant? Disappointed? "They should be somewhere in the heart of Alaska right now. Last year they sold their house in Brooklyn and bought an RV."

"What are they doing in an RV?"

"My father was a journalist and then a journalism professor. He's always dreamed of writing a book on the 'faces of America.' So he and my mom are driving around the country. He interviews local people of interest, and my mom does the driving and the editing."

"You see them much?"

Summer shook her head. "Not since they bought the RV."

"Good enough. Sharing time is over," Joey decided.

Summer opened her menu. "What's good here?"

They ordered food from Ed, and Summer settled back to enjoy her wine. The bar was starting to get busier. She recognized Willa at a table in the corner with Bobby from Peace of Pizza and another woman with turquoise and violet streaks in her hair. Willa waved and raised a pink frothy concoction. "Ladies night," she yelled over the music.

"Same here," Summer mouthed and held up her wine glass.

"Excuse me?" A string bean of a guy with freckles and

glasses touched the back of the stool next to Summer. "Would you mind if I joined you for a few minutes?"

"Ummm..." Summer looked at Joey for help. Joey looked entertained. "Sure?"

"Great." He took a skinny notepad out of the back pocket of his khakis and perched on the barstool. "So, I only have a few questions for you both." He produced a pencil from the pocket of his starched plaid shirt and flipped through a few pages scrolled with notes before finding a blank page."

Up close, he looked like he was twelve years old.

"I'm sorry. Are you old enough to be in here?" Summer asked.

"What do you mean you have questions for us *both*, Anthony?" Joey demanded.

He flushed to the tips of his ears.

"I'm twenty-eight, and I'll get to you in a minute Joey. Now, Summer, I have here that you're only in town for a few more days, is that correct? What's been your favorite thing about Blue Moon so far?"

Summer blinked. "Is this an interview?"

Anthony pushed his glasses up his nose. "It's just a little Q&A that will run in *The Monthly Moon*."

"You want to interview me because I'm here doing an interview?"

He seemed pleased by the question. "Exactly. Now back to the questions."

"Can I get you something to drink, Anthony?" Ed asked, swiping a towel over the bar.

"I'll take a diet soda, please. Now back to the questions. What do you think are the highlights of visiting Blue Moon?"

"I'd have to say it's the unique people that live here that has been the biggest surprise," she said diplomatically.

"Uh-huh, uh-huh," Anthony scribbled furiously. "Have

you had the chance to patronize many of our small businesses?"

"I've enjoyed Peace of Pizza and Blue Moon Boots. Shorty's is also turning out to be an interesting experience."

Ed dropped off Anthony's soda and winked at Summer.

"What kind of qualities are important to you in a man?"

"Excuse me?"

Anthony was frowning intently at his notepad. "You know like, smart, kind, good with animals, broad-shouldered, chiseled jaw..."

"I guess all of those."

"Great. And how many kids do you plan to have?"

Summer choked on her wine.

"Gee, isn't that funny? We were just talking about that, Anthony," Joey said. "I think Summer settled on an even half-dozen."

Summer's eyes widened as Anthony continued to scrawl notes. "Half-dozen," he mumbled. "Got it. Now according to your blog, you state that 'Farm life is a very large leap from Manhattan.' Is that a leap you'd be willing to make for love?"

"You know what? I think I have to go to the bathroom. Excuse me." Summer shoved away from the bar.

"No problem. I'll just squeeze in Joey's interview while you're gone. So Joey, now that Jackson Pierce is back in town, are you off the market?"

It was Summer's turn to laugh.

"Ed, we're going to need that food to go. Now," Joey called.

"Rumor has it that Jackson is back for good. What does that mean for you?"

"Ed!"

~

"PEOPLE DON'T REALLY READ this *The Monthly Moon,* do they?" Summer asked, watching the cornfields fly by her window. Their untouched, hastily packaged dinners were sitting in the bag on her lap.

"What do you think?"

Summer groaned.

"How do you think I feel? You get to go back to the safety of eight million strangers who don't give a shit what you do day in and day out. I *live* here," Joey grumbled. She passed the farmhouse lane and continued on, turning down the lane to the stables.

"Can Anthony be bought?"

"Not only is Anthony the editor-in-chief of *The Monthly Moon*, his parents are Rainbow and Gordon Berkowicz. He's second-generation BMBC."

"Crap."

Joey stopped the truck in front of a stone and timber cabin.

"Where are we?" Summer asked.

"My place."

Joey led the way up the porch to the front door where she fiddled with her keys. "Welcome to Casa Awesome," she said, pushing open the door.

The whole first floor was wide open. A seating area was arranged around the stone fireplace, and behind it was a wide plank table surrounded by charmingly mismatched chairs. The kitchen was compact but had all the essentials. Slate blue cabinets and white countertops broke up the wood tones of the walls and ceiling. The kitchen island was flanked by four backless metal stools and held a neat stack of magazines and books, all on horse topics.

"Two bedrooms up there," Joey said pointing to the loft that overlooked the living area. "Powder room is over there.

There's beer in the fridge. I figured we could eat on the back porch."

"Fine with me," Summer agreed. "We aren't going to get ambushed by paparazzi out there, are we?"

"If that happens, I'm getting my shotgun."

After a pit stop in the kitchen for utensils and beer, Joey led the way out onto the back porch. "We'll eat in the screened-in porch. I don't want to share my food with mosquitos."

She flicked a light switch, and an overhead ceiling fan and light came on.

"This place suits you," Summer said, taking in the vista. Beyond the deck, a brick patio ran the length of the back of the house and pastures rolled on as far as the eye could see. "You have a bathtub on your patio."

Joey grinned. "It runs, too."

"You take baths outside?" Summer asked incredulously.

"Who's going to see me? The horses?"

Summer imagined it. A warm summer night, a fire in the fire pit, and a good long soak under the stars.

"Okay. You may be onto something here."

Joey opened her container and dug into her lukewarm roast beef sandwich.

She pointed at Summer's salad. "No meat on that. Did Carter get to you, too?"

"Maybe a little," she confessed. "He and Dixie make a pretty compelling case." She reached for a fork. "When I write pieces like this, I try to live as close to the lifestyle of the subject as possible just to get a better feel for it."

"Method," Joey mumbled through a mouthful of mashed potatoes.

"What?"

Joey swallowed. "It's like method acting, only for writing."

"Exactly." Summer speared a cherry tomato. "So, think we gave Anthony enough to write his articles?"

"More than. He's very 'creative' with his facts. In a week, all of Blue Moon will be reading about how you've fallen for a farmer and plan to kiss Manhattan goodbye. And how I'm ready to have another Pierce brother's babies."

They both drank deeply.

"So how was the sex?" Joey asked as casually as if she was talking about shoes or recipes.

Summer choked on her beer. "Excuse me?"

"Those Pierce brothers know how to treat a woman right."

"Brothers?" Summer demanded.

Joey smirked. "After Jackson left, Beckett and I may have made out one night."

"No. Way. Does Jax know?"

"Probably not. And it was nothing," Joey shrugged. "Beckett was worried about me. I was in a tizzy over his brother leaving. It just happened. And then we came to our senses, decided we were better off as friends, and never spoke of it again."

"I've never made out with two brothers before," Summer said wistfully.

"It was a lot more than making out with Jackson," Joey said matter-of-factly. "Even at seventeen, that boy knew what he was doing."

Summer watched her straighten her shoulders and dig back into her meal.

"Why don't you call him Jax like everyone else?"

"I used to. I don't anymore." Joey kept her attention on her dinner.

"Too familiar?"

"Yeah, something like that. So back to sex with Carter."

"What's my scale?"

"One being 'I should have saved myself the self-loathing by staying home and watching Netflix' and ten being 'I heard angels sing.'"

"Oh angels. Definitely. A choir of them."

"Nice."

"With some fireworks, too."

"Now you're just showing off."

~

Joey dropped Summer off in front of Carter's house after nine.

"Are you sure you don't want to come in?" Summer offered, sliding out of the truck cab.

Joey's eyes flicked to the house. "Nah. I'm good."

"I had fun tonight," Summer said.

"Me, too," Joey nodded. "I'll call you if we need to go burn Anthony's house down or something."

"I'm in."

Summer climbed the porch steps and went inside. She followed the sound of male laughter through the kitchen—which looked like it had been destroyed in a tornado of testosterone—and into the great room.

Carter spotted her first and got to his feet.

"Lady in the house, gentlemen," Beckett said, dealing cards. "Let's clean up the language and tone down the farting and scratching."

"Oh, I don't want to interrupt any manly fun. I'm just going to grab my laptop and work upstairs."

"First, come meet the guys," Carter insisted. He pointed to the man with scraggly hair and Birkenstocks. "Summer, this is Bill Fitzsimmons. Fitz, this is Summer Lentz."

Fitz peered over his glasses at her and waved. "Hello. The brownies are safe."

"Thanks for tip," Summer nodded.

"Fitz is the prime example of the evils of excessive pot smoking, but he's a lucky bastard when it comes to cards. This," Carter said slapping the shoulder of a large blonde man wearing a backwards ball cap, "is Donovan Cardona. Don't let the idiotic look on his face fool you. He's sheriff here and a lousy card player."

Donovan unfolded his six-foot-four-inch frame from the table and stood up to greet her. "Nice to meet you, Summer. I've heard a lot about you," he said with a wink, shaking her hand.

"You must be on Facebook," she sighed.

"The department's been able to stop a few crimes before they happened thanks to that gossip group. I can see they weren't exaggerating how pretty you are."

Carter took Donovan's hat off and smacked him with it. "Don't even start," he said.

"That's assaulting an officer," Donovan said.

"Carter already called dibs," Jax said, breezing past on his way to the fridge.

"You called dibs?" Summer asked.

"You know, how about you just go on upstairs while I stay down here and kick everyone's ass?" And since everyone already knew, he gave her a hard kiss on the mouth before handing over her laptop and pushing her down the hall.

She held her laughter until she got to the top of the stairs. "So much for secrets," she sighed to herself. Summer flipped on the light in her room and was halfway in when she realized none of her things were there. Jax's tangle of possessions were exploding out of a duffle on the floor.

Curious, she almost called down to Carter, but instead, she followed her hunch into his room. He had hung up all of her clothes in his closet and stowed her suitcase. Her toiletries were neatly lined up on the counter in his bathroom next to the open box of condoms.

She caught her grin in the mirror.

When was the last time she had smiled like this? Or felt this light?

She couldn't remember.

But he wouldn't really want you if he knew the truth, would he? The little vile voice in her head whispered its poisonous truth.

Summer turned away from the mirror, from the words that scratched at her.

They weren't getting married. They were seeing where things went. And it was no reason to let herself get swept up in it. She had work to do, goals to accomplish, a battle to fight.

∼

CARTER FOUND her curled in his bed, asleep with her laptop browser open to an article on using an organic, plant-based diet to fight disease. Always working, he smiled, closing the laptop and moving it to the nightstand.

Her phone was still clutched in her hand. He gently pulled it from her grasp and plugged it into the charger.

Carter stripped down and slid into bed beside her. She didn't even stir when he pulled her into his arms and buried his face in her hair.

18

Summer woke in the gray dawn to the sound of rain on the metal roof and a soggy Carter crawling back into bed.

"Is it time to get up?" she murmured sleepily.

"No, baby. Go back to sleep."

Carter pulled her against him, and she snuggled in.

When she woke again, the rain still fell, and thunder rumbled in the distance. She was curled into Carter's side, a leg thrown across his. Her hand rested just above the steady thrum of his heartbeat.

He slept peacefully, she noted.

His face was a masterpiece. That perfectly straight blade of a nose. Lips that gave so much pleasure pressed in a line. Even in his sleep, he frowned. That serious look that, when turned on her, made her stomach feel like it was on a roller coaster. Inky lashes hid his steel gray eyes. And that beard. Oh, how she loved that beard.

It was her last full day here. She was going to make the most of it. Summer pulled the sheet down his body, taking her time and reveling in the view. He was built with strength and power from his broad shoulders to his scarred chest to the tapering waist and hips. He was perfection, and in this moment, he was hers to explore.

Summer trailed a light line of kisses down his chest, across his taut stomach, and lower still. He was already hard by the time she worked her way down those delicious slashes of muscle that brought her mouth to its destination. She felt him come awake when her lips parted to accept the head of his cock.

It was her name on his lips as his hips came off the bed, forcing him deeper into her mouth.

Summer slanted over him, tasting and licking. She gripped the base of his shaft with her hand and began a slow, torturous rhythm. He groaned and his hips flexed again, driving his cock deeper into her mouth.

The speed built with the need. She wanted to take him over the edge as he did for her again and again.

His fingers dug into her shoulders. "Baby, you have to stop."

She didn't listen. Summer wanted him helpless and shuddering.

Carter took matters into his own hands and wrestled her up his body. He flipped them, reaching desperately for the drawer of his nightstand. He returned to her triumphant, condom in hand.

Summer reached for it.

"No, baby. I want this to last, and for that to happen, you need to keep your hands to yourself."

She laughed as he hastily rolled it on before cuffing her hands overhead with one of his.

He rained kisses down on her, gentle nibbles down her neck, across her chest. His beard tickled the sensitive tips of her breasts.

Settling himself between her legs, he brought his mouth back to hers. Rather than the scorching inferno, his lips brought a slow burn. Summer opened her legs, inviting him in. His tongue teased her lips as the crown of his penis gently pressed against her.

Carter's free hand found her breast and began to knead. She sighed against his mouth as pleasure and need swamped her.

He plunged into her as his tongue took possession of her mouth. Smooth, slow strokes teased her, carrying her higher and higher.

Thunder rumbled outside the window.

Carter released her hands and carefully lowered his weight to her. She met his measured thrusts with eager hips. Rocking into him, she accepted everything he gave.

"My beautiful girl." His lips teased one sensitive nipple and then the other.

Her breath caught, and then their gazes.

She felt the tall, liquid wall building, cresting inside her.

"Carter," she whispered, frantic with need and fear.

"I'm with you," he said, nuzzling her neck. "Let it happen, Summer."

The dam broke, and she felt the climax flood every cell of her body. Carter was with her, pouring into her. They became one, the aftershocks forging them together.

It felt like hours later when Summer finally brought herself back to life. Carter was passed out on his stomach, an arm outstretched anchoring her to his side.

She reached for her phone on the nightstand and squinted at the screen.

"It's ten o'clock!" She shook Carter's shoulder.

His hand blindly reached out until it found her forehead and shoved her head back down on the pillow.

"Carter." Her voice was muffled by the hand that now covered her mouth.

She wriggled free and crawled on top of him to press her face to his. "We slept in," she whispered.

He opened an eye and then closed it.

She pinched him. He growled.

"Don't we have work to do?"

"I fed all the animals and paid Jax fifty bucks to turn off the irrigation systems so we could sleep in. Figured you were probably tired since we didn't get much sleep the night before last."

"You're the most amazing man on the planet. I'm going to make you breakfast," she announced. Summer pressed a kiss to his cheek and slid off the bed. She pulled on the shirt he had worn the night before and padded out of the room.

Carter dragged himself out of bed. He'd better go save his kitchen.

∼

THEY HAD oatmeal and fresh juice on the side porch, enjoying the rainy morning.

"What time do you have to leave tomorrow?" Carter asked.

"I have a production meeting at two at the office. So I'll need to leave here by ten."

"I was thinking we could have dinner just the two of us tonight."

"That would be perfect. I'd love that."

"You didn't let me finish. It turns out that my mother has other plans. We're having everyone over tonight and grilling."

"One last hurrah," Summer said sadly.

"It won't be the last," he promised.

She sipped the juice and swallowed hard. Tomorrow night,

she'd be in her own bed in her own apartment, three hours away from the farm, from Blue Moon, from Carter.

She thought she'd be excited about going home. It was where she belonged. Lord knew she had more than enough work to catch up on. And a good story to write. But there was no Carter Pierce in the city. And there was no senior editor job in Blue Moon.

They would just see where things went.

～

THEY SPENT the rest of the day in companionable silence, both working in Carter's office upstairs. Summer made headway on the article and handled magazine-related tasks while Carter muttered over spreadsheets and certifications.

They packed it in around four when the rain broke. With a kiss on her forehead, Carter left to take care of some things outside.

Summer used the opportunity to half-heartedly pack what she could. Choosing an outfit for tonight and laying out what she would wear in the morning. She carefully folded pants and shirts, tucking them into her suitcase.

She spotted the shirt Carter had worn the night before on the floor of the closet and with only a moment's hesitation tucked it into the bottom of her suitcase.

She would give it back. Eventually.

In the meantime, it would be her little secret.

She dressed for dinner in a white cotton sundress topped with her new denim shirt and proudly pulled on her boots for one last wear on the farm. *Would she have the occasion to wear them in the city?* she wondered.

She clattered down the stairs just as Carter came through

the front door carrying two covered bowls. He looked at her wolfishly.

"What?" Summer asked.

He dumped the bowls on the hallway table and snatched her off the stairs. Carrying her into the formal living room, Carter pinned her against the wall. "You look good enough to eat," he whispered against her ear, teeth snagging on her earlobe.

She shivered against him as his hands skimmed her curves. The front door opened again, but neither of them moved.

"I see Carter didn't get very far with the food." Phoebe's voice carried into the living room.

Summer couldn't quite catch her breath as Carter, ever so gently, lowered his mouth to hers. Completely at his mercy, she poured herself into the kiss. It was like touching the sun. The heat of it warmed her blood.

"What was that for?" she gasped when he pulled back.

"In case I don't get to do it again for the next few hours." He tucked her hair behind her ears. "Now get out of here. I can't get un-hard with you looking at me like that. And if I go into the kitchen with a raging hard-on, I'm going to scar my family for life."

Summer glanced down at the crotch of his jeans. "Later? Please?"

"I promise."

She moved out of his grasp, away from the wall. "Oh, and Carter?"

"Yeah, honey?"

"I'm not wearing underwear."

She heard the sharp intake of his breath as she skirted around the corner into the foyer. She was still grinning when she delivered the covered bowls to Phoebe and Franklin in the kitchen.

$\sim$

THEY GATHERED EN masse on the farm for Summer's last night there.

Even Joey graced them with her presence, though she kept a safe distance between her and Jax at all times. Undeterred, Jax made it his mission to get as close to her as possible. To Summer, it was like watching a slow motion chase.

Phoebe and Franklin canoodled by the stove in the kitchen while Beckett glared at them until Carter dragged his brother outside to help with the grill.

When the food was ready, they opened the doors of the little barn to eat at the enormous wood plank table. They stacked drinks and dessert on a smaller table against the wall. Citronella candles kept the bugs away and made for a more festive feel.

There was grilled chicken a la Beckett for the meat-eaters and tasty veggie kebabs with a tangy marinade. Garden salad, pasta salad, coleslaw, and baked beans rounded out the evening's menu.

Carter took the seat on her right, his hand resting high on her bare thigh at the very edge of her dress hem.

"What are you doing?" she whispered to him as dishes were passed around the table.

"Torturing you the way you torture me." His eyes glinted with lust.

Summer stifled a gasp when his hand moved another inch higher under the skirt of her dress. "Carter Pierce! You behave yourself at the dinner table," she hissed.

He took her hand, brought it between his legs, and pressed

it against his hard cock. "Do you see what you do to me, Summer?"

Conversations flowed around them as his erection throbbed under her hand.

"Should I see if I have the same effect on you?" His hand slid another inch higher, his fingers stroking her inner thigh.

Summer's eyes went wide. She was shaking her head when someone passed her the coleslaw. Summer very nearly bobbled the dish when Carter traced a long finger over her very slick folds.

She felt her muscles quiver, demanding more. Needing to be filled.

One-handed, he took the dish from her.

Another brush from the pads of his finger had her knees opening to take more. He withdrew his hand.

"More later, baby," he whispered, spooning coleslaw on to her plate.

Summer shut her legs and her mouth and tried to get a grasp on her sanity.

Joey had scored a position at the end of the table next to Beckett. But when he got up to get another beer, Jax slid neatly into his place and swapped their plates. Joey pretended not to notice but scooted further away until she was teetering on the edge of the bench.

"Jax, quit crowding Joey," Phoebe ordered. "Where are your manners?"

"We were literally raised in a barn, Mom," Jax teased. But he slid an inch or two away from Joey.

"Who wants dessert?" Joey demanded, jumping up from the bench. She hurried over to the other table and away from Jax.

Phoebe sighed and shook her head.

After generous portions of Joey's homemade apple crisp were sampled, the first murmurs of going home started.

"Before anyone leaves," Summer said, pushing back from the table. "I have a little something for all of you."

She rose and pulled the small gift bags out from under the beer table where she had stashed them. "I just wanted to thank all of you for welcoming me into your home. I never thought I'd say this, but I can't wait to come back to the farm next month."

She rounded the table handing out the bags.

One-by-one, they each pulled out forest green t-shirts with the new Pierce Acres logo on them.

"Summer, these are wonderful," Phoebe said, holding her shirt up to admire.

"She designed the logo herself," Carter said, grinning. He got up and dropped a kiss on Summer's cheek. "Let's see how they fit."

He pulled off his shirt and stuffed it in the bag.

Beckett and Jax followed suit. Joey gave her a thumbs up from across the table. Three shirtless Pierce brothers made for an impressive sight.

Summer had snuck a peek at tags for Carter and Jax, but she'd guessed for Beckett. Thankfully, they all fit.

Phoebe hugged her. "You're a sweet girl. Look how happy you've made my boys," she said, grinning at her sons. "Especially that one."

"Thank you for being so welcoming. I'm going to miss you," Summer said.

Phoebe hugged her again. "We'll be seeing you again. I'm sure of it." She moved to help Franklin pull his t-shirt over the polo he wore.

"Got one for Franklin, too, huh?" Beckett grumbled.

On impulse, Summer rose on her tiptoes and gave him a kiss on his cheek. "I'm going to miss you, Mr. Mayor."

"Come back and see us soon," he said, his face softening into a grin. He squeezed her arm. "And if you ever decide to upgrade your Pierce brother, give me a call."

"Beat it, Beckett," Joey teased. She held her t-shirt, logo up, in her hands. "Thanks for this," she said to Summer. "You didn't have to do that."

"You're welcome. I was thinking about getting you one that said Future Mrs. Pierce that you could wear around town."

Joey's eyes narrowed. "Very funny. I'll be sure to send you a clip of the 'I want to have six babies with Carter Pierce' article that's due out soon."

"Appreciate that. I'll frame it and hang it at work to remind me what real journalism looks like."

Joey frowned as if sensing danger. And Summer realized Jax was approaching.

"Well, I'll see you around," Joey said hastily. "I think I'm going to head home."

"Say hi to the horses for me," Summer called after her.

"Bring your boots next month. We'll go for a ride," Joey said over her shoulder.

"I should probably walk her home," Jax said, watching her go.

Summer put her hand on his chest and held him in place. "What you should probably do is give her some space instead of stalking her like a jungle cat."

"I gave her eight years of space."

"Give her time to get used to you being here."

Exasperated, he ran a hand through his hair.

"Jax, honey, will you help me pack up the leftovers?" Phoebe called from the table.

"Sure, Mom." He turned back to Summer. "I'll see you in the morning before you go, right?"

"I'll be here."

Jax leaned over and kissed her on the cheek. "I'll miss you when it's just me and that bearded lug here."

"Get your mouth off my girl," Carter ordered, wrapping his arms around Summer from behind.

"What can I say, you've got good taste," Jax winked.

"Carter, honey, we're going to pack up the leftovers in the kitchen and head out," Phoebe called, her arms full of plates and platters.

"Leave the dishes in the sink. Summer and I will clean up out here and take care of them later." He gave Phoebe a peck on the cheek and shook Franklin's hand.

Franklin pulled Summer in for a one-armed hug. "It was a pleasure meeting you, even under the unfortunate roof and robe circumstances."

"You make a mean ziti, Franklin. I'll be thinking of you when I'm back in New York trying to find a good Italian place."

"Anytime you get hungry, just come on back," he chuckled.

And just like that they were alone in the barn.

Wordlessly, Carter slid the door closed and turned to face her.

Lit only by candles, the room flickered with shadow and flame. He looked like equal parts angel and devil. How could something so breathtakingly perfect belong to her?

Summer didn't realize she was backing away until she felt the rough edge of the table behind her.

"You look beautiful tonight." He said it quietly. He hadn't touched her yet, and already her blood was humming.

"You look pretty good yourself," she said, smoothing the t-shirt over his chest to break some of the tension she felt rising in her body. It fit just as she'd imagined it would. Soft cotton layered over hard muscle.

He brought his hands to her waist and moved between her legs. She opened her thighs wider for him, dragging her hemline higher.

"Thank you for the shirts," he said softly.

"Thank you for... everything, Carter." She meant it. The past week had taken her to places she never expected. Sparked feelings she didn't know she was capable of having. She felt... hope. She wasn't ready for it to end.

Carter brought his fingertips to her face. After tracing along her jaw, her neck, they threaded into her hair.

"Kiss me, Summer." His whisper brought a tremor to her body.

She leaned into him, laying her lips on his, savoring the taste and texture of the raw power that he kept leashed.

He let her lead, let her gently deepen the kiss until it bloomed like a flower under the sun.

She ran her hands up his arms, over his chest, gripping his shoulders.

She felt him harden against her and cuddled into him closer.

"Do you know what I thought about all evening?"

Summer shook her head, letting him gently ravage her with his lips.

"This." He slid his hand under the skirt of her dress and, with a deft thrust, stretched two fingers inside of her. Summer felt her knees buckle at the invasion. Her thighs quaked as they tried to close against Carter's legs, but he merely moved in closer, forcing them farther apart.

He grabbed her hair, pulling her head back. "Open for me, beautiful," he whispered against her. His tongue and fingers entered her.

"I love how you touch me," she whispered against him.

Without breaking contact with her mouth, he freed himself from his jeans and brought the head of his cock to her wet center. He lifted her onto the edge of the table, spreading her legs wide.

He let her grip his shaft and guide it between her damp folds. Back and forth, she worked him with her hand sliding him against her until she trembled. His tongue rubbed against hers in a kiss so carnal it scared her.

"I thought about taking you like this," he murmured, moving his lips over her jaw, down her neck. "Then I thought about bending you over the table."

His voice caught as she brushed her thumb over his sensitive tip.

"What did you decide?" she asked, biting his bottom lip.

Carter growled low in his throat.

"This." He pulled back just enough to drag on a condom before lifting her in his arms.

He kicked a chair out from the table, and as he sank down onto it, he sank into her. She gasped against his throat.

"God, I love how you fit me," he whispered, lips skimming her throat.

Summer's legs hung over the sides of the chair, toes skimming the floor. Carter adjusted, shoving his jeans down further so he could open his legs.

She moaned at the friction it caused inside her.

"So perfect. So beautiful. Hold still a minute, baby." He held her hips in place when she started to move. "I just want to feel this. Feel you surrounding me, belonging to me." His fingers dug into her hips with the effort to stay still.

Summer shivered. She was so full.

"Let's take this nice and slow."

Carter untied the knot in her denim shirt and slid it from

her shoulders. He dipped his thumbs under the thin spaghetti straps of her white dress.

"Did I mention that I'm not wearing a bra, either?" she murmured, pressing kisses to his face.

His hands stilled on her waist.

"I'm glad you didn't tell me until now. Otherwise, I wouldn't have lasted through dinner," he said, trailing his mouth over her collarbones.

He slid the straps from her shoulders, and Summer held her breath as the material clung to her breasts for a moment before slipping down her body.

The candlelight flickered from behind her, casting shadows everywhere. But she could still see Carter's eyes, the hard glint of need when he leaned in to softly nuzzle at her breast.

Summer sighed and ever so slowly rocked her hips forward and then back. Carter moved inside her, with her. He ran his tongue over one sensitive tip and then the other. His strong hands lifted her so he could move with her.

"Slow, Summer. Slow," he whispered, his breath hot against her skin.

She rode him slowly in the candlelight until the wave of pleasure took them both to the peak before sending them drifting, spiraling down to earth.

~

THE MORNING ARRIVED TOO QUICKLY for Summer's taste. One minute she was wrapped in Carter's arms, and the next she was opening her car door, saying goodbye.

"Text me when you get home, okay?" Carter reminded her for the third time.

"I will. And we can talk tonight?"

"Nine o'clock," Carter nodded.

Summer swung her bag into the passenger seat and turned around to face him. She wrapped her arms around Carter's waist one last time.

"I don't know what to say. How to tell you..." she pressed her face into his chest.

His arms enfolded her again and he brought his chin to the top of her head. "Just say 'I'll see you soon.'" He was right. She fit him just right.

Summer nodded and sighed. "Okay, one more kiss."

Carter obliged and gave her a kiss that scorched her to her toes.

"See you soon, honey," he said, kissing the tip of her nose and her forehead.

"See you soon, Carter." Biting her lip, Summer pulled back and slid behind the wheel.

Summer slipped on her sunglasses and, blowing him a kiss, pulled away.

19

*S*ummer had expected to feel a bit of relief returning to the city, back to her routine. Back to everything that was so familiar to her. Instead, she was antsy and distracted. She spent her first week back—and a better part of the second—bogged down in the work that had piled up while she was gone and sneaking out of events to call Carter.

She had gotten a lot of compliments on her "glow" when she returned, which she told everyone had to do with the fresh air and sunshine. Not a sexcation.

Hmm, a sexcation. She scribbled a note to herself to see if any of the other big monthlies had covered that topic before.

She was rapidly becoming an expert on them. They had planned to wait two weeks before seeing each other again. They hadn't even made it one full week. He met her at the train in Rhinecliff on a Thursday, and they spent the entire night making love in a motel.

Dinner came from the vending machines. Carter put her back on the train at six the next morning, and it was back to work for both of them.

They had done it twice now.

The second time, there had been a delay at the station, and Summer arrived at the office in a panic having missed two morning meetings. It was a warning from the universe, she decided. Focus on work. Stick with the plan.

To cheer herself, she opened the email Joey had sent her a few days ago.

To: slentz@indulgence.com
    From: piercestables@netlink.com
    You're officially Blue Moon famous. Let me know next time you're in town and we'll go to Anthony's house to make sure he's never heard from again.

The email contained a link to the The Monthly Moon story, which skirted the rules of good journalism by speculating that, while Summer had left for Manhattan, it wouldn't be long before she returned to their fair community to permanently end her search for a husband after one of Blue Moon's most eligible bachelors won her heart.

It included a bulleted list of her qualifications for a good man and how Carter Pierce rated in each category. The only category he didn't rank highly in was "chiseled jaw." An asterisk educated the reader that his jawline was unable to be properly measured due to his beard.

Joey Grier was quoted as saying that Summer was looking forward to starting a large family.

The article ended with, "In related news, Ms. Grier is looking to rekindle her high school romance with Jackson Pierce. It looks as though two of the Pierce bachelors are officially off the market."

Summer rolled her eyes. If her father thought what she

did for a living was a disgrace to journalism, he would be horrified by *The Monthly Moon's* coverage.

She turned her chair to take in the view out the window.

She had felt off-balance ever since returning to the city. It was harder than she imagined to divide her time between work and a personal life. She wasn't exactly used to having a personal life, having dedicated so much of herself to her goals since college.

She was just getting used to a new normal, Summer told herself. She could make it work.

"Must be nice to have time to just sit and do nothing," the cat-like voice of Kira Nakano purred.

All five feet and ten inches of her leaned against the wall of Summer's cubicle. Everything about her was sharp. Candy pink nails that her manicurist shaped into points and black hair that hung to her shoulders in a razor's edge bob.

"What can I do for you, Kira?" Summer said, her tone as sweet as sugar.

"I just wanted to stop by and see how you're doing since your vacation." She examined the talons on her right hand.

"I was on an assignment," Summer reminded her.

"I just assumed it was a vacation since you've had so much trouble getting back into the swing of things," Kira said, pasting a phony look of concern on her face. "Missing those meetings earlier this week?" she tut-tutted. "Since you weren't there, I thought I'd get you up to speed. Katherine gave me the piece to do on Sylvia Van Brennan's new album."

Summer smiled sweetly. "Oh, the two hundred words on her holiday album? How nice. I bet that will keep you busy for a while."

Kira's eyes narrowed. "I'm also coordinating the anniversary issue contributors. Gosh, isn't that something you did last year?" She tapped a pink nail to her chin. "Maybe Katherine is just realizing that you don't have as much to offer as she thought you did."

"I guess that's for Katherine to decide," Summer answered shortly. "Maybe you should go remind her how invaluable you are."

Kira glared at her. "You're tan. All of that farm work is going to give you sun spots. You should see a dermatologist."

"Thanks for stopping by," Summer said. "You'd better run along now. You don't want to get behind with all your special projects."

"Ladies." Nikolai Vulkov sauntered into Summer's cube.

"Nikolai." Kira gave him a frosty nod before strutting out.

Summer shoved her hands through her hair. "Ugh! That woman makes me want to push her off a rooftop and then hit her with a bus."

Niko pressed a kiss to her cheek. "She has that effect on most people."

"You never... with her...?" Summer demanded.

Niko put his hands up. "I don't sleep with every beautiful woman I meet."

"You think snide nastiness is beautiful?" Summer snorted.

"Not everyone can be as sweet as you," he teased. "So I see you survived farm life."

"I have. And had a pretty good time doing it. How was Paris?"

"Same old, same old."

Summer grinned. "Jet-setting off to Paris for a shoot and then on to Blue Moon Bend. I can't wait to see you on the farm."

"Oh, like you're so at home there."

"I told you. I had a good time."

Niko's eyes narrowed. "Uh-huh. And what did you say Old MacDonald's name was?"

"Carter. Carter Pierce."

"You slept with him!"

Summer jumped up and slapped a hand over his mouth. "Shut up!" she hissed.

He dragged her hand down. "I knew something was different about you," he said triumphantly.

"Will you keep your voice down?"

He laughed. "Ms. I Have No Time for Relationships when it comes to models and investment bankers goes and falls for a farmer!"

Summer groaned and sank back in her chair. "Just what's it going to cost me to get you to keep your big, fat mouth shut?"

"Smuggle some vodka into the barnyard for me and we'll call it even," he smirked.

"You are insufferable."

"That's why the ladies love me."

"I'm throwing up now."

"It's good to have you back."

"Yeah, yeah. Get out. Leave me to my misery," Summer sighed.

~

SHE GOT HOME at the reasonable hour of nine that night and gratefully changed out of her work clothes into Carter's shirt. Summer had stayed late to get a jump on a few projects. Her conversation with Kira had reminded her of the dangers of taking her eye off the prize. If she slacked off, even just a little, someone would always be there to step into her shoes and take what she had worked so hard for.

She poured a glass of wine and carried it and her veggie stir-fry to the couch. Into the third week, and she was still eating like a vegetarian. It really wasn't bad. And if the diet had the positive health benefits it was supposed to, the sacrifice of bacon and burgers would be worth it in the long run.

She scrolled through the comments on her blog, noting that many of them were asking about Carter and the farm. Summer hoped she would do them justice in the article. The article that was due to Katherine in exactly two days.

She had a solid draft but wanted to take another pass at it with fresh eyes to make sure she was telling the best story she could.

Her phone signaled an incoming video call.

Carter.

She was already smiling as she answered the call.

"Hello, handsome."

He was on the couch, too, in his Pierce Acres t-shirt.

"Nice shirt," she grinned.

"I could say the same for you. I've been looking for that one." His voice soothed away the stress of the day.

"Oh, this old thing? I borrowed it. It smells like you."

"Right off the farm me or after shower me?"

Summer held the collar up to her nose and sniffed. "A little bit of both. I like it."

"How was your day?" Carter asked, leaning back against the cushions.

"It wasn't bad." She thought of Kira and Niko and decided not to mention either conversation. "Lots going on for the next issue. How about you?"

"You know I can read you like a glossy magazine, right? I'm not buying the 'it wasn't bad' answer."

Summer smiled. "Really? What am I thinking right now?"

Carter raised a dark eyebrow. "Honey, get your mind out of the gutter and tell me about your day."

She did, sparing him her wish to toss Kira off a building. "How is it everyone can look at me and know that we had sex?"

"If you figure it out, let me know because Gordon Berkowicz told me I had a 'healthy glow,' and Bobby took one look at me when I dropped off her delivery and started laughing."

"Did she say why?"

Carter shrugged in equal parts annoyance and amusement. "She said I was whistling and had a 'big, stupid smile' on my face." He held up his fingers as quotes.

"Awh, poor baby. Are those mean Mooners picking on you?"

"Yes," he frowned. "Come save me from them."

"I wish I could, but it looks like I'm going to be stuck in the city until I come see you for the shoot."

"If the motel is off the table—and I know how much you love animal crackers and stale candy bars for dinner—I was going to suggest I come to you."

Summer sat upright. "You'd come here?"

Carter ran a hand through his beard. "Yeah. If you're okay with it, I think I can get away for the weekend."

"This weekend?" Summer squeaked. "The whole weekend? Are you serious?"

He chuckled. "I take it you'd like that?"

"Well, I *guess*," Summer shrugged her shoulder. "I mean if you bring the animal crackers, I don't see why not. I have a gallery opening thing Friday night. Can you be my date for it?"

"What time does it start?"

"Eight."

"I don't think I'll be able to get away early enough."

"But after?"

"I'll be there."

"Is there anything you want to do while you're here in town?"

"Just you."

20

---

 ands on hips, Summer surveyed her apartment. Fresh flowers? Check. A fridge full of beer and vegetarian-friendly goodies? Check. Fresh sheets on the bed? Check. Box of condoms? Two actually. Check and check.

She was ready for an entire weekend with Carter. All she had to do was get through the gallery opening tonight, and then he would be here. She allowed herself a twirl to the happy strings of Vivaldi playing softly on her stereo.

Summer smoothed her hands over her dress. Perfect for summer in Manhattan, the silver crystal halter-top had a plunging neckline that ended just above the cinched waist. Blush chiffon fell to form a soft, layered skirt that floated away from her body ending several inches above the knees. Her blonde hair was pulled back in a low bun fed with thin braids.

She wished she was going with Carter tonight, but dragging him to an event like this would be the equivalent of harvesting lettuce. No one really wanted to do it, and afterward you'd feel tired, sore, and a little abused.

Summer grabbed her clutch and was in the middle of one

last makeup check in the mirror when she heard a knock at the door.

A peek through the peephole had her yanking the door open. "Carter!" Her heart did a cartwheel. She launched herself at him. "I thought you couldn't come until late tonight?"

"Surprise." He lifted her from the waist and carried her back inside.

The kiss was carnal, possessive. The heat of it singed her, igniting her on the inside. "I can't believe you're here," she whispered against his mouth, her lips teasing his. "How did you get in the building?"

"One of your neighbors downstairs buzzed me in. I helped her carry her groceries."

Of course he did, Summer sighed.

Carter finally pried her off him and held her at arm's length. "You look amazing," he said, taking her in from head to toe.

"I could say the same about you," Summer said, scrubbing her lipstick off his mouth. He was wearing a navy blue suit, sans tie, that looked like it had been created just to highlight his powerful body. His pants did nothing to hide his erection. "You look good in a suit. Did you borrow it from Beckett?"

"Just the shoes," he tugged his pant leg up to expose shiny loafers in a rich cognac tone. "A guy can't go to a gallery thing in jeans and a t-shirt with goat bites taken out of it."

"You're really going?" Summer squealed and clapped her hands. "This is going to be revenge for the lettuce."

"I think I can handle tonight. Especially with you dressed like that."

"You like?" She twirled around making her skirt billow out.

"Very sexy," Carter grinned and dragged her in again. His

fingers dipped into the neckline. "Maybe too sexy to leave the apartment."

"Nice try, Pierce. Now get that situation under control," she said pointing at his crotch. "Our Uber's here."

∼

CARTER WATCHED in fascination as Summer went to work. She navigated the polished concrete floor of the gallery with grace and purpose, juggling details and mini-crises without breaking a sweat. She drank nothing but water and remembered the name of every person who approached her.

She apologized profusely every time she had to leave his side, but Carter was content to watch her work. The event was an interesting concept. A new art gallery wanted a big launch for their grand opening and partnered with a magazine-favorite designer to host a small, exclusive fashion show in the gallery.

Clothes as art? Beckett would love this shit, Carter thought. He fished his phone out of his pocket and snapped a picture of an impossibly tall, bone-thin woman and a round, bald man examining a seven-foot canvas that looked like clowns melting in a campfire. He texted it to his brothers.

Jax responded first. *How much is that ketchup and mustard smeared masterpiece?*

Beckett's response was, of course, more people-oriented. *Someone get that woman a protein shake before she eats that little man.*

Carter smirked. *Just another Friday night in Manhattan.*

Jax sent a picture of two sets of bare legs propped up on Carter's coffee table as he and Beckett watched TV in the great room. *Just another Friday night in Blue Moon.*

You both better be wearing shorts, Hollywood. I don't want ball prints on the leather.

The next picture came in a minute later. Jax and Beckett were wearing nothing but shit-eating grins and strategically placed throw pillows.

I hate you guys.

Carter stuffed his phone back in his pocket when Summer returned to him with a beer in hand.

"Are you taking selfies?" Summer's eyes sparkled. She handed him the beer.

"Just checking on the farm," he fibbed.

"Everything okay?"

He thought of the couch he was going to have to burn. "Nothing that can't be fixed when I get back."

She leaned in a little closer, and he felt his heart rate ratchet up a notch. "I'm really glad you're here, Carter."

"Me, too," he said, running a finger down the flesh of her exposed back. "I like watching you work."

Raised voices reached them. "Speaking of," she craned her neck trying to get a better look at the commotion. "I'll be right back."

He watched the drama unfold from the safety of the bar. It appeared that a very good-looking man and a stunning woman were about to come to blows.

"Anastasia," he heard Summer's voice soothe. "You weren't supposed to be here until ten, remember? After Alexi left."

Voices rose and fell, and the woman with the thick Eastern European accent pouted with her superbly enhanced lips.

"She's something, isn't she?" A trim man in tortoise shell glasses and a pinstripe suit pointed his glass of champagne at Summer. "I wouldn't be surprised if she ended up running the place someday."

Summer now had Alexi and Anastasia posing for a

photographer together. They weren't smiling, but at least no blood had been drawn.

"Now she'll have the fashion world in a tizzy wondering if those two are back together again. I'm Quincy, by the way." He held out a slim, manicured hand and Carter shook it.

"Carter Pierce."

"The Carter Pierce of Summer's new article? Very interesting."

They watched as Alexi pulled Summer into the picture. The man's hand traveled down her back to cup her ass.

Carter started forward, but Quincy put a hand on his chest. "Hold on there, Tiger. She's got this."

Summer grasped Alexi's hand firmly and removed it from her ass. She thanked the photographer for his time and turned to the model with bad manners.

"Here it comes," Quincy said with the tiniest hint of glee. "The Summer Brush-Off. Sometimes it takes the dumber ones longer to get the message."

Carter couldn't hear what she said, but the color drained from the model's face. He began nodding profusely. When Summer was finished, the man made a formal bow and hurried away.

He caught a glimpse of the self-satisfied smile on her face before she composed herself.

"I see you've met Quincy," she said when she returned to Carter. Summer dropped a kiss on Quincy's cheek. "Quincy is our executive creative director."

"Yes, and Carter here farms the earth," Quincy said. "You didn't tell me he was gorgeous, Summer."

Carter shoved his hands in his pockets, and Summer laughed.

"You're embarrassing him, Quincy. Besides, there's a lot more to him than a gorgeous face."

"Oh, I can see that," he said, giving Carter the once over. "Have you introduced him to Katherine, yet? I can just imagine the ideas she's going to get once she lays eyes on him."

Carter shifted uncomfortably.

"Not yet."

"Well, my dears. I see some advertisers whose asses require kissing. It was a pleasure meeting you," he said to Carter. After another kiss on the cheek for Summer and one last look at him, Quincy toddled off.

"Sorry I abandoned you," Summer said, patting his jacket. "I was afraid World War Seventeen was about to break out between those two. They've been on again, off again so many times I can't even keep track. The last 'off again,' lawyers had to get involved." She sighed. "Did you get anything to eat yet?"

Carter shook his head. "I saw some tiny dots being passed around on trays, but it looked more like play dough sculptures than food."

"That's what happens to the food when you're catering for models and the people who manage them. You'd think the catering budget would be lower for these events, but it's just as expensive. Apparently beautiful people can only consume beautiful appetizers. We'll grab a bite on the way home. I promise."

"What's the story there?" he asked, nodding toward the handsy male model.

"Anastasia and Alexi?"

"He grabbed you."

She paused, long enough for Carter to realize she was thinking about brushing it off.

He took her hand and tugged her behind a thick brick pillar.

Summer squeezed his fingers. "Alexi thinks he's God's gift

to all women. Including ones who aren't interested in his pretty face and chauvinistic attitude."

"Is he a problem?"

She shook her head. "I handled it. I very calmly explained that if he didn't start showing me—and every other woman he comes in contact with—some respect, then *Indulgence* would be forced to recommend Ari Ray to advertisers for any and all upcoming campaigns."

"Who's Ari Ray?"

"Another model and Alexi's sworn enemy. Their feud is basically the plot of *Zoolander*."

He felt his lips quirk, even though he still felt like punching Alexi in his pretty face. She shouldn't have to fight these battles. And not just because she was his.

"Does this kind of thing happen often?"

Summer gave a dainty shrug. "There's always someone who's too drunk or too thick to get the message the first time around. The trick is finding a way to get your message across without pepper spraying every idiot you meet."

"Summer," he kept his voice low, controlled. "I don't like it."

"Imagine how I feel, Carter." Her blue eyes were earnest. "Would it be great to never have to worry about being groped or not having to be careful walking alone? Sure. But the problem isn't that I'm a woman. The problem is a small percentage of the population are—"

"Assholes? Dicks? Douchebags?"

She smiled. "All of the above. But you know what? It makes a girl appreciate someone like you even more."

Carter pulled her fingers to his mouth. He kissed them softly.

"I appreciate everything about you, Carter," she said, her

voice a husky whisper that sent his blood south. A feline smile spread across her face.

"Well look at you two hiding away in a corner." A man in dark jeans and a blazer over a casually rumpled button down leaned down to kiss Summer's cheek. "Hello, beautiful."

Summer's smile brightened. "Niko, what are you doing here?"

This was a man she didn't feel the need to pepper spray, Carter noted. Instead, she pulled him in for a tight hug.

"Katherine *suggested* that I make myself available. I had to break a date." He looked pained.

"Carter, I'd like you to meet Nikolai Vulkov. He's the relatively brilliant photographer who will be coming out to the farm with me."

"Right. The Wolf," Carter shook the offered hand. Nikolai shook like a man, a few degrees shy of bone crushing.

"You make the mistake of telling one pretty blonde what your name means in Russian, and she never lets you live it down," he lamented.

"If the fur fits," Summer said innocently.

"She's tenacious," Carter agreed.

"I'm not sure how you survived her following you around asking questions for an entire week."

Summer's chin lifted an inch. "Excuse me! I was a *delightful* houseguest."

"That I can attest to," Carter said, stroking a hand down her back out of Nikolai's view.

"Well, she did come back glowing. And smiling. And she's been staring off into space with a dreamy look on her face. It must be all that fresh, country air," Nikolai teased.

Carter gauged the situation. "I take it he knows?"

"Yep." Summer glowered at Nikolai. "He has a very big mouth, so we may have to kill him."

"We'll feed him to Clementine," Carter suggested, making Summer laugh.

"Who's Clementine?" Nikolai demanded.

"Oh, just a pretty little lady who's going to want to take a few bites out of you." Summer smiled sweetly.

"I'm actually starting to look forward to this assignment." He took a sip of his martini and glanced around the room. "I'd better get going. I need to make sure Katherine sees me here before I sneak out."

Nikolai said his goodbyes and headed out.

"Will there be any lettuce left to harvest when we come back for the photo shoot?" Summer asked sweetly.

Carter laughed. "Sorry, honey. But I'm sure we can come up with something equally horrible for him."

"That's what I like about you, Carter Pierce."

"My diabolical nature, or my inability to say no to you?"

"I think it's a bit of both."

They caught the attention of a waiter and were debating canapés when Carter spotted a very tall, angry looking woman stalking toward them. "Incoming," Carter said under his breath. "Who's this?"

"Oh, boy. You're getting the full experience tonight," Summer whispered back. "Kira. Don't you look... tall?"

Summer's tone had Carter on red alert.

The woman came to a halt in front of them in her five-inch stilettos. She towered over Summer and stood eye-to-eye with Carter.

"Aren't you going to introduce me to your date?" Kira asked Summer, her sharp gaze never leaving Carter.

He heard Summer hiss out her breath. "Carter Pierce, this is Kira Nakano. We work together."

Kira held out her hand to him as if she wanted it kissed. He shook it firmly instead.

"Hmm, rough. I like it rough," she said, running her tongue over her teeth.

For some reason, all he could think of was those Venus fly traps his mother used to grow.

Summer rolled her eyes. "Very classy, Kira. Don't you have a director or an editor to haunt?"

Kira tore her eyes away from Carter and glared down at Summer. "Don't get too comfortable at these events. When I'm senior editor, your presence won't be necessary at all." She stalked away, sending Carter another smoldering look over her shoulder.

"I feel like I need a shower," he muttered.

"That's the one I want to shove off a roof. I just haven't found a building tall enough, yet."

"You work with some very *interesting* characters," Carter said.

"Coming from someone who was born and raised in Blue Moon, that means a lot," Summer teased. "So there's one last person I need to introduce you to, and then we can start plotting our getaway."

She led him toward the center of the room where a small group of people clustered around a woman of medium height and medium build. Thanks to what Carter assumed was a very skilled plastic surgeon, her age was indeterminate. He put her on the low side of fifty, with a slick air of elegance. She was dressed simply, preferring to accent her black cocktail dress with bold jewelry. She wore her light brown hair in a sophisticated pixie cut.

Summer waited patiently for the conversation with some expensive suits to end. He saw the woman give her a subtle nod.

"I'd love to discuss this further, Raymond. Why don't you call my assistant and set something up for next month?" she said, skillfully bringing the conversation to a close. "Lovely to see you," she said, waving her audience off.

She turned her attention to Summer. "Now, what have you brought me, my dear?"

"Katherine, I'd like you to meet Carter Pierce. He's the owner of the organic farm we're featuring in the September issue. Carter, this is Katherine Ackerman, senior editor of *Indulgence*."

She held out a slim, cool hand, and Carter thought it wise to kiss this one.

"Summer turned in quite the article on you and your farm." Her plum-colored lips tilted up in a practiced smile. "Now I understand her fascination."

He could smell her perfume. A light scent that completed the subtle, elegant package. "Summer, dear, would you mind fetching me a drink?" she asked.

Summer accepted the empty glass that Katherine passed to her and winked at Carter as she hurried off toward the bar.

Katherine tucked her hand through Carter's arm, and together they slowly wandered to a wall featuring a trio of abstract canvases. Carter was more interested in the exposed brick of the wall than the splashes and slashes of paint.

"Tell me, Carter, why does someone who looks like you do spend his days in barns and fields when you could be doing so much more?"

The question put his back up. "What's more important than growing good food to feed people?"

She tilted her head to the side, and studied him. "Aren't you unexpected?"

Carter wished Summer would hurry the hell back. He was saved from answering by a woman with wildly curling hair and a sequined tunic over linen pants.

"Katherine," she said, extending both hands. "It's so good to see you again."

He saw it in the tightness around Katherine's mouth. She had no idea who this woman was. He could almost hear her mind racing through contacts as she took the woman's hands in hers.

Katherine leaned in for the double kiss on the cheek. "My dear, I'm so glad you could make it."

"So am I. Especially if it earns me an introduction to your arm candy."

"Mary Beth," Summer rushed up to their little group, clutching a glass of champagne. "Katherine was just saying she hoped you'd be here so she could introduce you to Carter. Carter runs an organic farm upstate. Mary Beth just started a community initiative that helps buildings design and develop rooftop gardens."

Carter offered Mary Beth his hand. "It's always a pleasure to meet a fellow gardener."

"Summer," Katherine said, pulling her aside. "Would you mind taking care of something for me?"

Carter and Mary Beth talked fertilizer and irrigation for nearly twenty minutes before she had to take a phone call. He was debating the merits of another beer when he saw Alexi strut his way into the men's bathroom.

It was an opportunity he wasn't going to pass up.

21

On the hunt, Carter stalked into the men's room after Alexi. The room was tiled from floor to ceiling in iridescent glass squares. The stall doors were murals of old Hollywood stars. Instead of urinals, a single long trough ran along the far wall.

Carter waited patiently for Alexi to finish at the trough.

When the man tried to get around him to the sinks, Carter simply got in his way.

"Do you have a problem?" His accent was heavily Slavic.

"Summer Lentz." Carter said, his legs braced apart.

"I do not know who this is," Alexi sneered.

"The woman whose ass you thought it was okay to grab tonight."

Recognition began to dawn in Alexi's eyes. "Summer, you say. She had no complaints at the time."

Carter felt his ire start to bubble over. "As a matter of fact, she did, and she expressed those complaints to you."

Alexi shrugged. "Women play hard to get. It is what they do."

Carter imagined plowing his eager fists into the

douchebag's face. "You ever touch her or any other woman without her permission again, and I will ruin your career." His tone was low, even, but the rage was there.

Alexi swallowed. "You are no one. You cannot touch my career." He drew himself up to his full height, still an inch or two shy of Carter's. "I touch who I want when I want." He drilled a long finger into Carter's chest.

"Wrong thing to say, asshole." Carter gripped the man's wrist and twisted. Spinning Alexi around, he shoved him up against Marilyn Monroe's bee-stung pout. He had Alexi's arm pinned behind his back at an angle that had the man whimpering.

"You ever touch Summer again, besides a polite hand-shake, and I will go to work on your face. First I'll break your nose. Then I'll shatter your jaw. And while your broken, mangled face is healing, who do you think will get all your jobs? All those campaigns?" Carter's grip tight-ened, and he gave Alexi enough of a shove that his fore-head knocked against the stall door. "Do you understand me?"

Alexi was sweating and keening against the partition.

Carter gave his forearm an extra tweak. "I said, do you understand me?"

"Yes, yes!" Alexi gasped, spit flying from his mouth.

"Now, I want you to go out there and apologize to Summer. And if it's not done to my satisfaction, I will find you, and I will hurt you."

The man gave a little whimper. "Okay. Okay. I will do so."

Carter released him. "Now, go wash your fucking hands," he ordered.

Alexi bolted for the sink, hands shaking.

"Well you certainly picked the right place for a pissing contest," Quincy said mildly from just inside the door.

Alexi ran past him, bursting through the door as if it were an escape hatch.

Carter straightened his jacket. "Quincy," he nodded and strolled out of the restroom.

His mood improved significantly when he spotted a sweaty and shaky Alexi in polite conversation with Summer.

Carter swelled with pride when Summer merely nodded briskly, not giving him any hint of friendliness. She offered her hand. Alexi glanced around the room and, spotting Carter, waited for his nod before accepting it for a perfunctory shake. He hurried off in the direction of the exit, bowling his way through a pack of executives.

Summer watched him go, a frown on her pretty face. Carter wandered her way.

"There you are!" Summer said with relief. "I was worried you got bored and wandered off or Katherine stole you away."

"She didn't catch on to our top secret relationship, did she?" Carter asked, stepping in closer.

"No, I think we're in the clear for now." Summer glanced over her shoulder.

"That was a nice save back there with Mary Beth, by the way," he told her.

"Thanks. Usually Katherine's assistant stays with her to help with names, but who knows where she disappeared to."

"I was almost enjoying Katherine squirming after she made me feel like a piece of meat."

"How dare she do that to a hot vegetarian," Summer said in mock horror.

"Well, you were very impressive and quick on your feet. I hope she appreciates you." Carter had a feeling she didn't.

"I hope you'll keep being impressed when I tell you the bad news."

"Does it involve extending the time between now and

when I get to peel that dress off you to see what you're wearing underneath?"

She bit her lip and nodded. "It's your own fault. If you hadn't impressed Katherine with your 'whole package,'" she waved her palm in front of him. "Then we'd be able to sneak out before the show."

"What does my *package* have to do with not being able to sneak out?" His package was currently straining behind his zipper at the idea of stripping Summer naked.

"She wants us—mainly you—to sit in the front row with her."

"I can tell by the look on your face that this is important, but I'm not exactly clear on why."

Summer laughed. "The front row is VIP-only. Usually at these events I don't even get to sit. I stand in the back. You and your sexy-as-hell everything just bumped a buyer for Saks and a Tony-nominee."

"I feel like you're still not speaking English."

"Have you ever watched the Victoria's Secret runway show?"

What red-blooded man hadn't? "I think I've seen bits and pieces of it."

"You'll be one of the people in the front row that the cameras are constantly panning over."

Carter swore. "This isn't going to be on TV, is it?"

Summer patted his shoulder. "No, but there will be photographers and videographers capturing your handsome face."

"I should have just waited for you at your place," he grumbled.

"But if you were waiting for me at home, you wouldn't know that the only thing I have on under this dress is a very pretty, very sheer thong."

He made a move to grab her, but she danced out of his reach and around another column.

He snagged her wrist and pulled her back against him in the dimly lit corner, the brick blocking them from the rest of the room. "You play dangerous games and think you're safe because we're in public."

She was breathing heavily. Her breasts rose, her lips parted.

He nuzzled against her neck. "You know what I could do to you here?"

She shook her head and angled her chin up, giving him more skin to tease.

"I could push you against this pillar." He nudged her forward until her hands met coarse brick. He kissed her behind the ear. "And I could slide my hand up your dress."

He gripped her shoulder and held her in place while his free hand roamed down between their bodies under the hem of her skirt.

"Carter!" A sharp whisper. A warning.

He skimmed his fingers down the gauzy material, following it from back to front. "I could slam my fingers into you right here." He pressed the pads of his fingers against the wet spot they found. "I could make you come."

"Carter." This time his name was a dark plea on her lips.

He pressed a kiss to the side of her face as his fingers worked in a tight little circle, teasing, tempting. She shuddered against him.

"I could do all that." His lips brushed against her ear. "But I won't."

Carter withdrew his hand and smoothed the layers of her skirt. "Yet."

Summer blew out a breath. "How do you do that?" She spun around and thumped him soundly on the chest.

"Do what?" He secured her hand, brought it to his mouth.

"Make me forget where we are and what I'm supposed to be doing. How do you make all that disappear so all I can think about is how empty I am without you inside me?"

It was Carter's turn to groan. He tried to adjust his erection, but it did nothing to relieve the pressure that had built so rapidly. He had wanted to tease her, not lose all control.

Now, she was watching him, cocky and proud of herself.

"You will be punished," he growled.

"We'll see. In the meantime, I hope you can control that before all those cameras are on you in the front row." She smiled innocently.

"I know I shouldn't, but I really like this mean, manipulative streak you've got going on," Carter sighed. "Now, please go away so I can get my blood back up to my brain. I can't look at you in that dress right now.

22

_____

*C*arter was able to pull himself together in time to take his seat on an uncomfortable bench between Summer and Katherine. Thankfully, he had the foresight to grab one of the gallery programs. He held it, rolled it up in his hand, and could use it to cover his crotch in case the situation got out of control again.

"Remember, don't smile, don't check your phone. Ignore the cameras. Just look at the clothes and frown like you're intrigued," Summer whispered in his ear as the lights dimmed.

"You owe me so much for this," he whispered back.

"I intend to pay up," she promised.

The show served as a distraction from how much he wanted to touch her. Lights pulsed in time with club music as model after model strutted down the raised runway dressed in clothing no normal woman would be caught wearing to the office or out to dinner.

The flashes from cameras were blinding. He didn't know how the models didn't get stunned by the light and trampled.

Carter couldn't help but notice that not one of the half-naked women parading past stirred him.

Summer had ruined other women for him, and if he hadn't already done so, he fully intended to ruin other men for her this weekend.

Katherine leaned over and whispered something about the color rose quartz being big for fall, which had the flashes from cameras dancing in his eyes again.

The show ended with the designer, a Korean man with a smile so perfect an orthodontist would weep, joining the models on the runway and offering the audience a bow and a double wave.

Carter stifled a sigh of relief as the crowd began to disperse. Katherine said a swift goodbye, kissing him on both cheeks, before departing.

"Okay, champ, pressure's off," Summer said, pulling him with her through a doorway and into an empty windowless gallery. "What do you think this is?" she mused, staring at the huge canvas of shapes and textures.

"A car crash," Carter answered, stepping in behind her and pulling her against him. He was hard. She could feel the length of his cock pressing into her lower back.

Wordlessly, she reached a hand behind her to grip his shaft through his pants.

A soft groan rumbled in his chest and Summer squeezed him harder.

"Two can play at that game," Carter said, quietly in her ear. One arm wrapped around her waist while his other hand slipped under the cup of her dress. His palm brushed her nipple and he gently squeezed her breast.

Summer's breath quickened. She shifted her hips back, grinding into him.

"Baby, you drive me crazy." His fingers tugged at her taut peak, making her dizzy with need.

She ached for more.

"I need to touch you, Summer." His fingers tugged harder. "Now. Somewhere without cameras."

Her gaze darted to the corner where the security camera blinked. "I think I know a place," she whispered.

They wound their way through the main gallery and down one hallway into another moving toward the back of the building. Summer prayed a silent prayer and turned the handle on an unmarked door.

It swung inward. "Oh, thank God," she whispered.

It was a small auxiliary kitchen that she had once used for a senior staff brunch. It was empty and dark now. A tiny window on the far wall by the refrigerator offered the only light.

Carter dragged her toward the window.

"There's no lock on the door," Summer hissed.

"I want to see you."

He pressed her against the stainless steel prep table, his erection throbbing against her stomach. "I can't wait anymore." His mouth claimed hers in a storm of heat and power. He overwhelmed her, and all Summer could do was cling to him. And as his mouth slanted over hers again and again, Summer's knees buckled.

He broke away and using his hands, turned her around to face the table.

A quick tug, and the ties of her halter were released. Summer gasped as her bare breasts pressed against cold steel.

Carter lifted her skirt, fingers skimming skin as they went.

"Beautiful girl," he whispered. With one hand at the back of her neck, the other grasped the top of her thong, a delicate web of fabric and sequins, and pulled it down just enough to leave her completely exposed.

"Please, Carter." Summer didn't know what she was begging for, she only knew need.

She heard his zipper and knew that soon she would be claimed. His hands left her, and she gasped. "Hang on, baby." She heard the rip of foil and his soft sigh as his hand slicked on the condom. Thank God he thought to bring one.

He didn't make her wait. Carter guided his shaft between her legs, parting her soft folds with his broad crown. She flexed her hips back against him and his hand returned to grip the back of her neck.

With aching precision he slowly entered her. Finally full, she sobbed.

"Hush, baby." His hand stroked her back and hip as he built a slow, gentle rhythm.

This. This. This was what she wanted, what she craved. With Carter inside her, stretching her until she was full, she was alive, and nothing else mattered.

Possessed.

She heard him groan, felt him pull back. "You're going to make me come too soon." He pulled out of her, his cock dangling against the back of her thighs. He pulled her underwear back into place.

"Please tell me you're not stopping," she whimpered.

"Turn around, baby."

Her shaking arms pushed off the table, and she turned in his arms on wobbly legs.

Lifting her up, he placed her on the edge of the table. "I want you to come with me," he said, his gray gaze drilling into her. He slid two fingers into her wet center. "Can you do that for me, baby?"

Summer nodded and opened her legs wider.

"Good girl. Now hang on to me, because this is going to be fast and hard." Carter pushed her thighs apart and yanked the thin scrap of her underwear to the side. He gripped his cock and stroked it once, twice, before guiding it to her core. His hands slid under her ass and lifted her as he speared into her. Summer instinctively wrapped her legs around his waist and gripped his shoulders.

His eyes didn't leave hers as he slammed into her again and again. Her eyes were half closed, but still their gazes held.

"I need to taste you." He ground out the words over clenched teeth. Carter lowered his mouth to her breast and with long, deep pulls drew her over the edge.

"Carter!" she gasped out his name as she felt herself tighten around him. It blazed through her like electricity.

He grunted against her breast, and she felt him jerk inside her, again and again. They clung together as their world fell apart.

~

THEIR TRYST in the kitchen took just enough of the edge off that they decided to order a very late dinner back at Summer's apartment.

"I can't believe you just ordered Chinese at midnight," Carter said peeling off her shoes. "Everything but the bars back home close by nine."

"Perks of city life, my country mouse," Summer said, leaning back against the pillows of the couch. His big hands enveloped her foot and absentmindedly began to rub.

Summer purred. "This makes me think of the back rub you gave me my second day on the farm."

Carter looked pained. "That was torture for me."

"For you? I was the one with spasms!"

He switched feet and started rubbing the neglected one.

"I was straddling you on a bed, touching you in an intimate place trying not to grind my hard cock into you while you moaned in a pillow. Fucking torture."

She threw her head back and laughed. "I'm glad I wasn't the only one suffering from trying to behave."

"You're starting to make me think you like torturing me."

"I like knowing that you want me."

The look he gave her, molten steel, had her stomach trembling.

"I'm so happy you're here," Summer sighed, running her finger tips across his chest and down his stomach, tracing lines and following curves.

Carter grabbed her wandering hand and pulled it to his lips. "I'm glad I'm here, too. I like seeing how you live here."

"It's no Blue Moon."

He laughed and nipped at her finger. "No, but you certainly have some characters here, too."

"They all seemed to be appropriately taken with you," Summer said, snuggling closer. "I think there will be some very eager readers when your article comes out.

"They only like me for my pretty face."

He wasn't far off, Summer thought. But the outside was what mattered in this industry, and being blessed the way Carter had been in that department only meant that his value sky-rocketed.

"Your friend Nikolai seems moderately human," he said.

"Yeah. He's a good guy. A womanizer, but a good guy."

"Did you ever..." Carter let the question hang in the air.

"Niko? No! Never," she laughed. "That's why we're friends. I'm the longest relationship with a woman he's ever had besides his mother."

His hands stilled on her feet. "Can I ask you something without you getting upset?"

"Maybe?"

"Why do you do this kind of work?"

"What do you mean?" Summer asked, resting her head on the back of the couch.

"You're smart, you're talented. But you're real. You don't fit here with the rest of them. They're all about advertisers and power plays and kiss-kiss, hate-hate, and here you are seeing people and stories. And what's more is I think you know you don't fit. I don't get it."

He got her. Carter saw her for the person she believed herself to be. There was no underestimating here. No thinly veiled disappointment. She wanted to hug him until he couldn't breathe, wanted to twirl around her living room with the thrill. How could someone she had just met know her better than everyone else in her life?

Summer bit her lip. "Can I tell you a secret that I've never told anyone?"

"Of course. Is it that you're really into dudes with beards?"

"That, and it's all part of the plan. I'm going to make senior editor and work there for two more years—three tops—learning everything I can, saving everything I can, and building my contacts. Then I'm going to start my own digital magazine."

"You sneaky, little—" Carter tickled her feet. "So you're not into any of this at all?"

"Well, I do love beautiful shoes and clothes. But do I care what anorexic, chain-smoking model is dating what heroin addict musician? Am I disappointed that I'll never have to drop everything that I'm doing to rewrite a blurb on our 'editor's favorite cover-ups' when an advertiser comes on board? Hell. No."

"Tell me about this magazine." Carter stroked her arm in lazy circles. "What's the angle?"

"Real life. Not four-thousand dollar must-have jackets for fall or sex tips from a former porn star—" She pinched him when he pretended to perk up. "It's going to be about real women living real lives and having real adventures. What do they care about, what do they do, how do they fuel their bodies, what and who do they love? We need role models showing us how to live, not supermodels."

Carter traced her nose with his finger. "You are going to disrupt the magazine industry."

"I intend to."

It felt so good to tell someone. Even better to tell Carter.

23

———

Summer was jolted awake by Carter's body going rigid next to hers. His breathing was coming in short, sharp gasps that punctuated the night's silence.

"Carter! Wake up." On her knees, she shook him.

When his eyes opened, she could tell he still wasn't with her.

"Wake up," she begged, blinking back tears. "You're safe. You're with me."

She saw it then. The recognition. The shame that flickered across his face. It hurt her to see his pain.

Carter sat up, swinging his legs over the side of the bed. He brought his head to his hands.

Summer wrapped her arms around him from behind, resting her cheek on his back. She could hear how his heart thundered in his chest. "Tell me."

He nodded.

Lights seemed too bright. So she lit candles and poured him a glass of water.

He paced. Naked. His mind still on the dream world he had just left.

Summer waited quietly. She sat cross-legged in the middle of the bed wearing Carter's discarded undershirt.

"It was another night and another mission," he said. His voice a rasp like there was too much pressure in his throat. "My team was a small tactical unit. Our job was to conduct raids on specific targets. There were some weeks during deployment that we were rolling outside the wire every night."

He prowled the room like a jungle cat in captivity.

"Mission after mission. We were good. We were tight. There were close calls. A lot of them. But we had ops down to a science. One night we were given orders to take a target in a small compound outside of Kunduz. He was in hiding with a small security team, and we were to extract them."

Carter paused, hands on hips. Staring as if looking back through time.

"It all went like clockwork. We breeched both buildings at the same time. He was in mine, and I was going to find him. We cleared the front room. There was no furniture, just trash everywhere. He was squatting in this place.

"The back room was locked. Just a flimsy hollow door. We were in in seconds. Me and Ramirez. And there they were. Two of them both holding pistols. We had him. We had them. But there was crying. I looked down." Carter looked down at Summer's bed.

"She was seven. Curled up, crying. Dirt on her face. Bare feet. Terror. The terror in those huge brown eyes. I tell Ramirez to grab her, and then—" his voice broke.

Summer tightened her hold on the pillow to keep herself from going to him.

"The target shot her. Right between the eyes." His finger grazed the skin at the top of his nose. "Started screaming that he would rather have her dead than with American pigs."

"I shot him six times before I fell. His buddy got me twice before Ramirez took him down."

Summer clasped her hands over the sob that tried to claw its way free.

"I laid there on the dirt floor, staring into her dead eyes and watching our blood pool together."

She went to him now. Offered him the only comfort she could. Summer wrapped her arms around his waist and buried her face in his back.

He forged on. "When I came home, I was a mess. I couldn't sleep because of the nightmares. I felt like I was never going to drag myself out of the abyss. The hate that I felt for that man scared me. I ended his life. I ended the hate that spewed out of him like a river. Sometimes the only thing that made me feel better was walking through those six bullets over and over again." He let out a shaky sigh, and Summer placed her lips on his back, tasting her own tears.

"And then I realized that me hating him was no different than him hating me. Fighting hate with hate gets you nowhere. That man was taught to hate his entire life. But me? I had a choice."

"You chose a better way," she whispered against his hot skin.

"I chose a better way," he repeated. "And things got better."

"But you still have the dreams," she said.

"Balance and control became very important to me. So sometimes, when I feel my control slip a little or when I get to feeling an intense high or low, the dreams come back. It's a weakness that I'm working on. I'm a work in progress."

She pressed her forehead into his back. "Carter, it's not a weakness. You're healing. There's a difference."

He was calmer now. His heart beat slower, but she still felt the tension in his muscles. Remnants of the dream, shards of a memory so sharp it still bled.

And she knew it as the truth before she said it.

"I love you, Carter."

She heard it. The intake of breath. And then he was pulling her around into his arms.

"I know it's too early. I know we just decided to see where this will go. We're supposed to wait months and really get to know each other before we say something crazy like this. But I love you, Carter Pierce. I love who you are and how you got to be you. Every story, every secret, everything I learn about you makes me love you more. And more weeks or months aren't going to change that."

He cupped her face in his hands.

Tears blurred her eyes until she couldn't see him through them. "You trusting me with this—" she clutched at her heart, at the ache in her chest. She started again. "You are the best person I know, and I love you."

Carter gently wiped her tears.

"Summer."

Her name on his lips carried so much emotion, so much weight, she had to lean into him. She saw the scars on his chest and torso and gently laid her lips on them. Once, twice. And then she pressed them to his heart.

"What took you so long?"

"What?" She leaned back and looked up.

"I've been waiting for you to catch up." Carter brushed his knuckles against her cheek. "I love you, Summer. I've loved you almost as long as I've known you. I loved you even before you let me put my hands on you."

"You love me?"

"Baby. How could I not? You're the one I've been waiting

for." He wrapped his arms around her, snuggling her head against his chest.

They rocked, side to side, in the candlelight, and Summer listened to the strong, slow beat of a heart that loved her.

∾

Saturday morning Summer yawned mightily and snuggled deeper into her pillow.

"Oh, no you don't." The bed sank as Carter sat on the edge. "Open your eyes."

"Mm," Summer muttered in the very comfortable pillow.

Carter slapped her on the butt, and she rolled over lazily. "Why are you torturing me awake at..." she squinted at the bedside clock. "Why didn't you wake me sooner?"

It was after eight. She needed to take her pills.

"Here." Carter took her hand and dumped three capsules and a tablet into it.

She stared down at them, panic rising in her chest.

He handed her a glass of water.

She kept her gaze down as she washed down the pills.

"You slept through the alert on your phone, so I followed the instructions on it. You're very thorough."

Summer was still silent. He couldn't know. Not after last night. He said he loved her. She wanted to hang onto that as long as possible. Maybe it was selfish of her, but if love turned into obligation and worry, it would ruin what they found together.

She needed just a few more weeks.

"Hey." Carter put his hand over the fist she had balled in the comforter. "You can tell me when you're ready, okay?"

Summer let out the breath she had been holding. She risked a look at his face.

Those serious gray eyes studied her. Hair tousled from sleep. He wore his Pierce Acres t-shirt and a pair of gym shorts. The body of a warrior and the face of an angel. And he was hers. She could tell him, and he would do what he thought was the right thing. He would stick. But she wanted more. Didn't she deserve more than a sense of obligation? Didn't he deserve more than an iffy future?

"Can I buy you breakfast?" she asked.

~

IT WAS CLOSER to brunch by the time Summer finished getting ready. Sex hair was much harder to tame than regular bed head. And walking out the door in the city was a different story than in Blue Moon. She could probably walk into Overly Caffeinated or OJ's in pajama pants, and no one would blink.

But go out in last season's "it" shirt here, and she'd be labeled immediately.

Over the commotion in her head, Summer had managed to pull herself and an outfit together and made herself Manhattan-brunch presentable.

Carter was sprawled on the couch in gray shorts and a tight black polo.

"Have you starved to death, yet?" Summer asked.

"I ate one of your throw pillows to take the edge off." Carter sat up. "Come here." He patted the cushion next to him, but when she got there he pulled her into his lap.

"Are you going to let things get weird because of last night?" he asked, resting his chin on her head.

Summer relaxed in his arms.

"There is no weirdness because of last night," she promised.

"So you aren't going to think of me as some sad, victimized head case?"

Summer wriggled in his lap to look him in the eye. "Carter Pierce!" Her laugh was genuine. "There is nothing about you that says victim or head case."

"Are you regretting what you told me last night?" he asked.

"Hmm, I can't quite remember what I told you." She tapped a finger to her chin. "Maybe you can refresh my memory?"

Carter flipped her over his knee, and Summer shrieked. Two well-placed smacks were enough to jog her memory.

"Okay! Okay! I remember!" she giggled.

Carter righted her. "I'm waiting."

She took his face in her hands. "I love you, Carter."

His grin was slow and sweet. "Let's go get something to eat so we can come back and I can spank you some more."

24

———

She took him to a pocket-sized place that served up a nice vegetarian brunch. They ate inside to avoid the late June sizzle and swelter. Afterward, they braved the heat for the hand-in-hand walk back to Summer's apartment.

"What would you like to do today?" she asked him.

His wolfish look told her exactly what he wanted to do.

"I mean in the city. Wearing clothes."

"What do you like to do on your days off?"

Summer laughed. "My days off?" She didn't have days off. If she wasn't in the office, she was working from home. If she wasn't working on magazine projects or attending events, she was blogging.

And if she wasn't doing any of that, she was doing laundry.

All things she should be doing today. Instead, she was strolling down the sidewalk holding hands with the man she loved.

And not feeling the least bit guilty about it.

"How about this? You suffered through my work days," Carter reminded her. "It's only fair that I follow you around and mess up whatever you're doing with my distracting sexiness."

She hip checked him. "I was a great farm hand!"

"You were okay," he winked.

"You know what? Let's pretend that we're regular New Yorkers with a Saturday all to ourselves."

"And what would these regular New Yorkers do?"

A slow grin spread across her face. "I have a few ideas."

$\sim$

SHE TOOK him to a Yankees game.

But not before they spent the afternoon enjoying the air conditioning of the American Museum of Natural History, where Summer let Carter the farmer educate her on the biodiversity of the New York State environment.

They took in a matinee at a second run theater that served beer and baked goods out of its concession stand. And then they carved out time for an early dinner at a crowded Irish pub around the corner before hailing a cab to their surprise destination.

Yankee Stadium.

Carter kicked back in his legendary blue seat with a prime view of home plate, a seven-dollar beer tucked into the cup holder.

"Very good surprise, Summer." He riffed the bill of the baseball cap he bought her.

"I had a feeling you'd enjoy this traditional New York pastime." She cheered with the rest of the crowd at the crack of the bat.

"I used to come here with my father and brothers," he told her, eyes scanning the field.

"Really?" She settled back in her seat and sampled the wine that came in a little plastic bottle.

"It was Mom's Father's Day gift to Dad every year. Pierce Men Day, she'd call it. I realize now that it was actually a gift to herself getting us all out of the house at the same time."

"Can't really blame her."

"We had some good times on those trips," Carter said. "Once, Jax got lost on his way back from the bathroom. We spent the entire fifth looking for him. Turns out he was entertaining some big wig with a box, and we got to watch the rest of the game from up there." Carter pointed at the glass walled suites.

"Do you miss him? Your father, I mean."

"Every damn day." Carter sipped his beer. "I barely made it home in time to say goodbye."

"Were you deployed?" Summer asked.

"Yeah. The Red Cross got Beckett's message to me." *This is it. Come home.* "I was on the next flight home. They got me as far as Albany. Jax picked me up and drove me to the hospital going ninety in the car the whole way. That's when it started to sink in."

Summer linked her fingers with his and he squeezed.

"He looked so... small in that hospital bed." He sighed. "Nothing like the John Pierce who could take all three of us when we ganged up on him in the pond."

"He must have been so proud of you, of all of you. The soldier, the lawyer, the writer."

"I didn't get to spend much time with him in his last years." A regret he still carried. "Neither did Jax. But Beckett was there for it all. He kept it all together until I could come home."

"And now you've all come home again," Summer reminded him.

Jax's brewery, Carter remembered. It was an idea that he'd put on the back burner. But it warranted careful consideration.

"I keep dumping all of my sad stories on you," he said, changing the subject.

"I like understanding how you turned into the fascinating, sexy man before me."

She said it without a hint of irony, and he bit back a sigh.

Summer was hiding something. Something big enough to scare her. But he would wait. And when Summer was ready, she would share. For now, he would enjoy a warm summer night with the beautiful woman who held his heart.

25

---

*T*he fireworks lit up the East River in a showy shower of color and flash.

Another holiday, another holiday party. Summer had planned to take two days of vacation time and spend them with Carter in Blue Moon. The town's Fourth Festival was apparently legendary.

However, when Katherine personally requested her attendance at the rooftop party hosted by a major department store, plans had to be changed. Especially when she mentioned that some senior staff members were starting to take notice of Summer's work. Things were falling into place, and in a few short years, she could follow her own dreams.

Carter was understanding.

But understanding didn't make up for the distance. In fact, it made her miss him more. The summer was high season on the farm, which meant Carter's free time was nonexistent. And combined with her renewed efforts to get back on top at work, they hadn't seen each other since his weekend in New York.

The phone calls and video chats weren't cutting it

LUCY SCORE

anymore. She missed him constantly and was surprised at the discontent she felt. This is what she had spent years working for, wasn't it? And yet here she was, feeling empty and alone on a spectacular terrace while the rich and beautiful partied poolside.

It was just annoyance at having to change her plans, she told herself.

Thankfully, the photo shoot was next week. She would get to spend two days on the farm watching Niko get assaulted by goats, determining what, if any, progress Jax had made with Joey, and spending as much time as possible with Carter's hands on her.

She could even extend it to three days if she planned carefully and used some vacation time, she mused.

Her phone signaled an incoming call, and her heart flip-flopped.

"Hi, handsome," Summer answered, her voice giving away her smile.

"Happy Fourth of July, beautiful." Carter's voice sent a rush of heat flooding through her.

She heard the booms and cracks on his end along with the oohs and ahs of the crowd.

"Where are you on this fine summer evening?" she asked.

"I'm in the square. Along with the entire population of the town," he grumbled. "Mom's idea, of course. It looks like a 1960s sit-in protest."

Summer laughed. "I can only imagine."

"I'd rather imagine you. What are you wearing?"

Summer laughed, glancing down at her festive red cotton minidress. "Stars and stripes underwear and patent leather red heels."

He hummed at that. "Great minds think alike. I'm wearing the matching loincloth."

"I'm really liking this mental picture." Summer snagged a bottle of water off the tray of a passing waiter.

"I wish you were here, Summer." His voice was low, sweet. She felt it like a caress and closed her eyes. For a second, it was just them.

"I do, too." She meant it. "I'll be there in a week," she reminded him.

"That feels like a year from now."

She laughed because it did for her, too. "I think we'll survive. I love you, Carter."

"I love you, honey. Here comes the finale."

She heard the booms through the phone. They watched together as town and city lit up in a blaze of festive color and sound.

~

THAT NIGHT, as the fourth ticked into the fifth, Summer lay awake thinking. When had a week become a lifetime? When had she ever let her life revolve around a man? Not since her father, she thought with regret.

And look how that had turned out.

The tiny, mean voice in her head put in its two cents.

Summer could still feel the cut of his disappointment. Still see the anger and sadness in her father's eyes. He had thought she was letting him down and wouldn't even listen to her as she tried to explain that she was trying to make him proud.

She was pandering to fools just like the rest of the fashion industry, he had told her. Didn't she want to do something important? Something meaningful? Did she only care about pretty dresses and celebrity gossip?

The words still had the power to cut her all these years later.

Summer rolled over to her side and switched her thoughts to Carter. *Was there any way this relationship could actually work?* she wondered. Moving to Blue Moon wasn't an option for her. She had a plan and was within striking distance of the next step. She couldn't just give it all up for... what? What would she do on a farm in the middle of nowhere?

Could she move closer? Make it less of a long-distance relationship? She thought of the train in Rhinecliff and shook her head against the pillow. Moving out of Manhattan would hurt her work in more ways than one. How long could they continue this way? Stolen moments, all-too-brief weekends. Constantly setting aside work to make time for each other.

What would suffer more? Their work or their relationship?

She took a sip of water from the glass she kept on her nightstand.

None of this could be decided tonight.

In September, she would have real answers, and with those answers, she would be able to build a future that suited her. But was it fair to Carter to keep going without answers? Was it fair to tie him to her when things could change forever in a few weeks?

∼

IT WAS JUST after one in the morning when Summer's headlights hit the farmhouse.

The Saturday night fundraiser had run long thanks in part to the lengthy speeches during the award portion of the evening. Summer felt a little guilty for bolting before dessert had been served, but she had paid her dues by logging in to a Saturday morning production video chat with several of the magazine's go-to freelancers.

What she did with her very late Saturday night, or rather Sunday morning, was her business.

It was a good pep talk, but she still couldn't shake the guilt. It seemed to be following her everywhere these days.

She parked in front of the house and carried her bag up the front steps. The front of the house was dark except for the soft glow of the porch light. The front door was open as always.

Summer left her bag at the foot of the stairs and followed the light that came from the kitchen.

She found Jax in gym shorts and nothing else working on his laptop in the great room. The TV was muted to accommodate the woman grumbling over the speaker of Jax's phone.

"Look, I know it's trite. I know it's been done. But the formula works, and we gotta figure out how to make this unlikeable hero likeable enough that the audience doesn't end up cheering for the bad guy," the disembodied voice explained.

"Uh-huh." Jax pulled up ESPN on his laptop. "How about you walk me through some of your ideas, Penny?"

Summer cleared her throat softly.

Jax rolled his head on the back of the sofa and grinned when he saw her.

Penny droned on about an opening sequence.

"Carter?" Summer mouthed.

Jax pointed upstairs and laid the side of his face on his hands miming sleep.

She winked and waved.

Jax shook his head and tapped his cheek until Summer moved in to give him a kiss. He ruffled her hair. "Welcome back," he whispered.

Summer headed back down the hall and grabbed her bag. Upstairs, she found Carter's bedroom door cracked open. She stepped inside and put her bag down, admiring the view.

He was sprawled on his back. The sheet bunched low on his waist, baring the glory of his torso to her.

All doubts and concerns that had hammered in her head for days now disappeared and were replaced with a sharp, desperate need.

As Summer stripped off her clothes, Carter's eyes flickered open. Opening his arms, he lifted the sheet and welcomed her to his bed.

Nothing else mattered.

~

SUNDAY MORNING DAWNED BRIGHT, and despite the lack of sleep the night before, the residents of Carter's bed woke with enthusiasm.

Summer felt a twinkle of pride when Carter pulled on the t-shirt she gave him. She dressed quickly in shorts and a pretty tank and followed Carter downstairs.

In the kitchen, Jax arched an eyebrow watching Summer struggle to tame her blonde tresses with a bun and Carter reach for the coffee pot with a self-satisfied grin. "You two look... rested," he commented.

"And you look like you got a nice, quiet night's sleep. Alone," Carter smirked.

"Dick."

"Asshole."

"Boys," Summer warned. She gave up on her hair and pulled on her Yankees cap.

"Yes, ma'am," they replied in unison.

"I can't begin to imagine the hell that you three put your poor mother through over the years."

"Phoebe Pierce isn't the innocent little angel you think she is. She tortured us in ways only a mother can," Jax said through a mouthful of cereal.

"Piano lessons," Carter supplied.

"Carpool sing-alongs on the way to school," Jax added.

"That time she got pissed at us and hid the TV remotes for a week."

"The Great Vegan Experiment of 1995."

"Trust us," Carter said, riffing the bill of her cap. "We learned torture from the best."

Jax dumped his empty bowl in the sink. "Give me five minutes to change, and I'll be ready to go."

He hustled upstairs, and Summer and Carter ate a quick breakfast. Jax came back down wearing his Pierce Acres t-shirt.

"Aren't you two cute in your matching shirts?" Summer cooed.

"It's our farmers market uniform," Carter grinned. "And technically, you're to blame for it."

"Yeah, you know, I think Summer could use a little brand-ing," Jax said, scratching his chin.

"Like the hot iron, flesh-searing branding?" Summer gulped.

"Well, we could go in that direction, or you could just wear this," Carter said, tossing her a green t-shirt.

"You got me a shirt!"

"Welcome to the family," Carter said, kissing the top of her head. "Go change."

26

---

*T*he entire town square with its wide brick sidewalks and leafy shade trees had been transformed into an open-air market. It wasn't quite eight yet, and already it was bustling. Vendors, including the Pierce brothers, erected pop-up canopies over folding tables that were soon covered in a variety of wares.

Summer helped unload and then stepped in to take over the setup when she realized they intended to just dump produce in sloppy piles.

"Trust me on this," she said, wielding a summer squash at Carter. "Presentation is important."

She organized the cucumbers, squash, and ears of corn into a cascading rainbow of color on the table before moving on to neatly stack beefsteak tomatoes in an upended crate on the ground. The green beans she lay in precise horizontal rows, edging the length of the table.

"Some galvanized tubs and crates would be better," she muttered to herself. "And little handwritten chalkboard signs for the names and prices."

"Huh," Carter grunted.

She turned from her work. Carter and Jax were standing, arms crossed, studying her display.

"That looks a lot better than what we usually do," Jax said.

"Your stand is going to be photographed today. It should look its best," she lectured, opening one of the paper sacks and weighting it with a beefy cucumber so that the Pierce Acres stamped logo was visible.

Summer stood back to admire her work and gave it a nod.

"Okay. Now what?"

"Now we wait for the crowds to descend demanding high-quality vegetables," Carter said, rubbing her shoulders.

"Well, look who decided to step up their game." Beckett strolled over, hands in the pockets of his shorts. "I can tell neither one of you style-less idiots did this." He swept Summer into a bear hug, lifting her off her feet.

"Summer classed up our stand." Jax picked up three tomatoes and started to juggle.

"It's more art directing," she laughed as Beckett put her on her feet again.

"If you can hang out here for a few minutes before going all Mr. Mayor on us, I'll take Summer on the grand tour of the market," Carter said to his brother.

Summer checked the time. They still had an hour before Niko was due to meet them.

"Sure, but it'll cost you. Bring me back a bag of those mini donuts," Beckett said, joining Jax behind the table.

Carter led Summer away by the hand as Beckett challenged Jax to juggle cucumbers.

"Are you sure it's safe to be seen together here?" Summer said, tugging at their joined hands.

Carter brought her hand to his lips. "I realized that as long as the BC thinks they won, they leave me alone."

"Have they won?" she laughed as they walked past a stand selling reusable shopping totes.

"They don't consider it an official win until there's a marriage license. So we've got some time before they crank up the pressure again."

Carter was just kidding, Summer told herself as her stomach pitched with guilt. They had known each other for a month. It was too soon in a summer fling to start talking futures.

"Where are these donuts Beckett asked for?" Summer asked as they looped past a handmade soap stand run by a woman wearing a turquoise jumpsuit and round Lennon sunglasses.

"Right next to Willa's vegan flip-flop stand," Carter said, nudging her forward.

"Vegan flip-flops?"

∽

THEY RETURNED to the booth with little bags of fresh donuts for everyone and two pairs of Willa's flip-flops for Summer. Willa had predicted a long and loving relationship. Summer still wasn't sure that she had been talking about shoes.

Phoebe had arrived and paused in her booth supervision to greet Summer with a big, heartfelt hug.

"So happy to see you again, Summer," she said, giving her one last squeeze. "Are you going to help me whip these boys into produce-selling machines?"

Summer stepped over a smashed tomato, the victim of a juggling mishap, she presumed.

"Nikolai will be here soon. I think I'll just watch you all work your market magic."

"Yeah. Mom's not going to let that happen." Carter said, digging out the cashbox. "It's all hands on deck here."

And it was. Within minutes the entire square was bustling with business. It seemed everyone in Blue Moon was either a vendor or a shopper. It was friendly, colorful chaos. She caught snippets of conversations about summer vacations, the closing of the local yoga studio. Apparently Maris was closing up shop and moving to Santa Fe.

Everyone knew everyone, and that included the Pierces. They answered questions about the farm and asked after everyone's Uncle Bill or family dog. Jax caught up with old friends from high school and their parents, spouses, and children.

The whole market had the festive feel of a summer picnic. And it wasn't long before Summer was drawn into conversations with Fitz, who was there for a bag of donuts, and Ernest Washington. Rainbow stopped by and officially introduced herself. She passed Summer a brochure on opening a new checking account at the bank.

Beckett took a break to catch up with the other vendors and make himself available to the rest of the residents. Carter called it his "kissing babies lap." He came back twenty minutes later with a carrier of coffees. "Overly Caffeinated traded me coffee for two dozen eggs. Can you bag 'em up for me, Summer?" he asked, handing over the coffee.

When Beckett left to deliver the eggs, Summer allowed herself a short coffee break to scope out the stand next door. It was an organic milk stand run by a local dairy farm. Their big draw was the frisky little calf they brought with them. Sassy trotted around her portable pen welcoming pats and scratches from treat-bearing visitors.

Jax caught Summer stroking Sassy's soft ears. "It's emotional blackmail," he told her. "How is someone supposed to just pick up a carton of growth hormone-laden milk at the gas station without thinking about happy, grass-fed Sassy?"

"At least they aren't selling steaks with Sassy here as their spokesperson," Summer said, giving her a final ear scratch before ducking back under the canopy. "That would be emotional blackmail and a terrible business strategy."

Summer moved in behind Carter to grab more paper bags and caught the tail end of his conversation with a frazzled looking woman with frizzy auburn hair. "So we'll see you at ten tomorrow. I really, *really* appreciate it," she said.

"Looking forward to it, Tracey," Carter said in a voice that made Summer believe he was lying through his nice, straight teeth. The woman hurried off carting a half dozen bags with her, and Carter turned around to look at Beckett.

"Absolutely not," Beckett snapped. "There's no fucking way you're dragging me into that mess again." He shuddered. "I still have nightmares about last year."

"Fine. I can count on my favorite brother here," Carter said, dropping an arm over Jax's shoulders.

"I get to be the favorite? Cool." Jax grinned.

"You won't think so when one of those baby-toothed monsters sets fire to your pants while the others try to pillage the farm."

"Does Beckett hate children?" Summer asked.

"These aren't just any children. They're Higgenworth Communal Alternative Education Day Care children," Beckett said, his eye twitching.

When Summer just looked at him, Carter stepped in. "They come from parents who don't like using the word 'no' and think that structure and discipline squash their delicate, little kid spirits."

"So they're holy terrors?"

"Exactly. And you, my beautiful girl," he wrapped his arms

around her and pulled her in, "get to see them up close and personal tomorrow morning when they come for their annual field trip."

"Stop making out, and get me some change," Beckett snarked.

"You're just jealous that you have no one to make out with," Phoebe clucked.

"That's low, Mom. Real low."

Summer counted out ears of corn and bagged tomatoes for Carter while he talked trailer hitches and rainwater barrels with patrons. She was so busy making change that she didn't notice that Nikolai had arrived until he shoved his camera in her face.

"I didn't recognize you in that getup," he said, tapping the bill of her hat. "Didn't know you were a Yankees fan."

Summer looked at his designer jeans and leather loafers and grinned. Wait until Clementine got a load of him. "Welcome to Blue Moon Bend," she said, drawing him behind the table.

"Sorry I'm late. I drove around looking for a parking meter before I realized there aren't any here."

She laughed. It was nice to see someone who was more a fish out of water here than she was. "Let me introduce you to everyone. We've got all four Pierces here." She made the introductions and gave Nikolai little pieces on his subjects. Carter the ex-Army Ranger farmer. Beckett the mayor. Jax the Hollywood scriptwriter. And Phoebe the mother with a master's degree in agricultural science.

Nikolai had an easy way about him that helped his subjects relax more in front of the camera. She needn't have worried about him warming up the Pierces. In no time, he had the brothers razzing each other and Phoebe smacking heads.

She helped Nikolai stow his gear before jumping out of

the stand. "I don't think portraits will work as well as candids here," she cautioned him.

Eyebrow raised, Nikolai peered at her over the screen of his camera.

"Sorry. Micromanaging," Summer waved her hands.

She let him work, let the Pierces execute their well-honed farmers market choreography. Laughing, chatting, bagging. Nikolai quietly capturing the way Carter tossed tomatoes into the open bag Phoebe held. How Beckett stepped in and seamlessly changed the subject when Jax's conversation with someone shifted to Joey. They functioned as a team and not just at the market.

It gave her a little twinge of envy to know she wasn't a part of it.

~

As the farmers market began to wind down early that afternoon, the Pierce brothers started loading up the now nearly empty bushels and baskets. The leftover produce went into Phoebe's car, which she would deliver to a church that fed the hungry and down-on-their-luck.

Carter pressed cash into Summer's hand and a kiss on her mouth and sent her off to grab take and bake pizzas from Maizie at Peace of Pizza's stand for a late lunch back on the farm.

With Nikolai following them in his rented SUV, they headed back to the farm where they enjoyed a casual, friendly lunch on the porch. Nikolai took the afternoon to shoot at the stables, and Jax tagged along. Presumably to put himself in Joey's way.

Summer volunteered to weed and water the flowerbeds while Carter and Beckett repaired a portion of fencing that had been damaged by a tree branch during a summer thunderstorm.

The humidity clung to Summer like a sweater, and in minutes she had worked up a satisfying sweat. It was such a pleasure to discover how good physical labor made her feel. It was comforting, the simplicity of clearing out what didn't belong and leaving order and beauty in its place.

She gave the front beds a good soaking with the hose before working her way around the side of the house where Carter and Beckett were just finishing up the new fence rail.

"Hey, Summer, when you're done there, we have a field of lettuce to harvest," Beckett teased.

She glared at him and fisted her hands on her hips.

"Now, Beckett, don't go picking on her like that," Carter said. "Summer can't help that she's a city girl who doesn't like getting dirty."

"Aren't you two funny?" she snipped. "You know, I don't mind getting dirty as much as you two mind getting wet."

She managed to spray Beckett in the chest with the hose and hit Carter full in the face before he gave chase. She dropped the hose and took off, looping around the front of the house and running for her life past the little barn.

She made it as far as the orchard before her lungs and legs gave out.

Crouching behind an apple tree, she tried to catch her breath. Her hands were coated with mud from weeding and sweat trickled down her back.

"Summer, where are you?" His sing-song tone told her she was in trouble if he caught her.

She smothered her laughter as he stalked past her, gaze roaming the orchard.

Carter never saw it coming. One moment he was the hunter, and the next the hunted. Summer launched herself onto his back, her muddy palm smearing across his face, through his beard, and up into his hair.

His counterattack was lightning fast and brutal.

He spun her off his back and tossed her over his shoulder as if she weighed less than a sack of feed.

Her victorious laughter quickly changed to nervous giggles when he started to walk and then run.

"Where are you taking me?" she yelped, trying to right herself.

He smacked her soundly on the ass. "Farm rules, honey."

She saw the wood of the dock racing by under his feet and realized what he was about to do.

"Carter Pierce, don't you dare," she shrieked.

Her protests did no good. Carter sprinted the length of the dock and launched them both off the end.

The icy pond water closed over her, and Summer tried to flail her way to freedom. But his strong hands were everywhere. She froze when one of those hands splayed across her bare stomach under her t-shirt. Their heads broke the surface, and she could see the fire in her eyes mirrored in his. He locked her legs around his waist, keeping one hand just under her breast.

"Summer." It was a warning.

"Carter." It was a dare.

And then his mouth was on hers. The frigid water forgotten, Summer opened for him. His tongue swept into her mouth, stealing her breath and sanity. His hands cruised up, taking her t-shirt with them. He tossed it over his shoulder where it landed with a sopping thump on the deck.

"Here?" she whispered against his mouth.

"I don't have a condom," he said, moving his lips over hers.

She pulled his t-shirt over his head and tossed it toward land.

"I don't want to stop," she murmured, diving into a kiss so hot it burned.

"Are you sure?" he asked her, nudging her chin so she'd look at him.

"I'm positive." She crushed her mouth to his.

One hand deftly unhooked her bra while the other yanked the straps from her shoulders.

She shivered as her breasts tumbled free, into Carter's waiting palms.

He propelled them toward the dock and closed her fingers around the ladder behind her. "Hold on," he ordered.

Carter dipped below the surface, and with a swift tug, her shorts and underwear were yanked free. He rose out of the water, droplets clinging to his hair and skin, and reached for her.

Even in the cool water, the heat from his body warmed her. He wrapped her legs around his waist again, and she felt him, hard and ready against her.

"Don't let go," he told her when she tried to release the ladder.

Her arms quaked, and her breath came in short gasps.

"Look at me, Summer."

She did as he asked and in his face she saw a raw, desperate need. In his eyes, something softer.

He entered her with one powerful surge that tore a cry from her throat.

"I could have you like this every day for the rest of my life, and it still wouldn't be enough."

His whispered words broke something loose inside her.

"Carter," she sobbed out his name. "I love you."

He answered her with his body. Giving until she could take no more.

In the water, under the sun, they loved each other.

27

_T_he Higgenworth Communal Alternative Education Day Care disembarked from their fleet of minivans at precisely 10:35 Monday morning.

"I'm so sorry," puffed Tracey, the center director, as she hauled a sticky toddler in a tie-dye t-shirt out of a car seat and handed her to Carter. "Ernie and Wahlon tried to escape again. Grandma Phyllis barely caught them before they climbed the fence. And then Katie Bell there threw up in the van, and we had to pull into the car wash to get everyone cleaned up."

Carter held Katie Bell out at arm's length, and she giggled, reaching for his beard.

"Don't let her get hold of that," Tracey warned, hefting a little boy out of his seat. "She's little but has fists like a vice grip." She passed him to Summer.

"Okay, HCAEDC adults," she called. "Let's do a headcount before we lose another one."

The five chaperones looked woefully unprepared for the chaos that a dozen tie-dye clad toddlers would wreak. Four of them were crying. Two were rolling around in the gravel yelling "Hulk smash!" A little girl was trying to fit her head through the spindles on the front porch. And Grandma Phyllis was sliding a flask back into her fanny pack.

"It's liquid Benadryl," she assured Summer, sneezing three times. "I'm allergic to—" She sneezed again. "Everything."

The little boy in Summer's arms turned and squished her cheeks between his chubby little hands. "Fis' face!" he shrieked. "Fis' face!"

She heard the click of Niko's camera.

"If you don't put that camera down and help us, I'm going to Hulk smash you," Summer said politely through her fish face.

Katie Bell took advantage of Carter's distraction and grabbed two fistfuls of beard. Niko's camera clicked again.

The headcount came out wrong three times until Jax came out of the house clutching a pigtailed little girl like a football under his arm. "I found her watching TV inside. I could only find one of her shoes."

Summer put her charge on the ground and hurried to Carter's rescue. She tickled Katie Bell until the little girl let go of her prize. Carter dumped her in a pile of kids and yanked out his cellphone. "We're gonna need all hands on deck for this."

The tour started off well enough with the adults, now including Joey and Phoebe, forming a circle around the rainbow-clad toddlers.

"This is not part of my job," Joey grumbled as a three-year-old boy walked behind her smacking her.

"Butt. Butt. Butt." Smack. Smack. Smack.

He wound up again, but Joey was faster. She whirled around and pointed a finger in his face. "Listen, Lucifer Jr., smack me or anyone else here one more time today and I'm feeding you to the goat."

Lucifer Jr. let out a satisfying scream and ran to the opposite side of the circle.

"There's supposed to be safety in numbers," Carter muttered.

"I think we need more adults," Summer whispered back.

"I wish you had herding dogs," Tracey called to Carter as she chased a little boy with glasses and a fishing hat back into the fold.

The man walking behind Summer—Grandpa Willis—caught up to the pigtailed girl who was taking off her shirt. "Mai Tai Joplin! We keep our shirts on in public, don't we?" Mai Tai shoved a finger up her nose and wandered off. "These are their field trip shirts," he said to Summer. "We make 'em wear 'em so we can see them if they wander off. One time we lost one dressed in camo for an hour in the corn maze. He had beheaded the scarecrow before we could get to him."

Summer pasted a smile on her face and hurried to catch up with Carter.

"What do you usually do on the tour?" Summer hissed to Carter.

"We used to take them to the horse barn, but Joey put an end to that last year when they ate the sugar cubes they were supposed to feed to the horses. It was horrible. It took the horses two days to recover from the hell that broke loose in that barn."

"You're kidding me."

"Look around you. Is that really a stretch? We also used to do hay rides, but two years ago Johnny 'Future Juvenile Delinquent' Delroy climbed up on the tractor and put it in gear. I still have nightmares about it," he shivered. "Now we just walk them around until they get sleepy, and then we send them back to the school for lunch."

"How long until then?"

"11:30."

She grabbed his watch arm and checked the time. "We're never going to make it."

"Stay strong, honey. I'll protect you as long as I can."

Carter's protection lasted all of three minutes until Johnny's little brother, Jimmi, picked up a handful of goat poop and threw it at Summer.

"Now, Jimmi, what have we told you about throwing poop?" Tracey sighed.

Summer looked down at her shorts and gagged. "I need to go get cleaned up," she told Joey. Nikolai's camera clicked, and Summer wanted to smash it into his face.

"There is no way in hell you're leaving the circle," Joey said, firmly gripping her arm. "They're trying to pick us off one by one. I'm not letting that happen. Now shake it off and stay strong."

"I've got an idea," Carter announced. "Close ranks, and I'll be back in five."

"Where are you going?" Jax demanded. "Never mind, I don't care. Send me instead."

"Just keep walking. I'll catch back up," Carter answered, jogging away.

Summer watched him go with a combination of envy and abject fear. "He's never coming back, is he?"

"He wouldn't abandon us," Joey said, but Summer heard the uncertainty in her tone.

They got the kids, skipping and running, past the CSA barn and around the eggplants and tomatoes without losing any when Carter caught up with them.

"Hey kids! Who wants to play in a fenced-in pasture with a locked gate?"

A dozen little ones cheered and stampeded after Carter as he jogged back toward the house.

Summer and Joey jogged to catch up. "This is so wrong," Summer said, watching Carter and Jax wade through the pack of children now safely locked in the pig paddock.

"This is the best thing that's ever happened to me," Tracey sighed. "I could go to the bathroom if I wanted to instead of holding it for eight hours. Or I could eat a sandwich without worrying that one of them figured out the key code to get outside again."

Grandpa Willis sidled up next to her. "Do you think the parents would go for this if we called it free-range play? We could pad the walls of the meditation room in the basement."

"I think it's worth a shot," Tracey nodded, mesmerized by the glimpse of freedom.

"And what does a cow say?" Carter yelled.

"Moooooooooo!" The kids shouted. Except for Katie Bell who barked.

~

"I swear to you," Carter said from under the ice pack on his forehead as he held Summer's feet in his lap. "Our children will never behave like that."

Summer shifted the pillow off her face and peered at him on the other end of the couch.

Carter Pierce wanted to have children with her?

"You still want to have kids after that shitstorm?" Jax asked, working on his second beer from the recliner. Both men were completely oblivious to the heart attack happening in Summer's chest.

"I refuse to believe that they are all demon spawn. We turned out okay, didn't we?"

Summer pulled her feet off Carter's lap and sat up.

"Where are you going?" Carter asked, swapping ice pack for pillow.

"I'm going to go see Joey," she said, heart pounding.

She met Beckett in the kitchen.

"Just stopped by to see if the place was still standing," he said, poking his head into the great room. "Hey, that's the pillow that touched my junk," he told Carter.

Carter hurled the pillow and a colorful insult as Summer hurried out the side door. She followed the grassy track that wound behind the barn and through the fields to the stables.

There Summer found Joey in the stable office, smacking the computer monitor.

"Come on, you son of a bitch, turn back on."

"Is this a bad time?" Summer asked poking her head in the door.

Joey gave the monitor another slap and sighed. "No. In fact, your distraction may have saved this computer's life." She kicked back in her chair. "What's up?"

"I need to ask you something about Carter."

If Joey was suspicious, she didn't let on. "Okay."

"Is he the type of guy to want kids? A family?"

Joey sat in silence for a minute studying Summer. "I want some water. You want a water?" she said finally.

"Uh, sure," Summer shrugged.

Joey grabbed two waters out of the mini fridge and tossed one to Summer. "Come on. I think better outside."

Summer followed her out the back of the barn. Charcoal and Lolly were in the pasture, both happily munching on grass.

"You pregnant?"

Summer choked on her water and had the horses' heads raising to see what the fuss was. "God. No. I'm not pregnant. I don't know if kids are in my future."

"And you're worried that Carter wants a family?"

Summer nodded. "Yeah."

"I've never heard him say in so many words that he wants a pack of rugrats."

"But..." Summer prodded.

"But look at what they come from. John and Phoebe raised them right and had a damn good time doing it. I wouldn't be surprised if they all planned to have big, sloppy families. It's just not something that guys talk about."

"That's what I was thinking, too," Summer said, tears pricking at her eyes. "But they don't know that not all families end up this way. And who knows if I can even have—" she stopped herself. If she wasn't telling Carter, she wasn't telling anyone.

"If you can even have what? Kids?" Joey asked.

Summer shook her head, waved the question away. "I need to get back. Thanks for the water."

She had gotten carried away. Swept up. That's what had happened, Summer decided as she followed the path from the stables to the house. It was all so romantic that she didn't even notice she was careening off track. This couldn't work. One of them would have to give up everything.

There he was. As if she had conjured him. Carter waited for her on a grassy rise behind the little barn. His hands shoved in the pockets of his shorts and on his face an expression of concern.

"Hey," he said, reaching for her when she approached.

Summer danced out of his grasp. "Hi." She hated herself. Hated her circumstances for what she was about to do.

"What's wrong?"

She took a trembling breath and began. "I'm concerned that we're moving too fast."

He shoved his hands back in his pockets and cocked his

head to the side. "Tell me why you feel that way." His voice was calm and neutral, and for some reason, that made it worse.

She needed it to be over and done with.

"I think we want different things, and I don't see why one of us should have to change to make the other one happy. It's just not working." The words tumbled out in an avalanche.

"Summer," he reached for her again and this time caught her by the shoulders. "Honey, tell me what's wrong."

"I don't want what you want." She could barely see him through the tears that swam before her eyes. "I need some time to think. Some time and space."

His grip tightened on her. "You're not telling me the truth."

She wasn't. But she dug in anyway. "I am."

"I want to build a life with you. A family, a future. I never thought I'd be able to say those words and mean them. But I am, and I do. I love you, Summer. My heart has belonged to you since the second I saw you standing in the driveway. Your eyes matched the flowers, and I knew then that you belonged here."

"Carter," her voice broke. "I know you think you mean those things, but you can't. You don't know everything."

"Because you've been treating this like an interview, not a relationship, Summer. I want to know you. I want to know everything." He threaded his fingers through her hair, and twin tears swam hotly down her cheeks.

"I can't give you everything you want."

"What do I want?"

Me. But he wouldn't. Not if he knew. The tears came faster with the panic.

"Summer, this has to be a two-way street. We can't move forward when you don't trust me."

"This would never be a two-way street, Carter. I would

have to give up everything I've worked for. My job, my life in New York. I can't just drop everything and move to a farm. This isn't what I want."

"I'm not asking you to. There's no reason why I can't move to the city."

"No!" The word cracked like a whip. "You can't give all of this up. There are things you don't know. Uncertainties. "

"Then tell me so we can work through it together."

"I can't—don't want a family. I want what I've been working for. I'm so close, and I can't give that up. Not for you, not for anyone. Look, I'm sorry, but this is just moving too fast. I can't get my head around what you're saying. I need time."

She saw it. The pain—keen and bright—in his eyes. She was destroying him while trying to save him.

"Summer." The pain was there too, sharp in his tone.

"Please, Carter," she sobbed. "Please let me go."

She ran the whole way to the house. Through the filter of tears, she didn't see Beckett just inside the door until it was too late.

"Whoa! Where's the fire, honey?" He grabbed her shoulders and steadied her. "Summer? Are you okay? Are you hurt? Where's Carter?"

She couldn't say anything, just shook her head. He looked so much like Carter. All good men, the Pierces. She couldn't take it. Summer buried her face in Beckett's chest and sobbed.

"Jesus, Summer, you're scaring me," he said stroking her back.

"Carter loves me and wants me to stay." She choked out the words.

"That sounds horrible," Beckett said, rocking side to side.

"It is. He doesn't know. If he did he wouldn't want me. Or worse, he'd feel obligated to stay with me."

Carter wouldn't run. He'd stick. He'd be there for every

single low. Instead of starting a family and looking forward to a future, he'd be facing the constant unknown of an ending that could come too soon.

"What doesn't he know?" Beckett asked gently.

Summer pushed back and looked up at him. "I have to go home, Beckett. Will you tell Niko for me?"

"Tell him what?" Beckett tightened his grip on her shoulders.

"Just tell him I had to go home."

She extricated herself from his grip and ran up the stairs.

28

Carter stared at the ripples on the surface of the pond, willing the water to absorb the hurt. He didn't turn when he heard the footsteps, only skimmed another rock over the surface.

Beckett joined him at the water's edge and squinted up at the impossibly blue sky.

"Shitty day," he said finally.

Carter nodded and picked up another rock.

"She loves you, you know."

Carter sighed, sending the stone hopping. One. Two. Three. "I know."

"That counts for something."

It did. And somehow that made it worse. Life was precious, fragile. There were no guarantees. And fighting something beautiful and good because of fear? It was senseless.

"She's scared." Voice flat, he shoved his hands in his pocket.

"You certainly have an interesting effect on women," Beckett sighed. "Where are you now?"

It was a question that was born when Carter came home. Plagued by nightmares and panic attacks and a dark emptiness, Beckett had been there to gauge him every day. Jax had checked in by phone twice a day for the six weeks after his return and flew out for a week in the middle of it. Their mother made him lunch every day and sat with him while he ate even when he didn't want to.

Every day, sometimes several times, Carter ranked his state of mind.

Where am I now?

At first, it was hard to be honest. It hurt the ones he loved to know his pain. It was terrifying to be so vulnerable. But day by day, that vulnerability had turned into a strength deeper than any he had ever known. It was built on something real, something honest. There was no lying to himself or his family.

After a few months, most of the shadows had been chased out.

The ones that remained were reminders of how precious life and hope were.

He still asked himself the question every morning. Only now it meant something different.

"I'm okay," he told his brother. "I know she loves me. She just needs time and trust."

"How much time are you going to give her?"

Carter shrugged and shoved his hands in his pockets. "As much as she needs."

Beckett slapped his hand on his back. "You know we're going to hover for a while, right?"

Carter nodded quietly. "Unnecessary, but appreciated."

"You let me know what you need."

"I could go for an IPA."

"I'll grab the six and meet you by the fence rail on the road. We can probably get that mowed in an hour."

❧

BECKETT WAITED until he was out of earshot before yanking his phone out of his pocket and dialing.

"Code Shit," he said when Jax answered.

❧

"WHAT?" Joey's tone held the frost of a winter's morning in Antarctica on the other end of the phone.

"Shut up and listen," Jax ordered. He didn't have time to coax out the gentleness he knew she still carried. "I need you to call Carter and get him over to the horse barn this afternoon."

"Why?"

"Just get him on a fucking horse and don't ask him any questions."

She swore quietly. "How bad is it?"

"Not great, but he'll be okay. Consider it a preemptive strike."

"Okay. Thanks for the head's up."

"Thanks for the help."

"Jackson?"

"Yeah?"

"I'm glad you're here this time."

He frowned as the prickle of guilt caught him. "Me too."

❧

CARTER FOUND Nikolai sitting on the ground playing fetch with the pigs and shooting close-ups.

"She fucking smiles like she knows how lucky she is," he said, glancing up from his screen.

Dixie trotted over, ears flopping, and Carter ran a hand down her back.

"Summer left."

Nikolai squinted at his screen as he flipped through shots. "I know. Beckett told me."

"Any ideas on what happened?"

He stood, slinging his camera around his neck. "I have one."

"But you can't say," Carter predicted.

Nikolai nodded. "She's got stuff going on that she doesn't talk about to anyone."

"But she told you."

He shook his head. "No. I found out, and she couldn't deny it. Swore me to secrecy. She's very careful about who she lets in, and there's still times when I know she's pissed that I'm in."

"She doesn't want to let me in."

Nikolai stood and put his hand on Carter's shoulder. "Look. I've known her for a few years, and I've never seen her happier than she is here with you. In the city, she's a fucking machine marching toward her goals, working seven days a week. Here, she laughs. She doesn't carry her phone everywhere. She sits on the porch and drinks iced tea instead of spending three hours a night reading emails and writing blogs. She looks at you like you invented puppies and manicures."

"This stuff that she's got going on, is there an end in sight?"

"I hope so. Or this summer was just a brief reprieve."

"Do me a favor," Carter said, frowning up at the sun. "Keep an eye on her for me. Keep her safe."

~

NIKOLAI TALKED Carter and his brothers into posing for a few outdoor portraits that afternoon before heading back to the city. And Carter couldn't help but hope he was going straight to Summer to talk some sense into her.

He knew it was a setup when Joey asked him for help with the evening riding classes. He also knew it wasn't a coincidence that his brothers decided to call for pizza and hang out to binge watch the first four episodes of the latest zombie apocalypse show.

Joey survived two episodes before calling it a night. She didn't even snipe at Jax when he offered to drive her home. She did, however, insist that she get to drive his new car. "Look at that," Beckett snickered when they left. "All Jax had to do to make time with Joey was scare her with the threat of zombies in the cornfield."

"Maybe he's not such an idiot after all," Carter conceded.

"No, he's still a fucking idiot. Why do you think he left?"

Carter shrugged. "Scared? I don't know. I think the accident had something to do with it."

"Think Joey will ever forgive him?"

"I think he has some work to do before that's a remote possibility. He owes her that." Carter stood up, a subtle buzz from the beer crept into his head. "Let's adjourn this meeting to the porch."

Beckett reached for the empties. "I second that motion. And move to switch to that bottle of scotch you have stashed in the pantry."

"Motion carries," Carter nodded. "Now let's move on to the discussion item of the brewery."

When Jax returned, he found them rocking in silence sipping scotch.

Beckett passed him a glass.

"It doesn't look like you have any slap marks on your face," Carter commented.

Jax ran a hand over the stubble on his jaw. "I didn't make a move on her this time."

"Maybe you're wisening up, Hollywood?" Beckett snickered.

"Is wisening a word, Mr. Mayor?"

"I'm the mayor, and it's a word if I say it's a word."

Carter raised his glass. "I'm with the mayor on this one."

"Jesus, I need to catch up." Jax drained his glass and blew out a sharp breath.

Carter passed him the bottle. "Hurry up. You need to be in the same state of inebriation as your partners."

Jax's grip tightened on the glass. "Partners?"

"The brewery. If you're sticking, we're in. But if you're even considering the slightest chance that you're going to haul ass out of here again, then I want nothing to do with it," Carter said.

Jax topped off their glasses. "I'm sticking."

Carter could hear the earnestness, the excitement in his tone, and knew. It resonated. Whatever demons made his brother run away would be faced. He would stick.

He nodded. "Then we're in." He raised his glass. "To John Pierce Brews."

"After Dad," Jax cleared the emotion from his throat. "Shit. That sounds good."

"It sure does. Now don't fuck it up," Beckett said, bringing his glass to theirs.

"To John Pierce Brews," they toasted.

"Let's call Calvin tomorrow and get him out here to look at the barn and see where we need to start."

Jax nodded. "As soon as the hangover wears off, I'll call. What were you thinking with scotch, anyway?"

"I texted Mom and asked her to come over and make us breakfast in the morning," Beckett said. "It was as long as I could put her off, Carter. She wants to make sure her baby boy is in one piece."

Carter rubbed a hand over the center of his chest. "Great. Now she's gonna know that her kids are adults and still can't hold their liquor."

"Speak for yourself," Beckett said, standing up to pirouette in a sloppy circle. "I'm sober as Great Aunt Margaret."

"Are those sweat stains or are you spilling scotch?" Carter teased. There was no relief from the heat of the day. It just settled into a night so thick with humidity he imagined the fireflies had trouble staying aloft.

"You remember what we used to do when we were kids when it was hot like this?" Jax asked, smiling with the memory.

Air conditioning was relatively new to the farmhouse. And many a night in their childhood had been spent engineering complex sheet and fan ventilation systems. But on the nights when even fans didn't help, the brothers snuck out and raced to the pond.

"You remember the time Dad caught us and jumped in in his pajamas?" Beckett said wistfully.

The image of their father swan diving off the dock in his t-shirt and underwear loosened something in Carter's chest.

"That was one of the best nights in my life."

"Ranks right up there with the night I talked Moon Beam Parker into the backseat of Mom's SUV."

"Or the Christmas we all got paintball guns," Jax remembered.

"Do you still have that scar?" Carter grinned.

"It's my badge of honor," he said, rubbing a hand absently

over his temple. "I can't believe Mom didn't kill us. Christmas night in the ER."

"Head wounds tend to bleed a lot. I told you not to move," Beckett smirked.

"I didn't move! Your aim just fucking sucks."

"I still maintain that the sights were off. Besides, the fruit-cake hit the ground. That's all that matters."

Carter put down his empty glass and stood up. Bracing himself against the porch railing, he yanked the t-shirt over his head and tossed it in Beckett's face.

"Last one to the pond has to start the eggplant tomorrow."

He vaulted over the railing and sprinted for the pond. Behind him, his brothers pounded down the porch steps after him.

≈

WHEN PHOEBE LET herself into Carter's house the next morning, she discovered all three of her sons in various states of undress, sound asleep in the great room. Carter was on his stomach on the long L of the couch, a blanket pulled over his head and upper body.

Beckett was sleeping open-mouthed in the chair, his legs propped up on the ottoman.

Jax was snoring on the floor, his legs under the coffee table, an empty beer bottle clutched in his right hand.

As quietly as possible, she pulled a barstool over to stand on and opened the camera on her phone. If nothing else, this could be the family Christmas card, she thought, snapping the photo of her unconscious boys.

Her boys.

She loved them fiercely.

Their loyalty to each other was unshakable. Neither time,

nor distance, or even disappointment, could dim it. And though her heart ached for Carter, she knew he would stand strong. She only hoped that Summer would find the strength to embrace the love that had been offered to her. Whatever her secret, family and a life full of love was the answer.

Phoebe tiptoed back to the kitchen and slid the hash brown casserole into the oven.

≈

THE SCENT of coffee drifted into the great room and teased Carter awake. His head pounded, and his heart hurt. But he was here. He glanced at his phone, not daring to hope, but still felt the pang when there were no new messages.

He shuffled out to the kitchen.

"Good morning," he murmured to his mom, thankful when the words didn't split his head in two.

She kissed him on the cheek and pushed a coffee mug at him. "Rough night?"

"Jax was the one who puked."

Phoebe rolled her eyes. "A mother only has so much pride to go around."

She pushed him toward a barstool and started pulling plates out of the cabinet. "Do you want to talk about it?"

"I assume you don't mean Jax vomiting scotch in a flowerbed?"

She raised her eyes heavenward. "I hope it wasn't the zinnias. They're so unforgiving."

Carter got up and retrieved a container of coconut water from the fridge. "I told her I wanted to spend the rest of my life with her." He took a deep swig to wash down the tightness in his throat, remembering her face. "She wasn't of the same mind."

"Bullshit."

"Do you kiss your sons with that mouth?" he teased.

"That girl loves you so much it was exploding out of her."

"She got scared, Mom."

"That's what worries me. You have us," she said waving her hand in the direction of his snoring brothers. "You have the farm, the animals, all of Blue Moon. Who does she have to walk her through scared?"

"Nikolai went back yesterday. I think he was planning to talk some sense into her."

"He's a good boy, but she won't listen to him."

Carter nodded. "No. She won't," he agreed. He took another hit of coconut water and chased it with a gulp of coffee.

"So what do we do?" Phoebe asked. It was the follow up question to "Where are you today?"

"We wait."

"We hope?"

"We wait, and we hope," Carter sighed.

29

Summer logged another marathon day in the office dealing with a thousand mini crises—none of which really mattered in the grand scheme of things, but at least they gave her something else to think about.

Something besides Blue Moon Bend and Carter Pierce.

She pushed back from her desk and moved to the window. It wasn't the view from Pierce Acres kitchen, that's for sure. As a sunset bloomed above, Manhattan bustled below. Traffic snarling and weaving. Nameless pedestrians hurrying from building to building.

She loved it. Didn't she? The energy. The frantic pace. The sense of urgency that never ceased. It was where she chose to be.

Sure. There were no flop-eared pigs or bad-tempered goats here, but the city held its own appeal. A nightlife that never slept. A few million strangers, all with their own stories.

It was for the best, of course. This is where she belonged. It never would have worked with Carter. She did the right thing by ending it when she did.

Why was it that her heart wasn't buying it?

"Missing those rolling pastures?"

Nikolai's voice pulled her from her reverie. Her friend dropped into her unoccupied desk chair.

"Don't, Niko."

He held up his hands. "I'm not trying to rub it in."

"You of all people think I made a mistake?"

"Stop putting words in my mouth. And what do you mean by me 'of all people?'"

"You love this city as much, if not more, than I do. A never-ending parade of beautiful women. World-class artists, musicians, designers, all cohabitating on one tiny island. Food from every country available for delivery. And you think I miss Blue Moon."

"Manhattan doesn't have Carter."

She glared at him. Somewhere along the line, Niko had fallen onto the Team Carter roster. "Why are you pushing this?"

Niko stretched his long legs out, touching the far wall of the cubicle and blocking her exit. "How long have we known each other?"

"Three, three-and-a-half years?"

"And in those three or three-and-a-half years, I have never seen you as happy as I did last month. Covered in dirt, harvesting vegetables, playing with farm animals. Looking at Carter. You love him. You love that family, that farm, that town. Yet here you stand."

"You know why," she spat out the words.

"No. I don't." Nikolai stood up, arms crossed. "You won't let me in. You won't let anyone in." He was just below a low roar now.

Summer grabbed him and dragged him into an empty conference room where she shut the door. The glass walls wouldn't hide the fact that they were arguing, but at least the ears of the office would be left guessing as to what about.

"I have cancer, Nikolai."

"I know that, Summer. And the fucking word you're looking for is *had*, not have."

Her six-month tests had been clean. And though her doctors were cautiously optimistic, remission was a fickle thing. "It could come back at any time."

"Or you could get hit by a bus crossing 33rd."

"You don't understand."

"Then help me. Tell me why you beating cancer means that you can't be with Carter."

"He wants a life and a family. I don't even know if I can ever have kids. One of the side effects of treatment. And what if I do, and it comes back? What if I don't get lucky next time?"

"So you make the choice for him? Goddamn it, Summer, you are a smart, capable woman, but that's the dumbest fucking thing I've ever heard." Nikolai waved his arms in exasperation.

He grabbed her shoulders. "What if it does come back? What are you going to do then? Hide it from everyone again? Try to do it all on your own? Until someone catches you in a weak moment when you're so sick from your meds that you can barely stand up? What if it comes back, and this time it kills you?"

Summer winced at his words.

"Niko—"

"You want to do that alone? You could have Carter at your side, helping you, but you think it's better to go it alone."

Summer wrenched free. "He deserves better!" She was shouting now and didn't care. "He deserves someone who is going to be there in fifty years and sit on that porch and watch the grandkids play."

"No one gets that guarantee," Nikolai said it quietly. "Not even people who don't have cancer. People die every day. People lose loved ones every damn day. And you think by not being someone's other half, you can protect them from that? Bullshit."

"I'm scared, Niko." The fight had gone out of her.

He wrapped his arms around her, and she could smell leather and cologne. "I know you are. I would be, too. You're facing two of the scariest, shit-your-pants things in life: cancer and love."

She snickered. "Oh my God, you really should be a writer."

"Look, brat. I love you to pieces. I hate to think that you're too scared to be happy."

Summer sighed and flopped down in a chair. "I will think about your curse words of wisdom."

"That's all I ask."

"Did you know your accent comes out more when you're mad?"

"Just be glad I didn't break out any Russian swear words. Your fragile American ears would never be the same." He leaned against the table. "When are your tests?"

"The eighth." It was the day the magazine's September issue came out with her story on Carter and the farm, she thought.

"I get the results the next day."

"Do you want me to go with you?" Niko offered.

Summer shook her head.

He glared at her.

"I'm not being stubborn." She was. "I just want to do this on my own." For better or worse, she wanted to see this through. If she could get through this, that meant she could conquer anything. Including a senior editor position.

If that's what she still wanted.

"Do you really believe it's back?" Niko asked, crossing his arms.

"I want to say no," she said, tracing a finger on the glossy tabletop. "I want to say I know that I kicked its ass. I feel good. Strong. But I just don't know. I don't want to get my hopes up and then have them crushed."

"Hope doesn't have to be a scary thing."

"When did the Wolf get to be so warm and fuzzy?"

"I think they put something in the water upstate."

"Yeah, I think so, too."

∼

NIKO HEADED off to meet a smoky Italian at a jazz club, and Summer wrapped things up at her desk. Darkness had fallen, but the city still lived. And so did she. If her one-year tests were clean, then there was cause for some actual, tangible hope. Then she could start to entertain what a future could look like for her. And whether or not she could make room for Carter Pierce.

But until she had her test results, she wouldn't drag him into it.

She was shutting down her laptop when a lean, young blonde called her name.

Shauna was Quincy's personal assistant. She was holding a garment bag draped over her arm. "Quincy sent this up for you to wear tonight." Her perfect beach waves would have made a mermaid jealous.

"Thanks, Shauna." She had almost forgotten about the benefit tonight. Trust Quincy to remember for her. She took the bag from Shauna and hung it from the hook on the cubicle wall. She unzipped it a bit.

"It's the fuchsia Elie Saab you liked from the shoot last week. Quincy stashed it away for you."

It was beautiful and would look perfect with a carefully mussed chignon. But her pulse had yet to stir. When had she lost her lust of high fashion? Was this just a side effect of the sadness that plagued her?

"Thank you, Shauna. I don't suppose—"

"Shoes are in the bag. He took pity on you and went with gold gladiators that wrap up to the knee so you won't have to spend the entire evening sitting."

"He thinks of everything."

"So, how's that gorgeous farmer of yours?" Shauna asked. Summer could hear it, that sharp edge. The need for a tasty morsel. Well, she'd just have to dine somewhere else.

Summer gritted her teeth and zipped the bag. "He's looking forward to seeing the story this month," she snapped. "I guess I'd better go get ready. Thanks for bringing this down."

She brushed past the hungry assistant and made her way to the ladies room.

After the fashion show in June, the office had been abuzz about Carter. A few staffers had dropped some not-so-subtle hints about whether he and Summer were an item or he was just an evening's eye candy.

She had yet to tell anyone what had happened in Blue Moon and why she had returned so suddenly.

But the hive still gossiped.

~

THAT NIGHT, she crawled into her apartment just shy of one in the morning. She hadn't wanted to stay so long. But the music and the conversations were more of a comfort than the silence of her apartment, the emptiness of her bed.

She slipped out of the gown and pulled on a cozy robe. She'd just check her email one more time before bed.

A quick scan told her nothing had to be addressed before morning. Except for Niko's email. Subject line: Farm art.

Summer told herself not to click on it, but her finger didn't listen.

Finished editing. Thought you'd like to see some of the art for your story.

- N

He'd attached a link to an online gallery, and Summer was opening it before she could talk herself out of it. She could look at his pictures. She was a professional. It wasn't too painful for her. Her memories of Carter and the farm and Blue Moon Bend were something to be treasured.

The first shot punched a hole in her heart. Carter was standing knee-deep in a field, his legs braced apart. His arms crossed. His uniform of well-worn jeans and t-shirt clung to all the right places. A warrior in the garden. Behind him, the farm rolled out until it met the blue-skied horizon.

It was perfect. Her editor's mind immediately labeled it the lead art while her lover's heart ached.

One thing was for sure. Once this story came out, Carter wouldn't be lonely for long. Women would beat a path from Manhattan to the gate of Pierce Acres just to catch a glimpse of this perfection.

He would hate that, she thought with a tight smile. He'd probably look at this picture and not see what every woman in the world would.

She sighed and clicked through the rest of the gallery.

There were shots of the Pierce brothers together, looking rugged and gorgeous. One of Phoebe at the farmers market. The farmhouse. Clementine and Dixie. Even Joey in the middle of a riding class. The farm was in summer bloom with color and growth everywhere.

It looked like heaven. It looked like home.

She caught her breath. The very last picture would never make the story.

It was her with Carter in the orchard, arms wrapped around each other, dirt everywhere. She was looking up at him, laughing. He was grinning down at her. She was on her tiptoes in the beloved boots she had now buried in the back of her closet.

Summer had no idea Niko had been there to capture the moment. And what a moment it had been.

30

_____

*S*he almost didn't look.

That glossy copy of *Indulgence* lurked front and center on her desk with the cover proudly proclaiming an inside feature on organic farming and the "new gentleman farmer." She had proofed the drafts, hadn't she? There was no reason to review the final piece.

Except that she was being childish.

And she wasn't a child. She was a grown woman who would be faced with situations more complicated than looking at an article on an ex-lover.

She would read it after she answered some very important emails, she decided. Summer stowed her bag in a desk drawer and distracted herself by booting up her laptop. She returned a few emails and tweets and listened to her voicemails. She ripped off the bandage from her blood test and tossed it in the trash.

But still the issue lurked.

"Oh for Pete's sake," Summer sighed and yanked the magazine off her desk.

She thumbed through it, past the winter coat guide and the four-page advertorial for a well-known designer's upcoming holiday collection. And there he was. A two-page spread of Carter Pierce standing arms crossed, knee-deep in soybeans. Niko certainly made the most of what he had to work with.

Carter looked like an earth-bound god.

Summer was sure this picture would be hanging up in cubicles throughout the building, possibly even the city. She skimmed the lead and frowned.

In an otherwise sterile digital world, hot gentleman farmer Carter Pierce and his bachelor brothers teach us the benefits of getting dirty. Very dirty.

"What the hell is this?" She turned the page so quickly it tore. Gone was her insightful article on health, wellness, and community in Blue Moon. And in its place was a splashy, tawdry pictorial.

Her desk phone rang, and she ignored it, skimming the scant copy.

And the best part, ladies? They're all single.

Her cellphone rang. "What?" she demanded.

"Who got their tabloid talons on this piece?" Nikolai growled in her ear. "What the hell is this trash?"

"This is the first time I'm seeing it. When I looked at the final proofs last week there was no mention of Carter's 'farm boy broad shoulders.'" She felt sick to her stomach. Her name was on the article. People were going to think she wrote this.

Carter was going to think she wrote this.

"Oh my God. This is obscene, Niko! It's like soft porn."

"Katherine called me a few days ago and asked if I had any shirtless pictures of him or his brothers. I thought she was fucking joking!"

"Obviously she wasn't fucking joking!"

"Did you read the whole thing?"

"There's only like three paragraphs."

"Read it."

"'Struggling with PTSD, we think this sexy vet could use some comfort—' I'm going to be sick. I'm going to be sick and murder someone. Oh God, Niko. They sent him copies. I know they sent him copies. I have to go. I have to call him."

She cut off Niko's reply and dialed Carter's cellphone. There was no answer. She tried the house phone and again there was no answer.

She tossed her phone on her desk and made her decision.

She snatched up the magazine and stalked out of her cubicle. Katherine's office was one floor up, and Summer fumed the entire way there.

She breezed past Katherine's unsmiling assistant, a six-foot tall waif with hair the color of midnight.

Katherine was on the phone. She laughed, a silvery little tinkle. "I'm sure I can put you in touch with them. As far as I know they have no representation yet... Yes, it's like finding oil in the last place you would expect it."

Summer tossed her copy of the magazine onto Katherine's glass desk and crossed her arms.

"Felipe, I must go. I'll have my assistant give you the information... You too, darling." She hung up the receiver and steepled her manicured hands. Last winter's nip and tuck was tastefully done, leaving her face looking refreshed and youthful. The rich red of her lipstick never smudged. Summer often wondered if it was tattooed on.

"What can I do for you, Summer?"

"You can explain why you took a piece that was about something deep and meaningful and turned it into this trash," she said, drilling her finger into the open page.

"Excuse me?" Katherine's frosty tone was meant to stop perceived insolence in its tracks. But it had the opposite effect on Summer.

"You heard me. Where is the story I wrote, and why did you slap my name on this bullshit?"

"Darling, I don't think you understand how things work here. Need I remind you that you are an *associate*." She enunciated the word as if speaking to a toddler. "You work for me. I have the final say in what goes into this 'bullshit,' as you so eloquently call it. You turned in a weighty piece that would have readers tossing it in the recycling bin. You've been in production meetings. Advertisers want sex. What you wrote was a boring ode to an obsolete way of life."

"What about the readers?"

"The readers want what the advertisers tell them to want. They don't want some sappy love story about a simpler way of life. No one wants that. They want bigger, shinier, more." Her voice was as sharp as the corners of her desk. "They want this," her finger tapped Carter's bare chest.

"You made what they do into a joke."

"No, I made their lives." Katherine brought her purple tips to the glass top as she rose. Her wrap dress hugged a trim figure made possible by the finest plastic surgeons in Manhattan. "I've been fielding calls all morning from agents wanting to represent them and designers wanting to use them. There's no more playing in the dirt for these men. We just made them famous."

"There was no 'we' in this. And there is so much more to life than chasing fame."

"That's right. There's documenting it. That is what we do. We hand these people the American dream and watch what they do with it. Do you know what we love more than America's sweetheart? America's sweetheart on a very public downward spiral." She held up the magazine. "It's vicious. I'll be the first to say it. But in order to thrive in this business, you have to have the stomach for it."

"You put my name on this." Summer glared at her over the desk.

"And you should be thanking me. The digital piece has been getting more hits than the cover story. This could be the fast track to getting what you want, my dear, so be very careful how you proceed. You can either give my assistant Carter's contact information while I talk to a few select people about a new senior editor position, or you can think about how it would feel to go back to copy editing."

Summer leaned over the desk, her fingers leaving smudges on the glass. "Actually, there's a third option that I feel really good about. You can take your sexy advertising and your emergency moisturizers and your constant need for ass kissing and shove it. I quit!"

She turned on her Manolos and stormed out, past the assistant, past the creative department, past Quincy calling her name in the hallway.

She took the stairs back to her floor. In her cubicle, she shoved her laptop and phone in her bag. There was nothing else there. No personal mementos, no trinkets. Just an empty desk. It had been on purpose. No personal items until she was in an office. And then it would be carefully chosen pieces that reflected the importance of the position and the responsibilities she would carry. She snorted.

Summer put the bag on her shoulder and marched to the

elevator. Phones started ringing, and heads were popping out of cubicles.

"She's at the elevator," someone whispered loudly into their phone.

It was the *Indulgence* version of Blue Moon's online gossip group. And it made her smile.

She was still smiling when the doors closed on the floor of gawkers.

She pulled her phone out of the bag and dialed Murray, part of *Indulgence's* elite legal team.

"Hey there, Summer. I just heard."

"Good, then I'll keep this quick. My blog, is that mine or does it belong to *Indulgence*?"

"You started it before you had the job. It's yours."

"How about an article that I wrote for *Indulgence* that they chose not to use."

"I'd double check your contract on that, but if they chose not to exercise their rights to it, then it's possible you could resell it."

"What if I don't want to sell it?"

"You want to keep it for personal use? That's probably a little less murky. Read the fine print and text me if you need clarification."

"Thanks, Murray. It was nice working with you."

"You, too, Summer. Good luck."

She was halfway home when her phone rang in her bag. Nikolai. She silenced it and let her momentum carry her the rest of the way home.

$\sim$

SHE BURST through the door of the apartment she could no longer afford and dumped her laptop on her coffee table. She would fix this. All of it.

Summer wrote from the heart, letting the words flow.

I've spent my years since college mapping out a career path that would bring me the trappings of success that I so desperately wanted.

An apartment with a view...

A collection of shoes that makes other women sigh with envy...

A wardrobe by all the right designers...

The right circle of interesting friends...

My name on insightful articles perfectly crafted to tell you the stories that deserve your attention...

I sit here in my apartment with its charming bay window that overlooks a neighborhood grocery store and barbershop in my Manhattan-approved this-season's-hottest outfit with my barely worn Manolo Blahniks sitting on the floor next to me. My circle of "friends" consists of advertisers, designers, and industry insiders who are all very busy and terribly important.

Many of you have probably seen the "Hot for Farmer" piece under my byline in a magazine that, from now on, shall remain nameless. It's getting big hits online. Enough attention that maybe a new position could open up for me.

By all previous measures, I've made it. I am a success. I have everything I ever wanted.

So what if my "friends" are advertisers that require schmoozing, designers who can't remember my first name, and a handful of acquaintances who know nothing more about me other than where I bought my last pair of shoes? Who cares that I spend every minute of every day trying to write things that will make you buy something? A magazine, a beauty product, a fabulous winter parka. Does it matter that the shoes hurt my feet? Or that I haven't spent a Saturday night doing what I wanted to do since college? It's fine. Right? I have everything I want.

I also have cancer. One year ago, I was diagnosed with adult Hodgkin lymphoma. I spent weeks sneaking off for treatments and hiding my reactions to them. If work found out, paid medical leave could have been the kiss of death to my senior editor aspirations. I didn't even tell my parents. I didn't want them to worry. But mostly, I didn't want to be vulnerable.

But that's what cancer makes you. Vulnerable. And scared. And I let it isolate me. After aggressive treatment through a clinical trial, I went into remission. Six months out, my tests were clean. Tomorrow, I find out if I can say "had" or "have." Tomorrow I find out what the future holds.

Recurrence is always a concern, and so are the side effects of the treatments, including infertility. I hadn't given kids and family much thought. At least not until I met a man with a heart as big as the blue moon. One who made me start asking myself questions instead of just firing them at other people.

If you've been following my blog, you know that this summer I had the pleasure of spending time in Blue Moon Bend, N.Y., on Pierce Acres, a family-owned and run organic farm.

And it was in Blue Moon that I fell in love. With the town, with the people, with the sense of belonging and community that residents there are born with. There is no jockeying for position, no backstabbing, no trying to get ahead. Just neighbors helping neighbors. People trusting each other.

I fell in love with the town and I fell in love with a man.

Those photos? They don't do him justice. You can't see the soul of a man through glossy pictures. You can't see the brave heart that carries the scars of a warrior. You don't get a hint of the noble character, the steadfast loyalty to family and country. You aren't able to understand what happened when he discovered the healing power of a foundation of vulnerability and honesty.

So I fell in love, and I got scared. And I ran back to the city where I felt safe in my anonymity, my path.

And here I sit with a manufactured, runaway digital success. Alone.

So I quit. And I'm going to do something bigger and more beautiful than even I dreamed possible. I'm going to write about real things, about health and wellness and community. I'm going to share the stories of people who have fought and won against disease, who have created a new way, who are making a difference, of the men and women who are shaping our future. Those are the people I want in my life. The people you should want in yours.

I went to Blue Moon to write about goats and organic tomatoes. Instead, I fell in love, and everything changed. I met a pig and went vegetarian. I realized the healing nature of mother nature from the food we use to fuel our bodies to the sunshine that warms our skin and the fresh air that makes you take that first deep breath when you walk out the door in the morning. Most importantly I learned that our real strength is in vulnerability. In facing and living the truth no matter who's watching. That is where we are strongest. I learned this from Carter, and you should have, too.

Carter, I owe you a huge apology for taking your trust and then letting someone distort your story. I owe you an even bigger apology for running away when I got scared. I never meant to hurt you. I can't ask you to forgive me, but I can show you what I wanted everyone else to know about you. Here's the piece I originally wrote, which was rejected by the editors who substituted it with their own content.

I'm sorry, and I love you.

Summer copied and pasted her article into the post and added some of the pictures she took during her time in Blue

Moon. She headed the post with Carter's first selfie. Two quick rounds of proofreading, and she hit Post.

She closed the lid of her laptop and sighed. It was done. She was going to put on her boots and go for a walk in the park... and then maybe panic about the future that she had just wiped clean.

31

A low roll of thunder woke Summer the next morning, instantly reminding her of the rainy morning she had spent in bed with Carter. Her next thought—and another regret—was of the better part of the bottle of wine she had polished off before bed.

She sat up and reached for her phone.

10:20?

She had forty minutes to get dressed and cover the twenty blocks between her apartment and her oncologist's.

Summer scrambled out of bed and dragged on a pair of jeans and a stretchy short-sleeve sweater. She was reaching for a pair of sandals when the boots caught her eye. If anything would give her luck today, Carter's boots would.

She pulled her hair back in a low messy knot on her way out the door.

Thanks to some ill-timed, poorly placed construction, Summer had to jump out of the taxi a few blocks early and race through the misty rain before scurrying up the office stairs with a minute to spare.

"Good morning, Summer," the receptionist greeted her warmly. "We've been talking about you non-stop all morning!"

Summer signed in. "Really? Why?"

"There she is!" Summer's oncologist, Dr. Armenta, swept into reception. Tall and slim, she moved like a ballet dancer. "I'm dying to know, have you heard from Carter?" Her eyes sparkled behind her wire-rimmed glasses.

"How do you—"

"Your blog!" The receptionist chirped. "We all read it yesterday. It's all everyone is talking about. We're so excited for you!"

"Well, come on back, and we can talk," Dr. Armenta said, taking Summer's arm.

She led her back through the suite to her office. "I love your boots. Can I get you a drink?"

Summer sank down in the first visitor's chair facing the desk. She'd sat in this exact seat for her six-month results, so she might as well continue the tradition.

"Before we begin, I have to tell you how proud I am of you," she said, folding her hands on her desk. Her unruly red curls were escaping the braid that lay over the shoulder of her white coat. "You know that I didn't agree with your desire to handle your diagnosis and treatment alone."

Summer winced and nodded. Dr. Armenta had made it clear on several occasions that she thought Summer was making a mistake.

"Support plays a very important role in healing. And I was concerned by your choice to cut yourself off from that support," the doctor continued. "So you can imagine my delight when I read your blog. The entire staff was texting back and forth last night. You went from having virtually no support network to thousands of supporters."

"I have?" Summer frowned in confusion.

Dr. Armenta smiled. "Haven't you been monitoring your blog?"

Summer shook her head and again thought of the Chardonnay that had gone down so smoothly last night.

"Well, then I don't want to ruin the surprise," Dr. Armenta said. "Let's start with how you feel today."

"I'm fine, thanks. I'm nervous." She let the words tumble out of her mouth. Honesty. Vulnerability.

"There is nothing to be nervous about. We're in this together," Dr. Armenta said, turning her computer monitor to face Summer. "These are your white blood cells from a year ago when you were diagnosed."

She moused over the screen showing the abnormal cells. She clicked to another image. "Now, these are your results from six months out. Clean." She opened one more image. "And this is where you are currently."

～

SUMMER MADE it down the steps of the stately brownstone and onto the sidewalk before the tears came. They warmed her cheeks just like the September sunshine that had broken through the clouds. She was crying in public, and she didn't care.

Overwhelmed, she didn't even care that a watery blur of a man was standing there watching her from one building down. She was overdue for this and wasn't going to rush herself through a good cry.

"Summer?"

"Carter?" she swiped tears from her eyes. There he was in the flesh. Wearing his trademark jeans and a t-shirt, he had a bouquet of wildflowers clutched in his hand. "Carter!"

She didn't even realize she was running until she heard

her boots on the concrete. He caught her in mid-leap, boosting her up and holding her close.

Summer brought her hands to his face.

"Hi," she whispered.

"Hi."

"How did you find me?"

"Nikolai snagged the name of your doctor out of a calendar appointment once in case he ever needed it."

"Sneaky bastard."

"Tell me everything, honey."

She kissed him hard on the mouth. "In order of importance: I love you. I'm so sorry. And I'm cancer-free." She punctuated each announcement with a kiss.

Carter crushed her to him, burying his face in her neck.

"I love you so much. When I read..." he stopped, trying to clear the emotion that was clogging his throat.

"Everything is going to be okay. Better than okay. I'm so sorry for not telling you. Can you ever forgive me?"

"I think I can find it in my 'big as a blue moon' heart to find some forgiveness. But you have to promise me you won't ever keep something like this from me again or I'll feed you to Clementine."

Summer cupped his face in her hands. "I promise you, Carter Pierce, that I will trust you and love you and drive you crazy from this day forward."

"Nothing would make me happier." He spun her around, teasing a laugh out of her throat.

A dog walker with a Chihuahua and three Yorkies scurried past them without looking in their direction.

He grinned, big and bright. "You realize what this means to the Beautification Committee, don't you?"

"I think we're going to make that committee very, very happy," she said, kissing him again. She pulled back to look into his eyes. "Carter, there's something else you need to know. It may change how you feel."

His fingers tightened on her hips. "Summer, you're about to say something that isn't going to matter to me in the least, and I'm going to get pissed again."

"Infertility can be a side effect of some of the treatments I had. I might not be able to have kids." She blurted out the words before they could get stuck in her throat.

"I was right. You're pissing me off."

"I'm so sorry—"

He let her slide to the ground, but when she tried to take a step back, he grabbed her by the shoulders.

"Summer. We haven't even talked about kids. How do you know I want them?"

She shrugged under his hands. "You're a Pierce. You're destined to be a family man."

"And you think I'd rather choose a life with someone who can get pregnant with children I don't even know if I want instead of you, the stubborn, illogical woman I love more than anything?"

"I'm making a mess of this," she groaned.

"Yes, you are. But you're new at this, so I'll cut you some slack," Carter said, pulling her into him. "For the record, I haven't given kids a thought. Could I see us with a family? Sure. Someday. But it doesn't have to be now, and it doesn't have to be the way everyone else does it. There's more than one way to make a family."

Summer looked down, but he nudged her chin up. She saw only love in his eyes.

"Honey, I'm not upset that we might not be able to have kids. I'm upset that you think it would change how I feel about you."

She smoothed the t-shirt over his chest, enjoying the feel of him under her hands.

"I'm so sorry for so many things. For not telling you about any of this. For running away when I got scared. For underestimating you."

He wrapped his arms around her and tucked her head under his chin.

"Summer." Her name on his lips was like a caress, and she knew she was forgiven. "Jax read your blog last night and came tearing into my bedroom yelling and carrying on. All I caught was 'Summer' and 'cancer.' It scared the life right out of me."

She winced. "I was so scared. I've been so scared for so long that it started to feel normal."

"Where are you now?" he asked.

She smiled against his chest. "Right where I want to be. In your arms with a wide-open future in front of us. There's just one thing that I want right now."

"What's that? Name it, and I'll make it happen."

"I want to go home. Will you take me home?"

"Of course."

"We can swing by my apartment first so I can pack."

Carter leaned her back to study her face. "Home to Blue Moon?"

"Home to Blue Moon," she nodded.

He swept her up in his arms again, spinning them around in a circle. Summer laughed.

"As soon as I introduce you to Dr. Armenta. She's a big fan of yours."

She felt a vibration against her hip. "Oh my God! My phone's been on silent since yesterday," she said, reaching for her pocket.

"You have about thirty missed calls from me," Carter said, lowering her to the ground.

Summer dragged her phone from her pocket. Her eyes widened as she read the caller ID.

She glanced at Carter as she swiped the screen to answer. "Hi, Dad?"

32

———————

Two weeks later.

*S*ummer wiggled in excitement on the stool.

"Listen to this one, Carter," she said, clapping her hands.

Carter grinned from the stove where he was pouring the evening's leftover vegetable soup into glass containers. "I'm listening."

Summer cleared her throat and began to read the email out loud.

Dear Ms. Lentz,

We at Eve's Garden were thrilled to read about your plans to start a digital magazine that focuses on real life health and wellness. As a creator of an entirely natural and cruelty-free cosmetic line, we would love to discuss advertising opportunities with you...

"There's a dozen more of these just from today from eco

clothing designers, wellness spas, even frozen food produc-ers," Summer said, scrolling through her inbox. "I just can't believe this is happening!"

Carter tucked the soup containers into the refrigerator and joined her at the island. "You know why this is happening, don't you?" he asked, arching an eyebrow.

He nipped her off the stool and placed her on the counter.

"You'll have to remind me. It keeps slipping my mind," she said, cheerfully wrapping her arms around his neck and drawing him in.

"It's because when you're open and honest about who you are and what's important to you, things fall into place."

"Some things don't seem to be falling," Summer said, play-fully running a finger over the bulge in Carter's pajama pants. She bit her lip when she saw the light in his eyes.

"Summer, what time is it?"

She pulled his wrist to her face to check his watch.

"It's almost ten."

"And what's our rule about working at night?"

He was playing with her now, and she liked it. "You mean the rule where I'm not supposed be on electronics after nine?"

Carter nodded slowly, and she felt her pulse pick up. Oh-so-casually she reached over and shut the lid of her laptop. "Oops."

He arched an eyebrow. "You think that's going to keep me from punishing you for breaking the rules?"

"Oh, I'm *so* scared," Summer teased.

Carter leaned in closer until she put a hand on his chest. "What's that?" she asked, her gaze darting to the side door.

When he looked away, she slid off the counter and started running.

He caught her in the great room, bringing her down to the floor with a neat tackle around her knees. In a fit of laughter,

Summer clawed at the couch trying to escape. But she was no match for Carter.

In seconds he had her kneeling on the floor, her face pressed into a couch cushion.

"I think you need a refresher on the rules," Carter said, holding her in place with one hand while his other roamed freely.

When his fingers hooked into the waistband of her shorts, she shivered with the thrill. And when he pulled them down her thighs, exposing her flesh to his hungry gaze, she whimpered.

He caressed and stroked until she was sure he could hear her heart pounding in her chest.

She tensed, remembering. "Where's Jax?"

Carter slapped the curve of her bare flesh. "I'm getting you naked, and you want to know where my brother is?"

"I want to make sure your brother isn't going to come in here and see you getting me naked!"

"He's with Beckett. They're working on Beckett's guesthouse so he can rent it out." His fingers trailed a path up her back, pulling her shirt with them. "Now, if you're finished with your questions, I have a few of my own."

Summer moaned as his lips burned a fiery trail down her back. He paused to nibble lightly at the dimple next to her spine.

"Question number one," he said, nibbling the curve of her hip. "Are you happy?"

"So very happy," Summer said to the cushion.

"Good answer," Carter said, teasing her sensitive ribs with his tongue and teeth. "Question number two. Why don't we use electronics after nine?"

Summer shivered under his mouth. "So... so we can spend quality time together without unnecessary distractions."

"Good girl," he murmured against her. "Question number three. How do you want to spend said quality time tonight?"

He had been so gentle with her since they left the city, making love to her like she was something precious, fragile. And as beautiful as it was, she wanted him to break through that steel-fisted control. She wasn't delicate or fragile, at least not anymore.

"I want you so deep inside me that I can't tell where I stop and you begin," she told him.

She felt him tense and tremble with lust. "Summer."

"Show me how much you want me like this, Carter."

Gone was the gentle pressure of his touch, and in its place was a controlled violence. His strong, callused hand stroked down her back and lower still until his fingers found her center.

"God, you're so ready for me," he whispered through gritted teeth, using two fingers to slowly, reverently part her folds.

"Don't make me wait, Carter," Summer begged. "Please."

With a fierce surge, his fingers stretched into her. Her sigh was a sob of pleasure. Carter fisted his other hand in her hair and worked his fingers in and out of her aching tightness.

"Come to bed with me, baby," he ordered.

"No," she countered, pushing back against him. "Here. Like this."

She heard the rumble deep in his chest as he withdrew slightly only to plunge back into her. Again and again until she pulsed with desire. She felt his erection like molten steel as he leaned into her. He was dominating her, and she wanted more.

He pulled out of her, leaving her empty and aching. But his fingers were replaced with his blunt crown. He entered her on a groan, forcing himself into her core. Summer cried out at the invasion. She never wanted to get used to the feeling of being claimed by him.

He stayed there, fully sheathed in her, for just a moment. She felt him fighting the urge to let go and take.

She shifted back into him, enjoying the exquisite pressure that was already building inside her. She would never have enough of this, of him. He filled her body and soul. He was everything she had been missing.

"Carter." His name was a prayer of thanks from her lips.

He began to move then in short, violent thrusts that stripped away all control. Flesh slapped against flesh in a race to the finish. Summer found herself there at the razor's edge of desire, but she wasn't alone. He was with her, as always.

She felt Carter's hand glide between her legs. Fingers teased her until she spiraled over in a beautiful eruption of power, of love, of passion. She felt him tense against her, felt him shudder inside her as he joined her with his own climax.

This was love.

～

STILL JOINED, they sank to the floor. Carter curled around her, stroking her, whispering dark words of love. She fit here, in his arms, here in this house.

Her entire wardrobe had neatly transferred into Carter's closet. The furniture she brought with her from the city was stored on the second floor of the little barn, which would soon be turned into the headquarters of her digital magazine. With construction already started on the brewery, Carter had culled out a small crew to simultaneously rehab the second floor of the barn into a spacious loft office.

Summer still took little moments in the day to remind

herself where she was. Everything had moved so fast that she was determined to slow it down and enjoy every moment of it.

The man that she loved had carved a space for her that fit so perfectly she wondered why she ever fought it. Her life's dream was being realized, she had begun to repair the relationship with her parents, and she was planting the roots that she never knew she so desperately wanted.

And she was *finally* an official member of the Blue Moon Gossip Group.

Life was better than good.

A horn sounded outside, breaking her reverie.

Carter jolted beside her.

"Who is that?" Summer wondered out loud, annoyed at the interruption. "It sounds like a tractor trailer truck."

"Someone who wasn't supposed to be here until tomorrow," Carter grumbled. He eased out of her. "You'd better get dressed, honey. We've got company."

They hastily pulled on clothes and headed out onto the front porch.

"Isn't this pretty late for a visit in Blue Moon?" Summer asked as Carter held the door for her.

If he answered her, she didn't hear him. Her attention was on the hulking RV parked in front of the house. Her mother threw open the passenger door and waved.

"Surprise!"

"Mom?" Summer gasped. "But you're supposed to be in Alaska!"

"Well, then your father is never going to let me navigate again since we took a very wrong turn and ended up here."

Carter nudged Summer forward until she hurried down the steps and met her mother for the hug she didn't know she had been missing.

"I can't believe you're here!"

Her mom released her and reached for Carter. "It's so nice to finally meet you in person, Carter," she said, wrapping her slim arms around his shoulders.

"I get the feeling you two have been scheming behind my back," Summer accused.

"The three of us actually," a booming voice interjected.

"Hi, Dad." Summer took a tentative step toward the man in the moose sweater.

He opened his arms to her, and she flew into them. "There's my girl," he said in a voice choked with emotion.

Still larger than life, Phil Lentz seemed softer somehow. The lines of his face were cut a little deeper, his hair a little wispier.

"I can't believe you're here," Summer said again, this time sniffling.

Her father set her on her feet. He extended a hand to Carter. "Carter. Thanks for having us."

Carter shook his hand. "You're very welcome. I'm glad you could make it."

Summer slipped out of her dad's grasp and threw her arms around Carter's waist. "Thank you," she whispered against his shirt. His arms came around her, and she felt his mouth on the top of her head. Wrapped in the embrace of the man she loved, she missed the teary smile her mother shot her father.

"I love seeing you so happy," Carter whispered in her ear. "I'd give anything in my power to see you smile like this."

"You've already given me everything. I can't wait to spend the rest of my life evening the score."

EPILOGUE

*C*arter Pierce swore ripely when his grip on the wrench slipped and knuckles met cabinet. To add insult to injury, the pipe spat another drop insolently in his eye.

"Everything okay under there?" his mother and current task master, Phoebe, asked from her position at the kitchen island.

He shook out his throbbing hand and tightened his grip on the bastard wrench. "Just peachy, Mom."

"The sarcasm is strong with this one," Elvira Eustace, Phoebe's best friend in the world, quipped into her wine glass.

Two good turns later, the leak was vanquished. Carter slid out from under the sink and tossed the wrench back in his tool tote.

Phoebe shoved a plate of cookies at him, a sweet smile brightening her pretty face. Her hair was cut in a sleek chin-length bob. A new look for her. But the glasses and the blue eyes behind them were the same.

"Have I told you you're my favorite son?" she asked playfully.

Carter rolled his eyes and turned on the faucet to wash his hands. "When I got here and told you not to worry about calling a plumber. But I also heard you sharing the same sentiment with Beckett last week when he updated your will and Jax yesterday when he was kissing your ass by mowing your lawn."

"But you know I really mean it with you."

He grinned at her. It was an old game she played with them all. And somehow, she made him and his two younger brothers feel like it was true. They were all her favorite.

Carter dried his hands on the rooster dish towel looped over the oven handle and snatched a cookie off the plate. "Isn't it a little early to be drinking?" he asked, eyeing the wine glasses she and Elvira were clutching.

"We're retired, and it's five o'clock somewhere," Elvira announced.

"Yeah, well in Blue Moon it's 12:01."

"Of course, it is. Otherwise it would have been Bloody Marys," Phoebe explained, helping herself to a cookie.

"How's life, my favorite son?"

Carter fired up Phoebe's coffee maker and shoved a mug under the spout. "Life is just about perfect," he said, noting with a glance around his mother's kitchen that his life wasn't the only one on the upswing. Phoebe and her husband, Franklin, had built this house on the family farm with the intention that it would comfortably hold every member of their loud, extended family. The wide open first floor—with kitchen spilling into living and dining spaces—and upstairs bunk room accomplished just that.

"I saw Summer and the twins in town getting custard this week. You have a beautiful family." Elvira raised her glass, her eyes twinkling.

"I certainly do." He thought it funny that even after all this time he still got a thrill when someone mentioned his wife's name. It was a daily reminder that he'd landed the woman of his dreams—once she'd gotten out of her own damn way—and built a life with her.

"You look at Summer the way John looked at your mother," Elvira sighed.

John Pierce, Carter's father, had been a man among men. He'd raised his sons on the tenants of integrity, respect, and service. And when he'd died, their community grieved with them.

Phoebe smiled fondly at the memories. "Your father certainly had a way of making me feel very special. Whether he was doing the dishes for me or we were sneaking some afternoon delight in the coat closet—"

"Mom!" Carter mopped the coffee out of his beard.

"Carter!" Phoebe rolled her eyes. "You're over thirty. You don't need to pretend to be so prudish about sex."

Elvira joined in on the ribbing. "It's true, Carter. You really need to expand your horizons. Why just the other night Phoebe was telling me that Franklin likes to—"

Carter clapped his hands over his ears. "For the love of God, I'm begging you both to stop." He knew his mother and her husband had an active sex life. The first time he met the man, he'd been crawling out of Phoebe's bedroom window onto the roof of the front porch. He loved that she was happy again. He just didn't like to think about the specifics.

They exchanged sly looks, all innocence. "Sorry," they chorused.

"So how is Summer?" Phoebe pressed. "You two have been so busy lately. I hope you're still making time for each other."

"She's good. Better than good. We're great." And they were, he thought. Between the twins and the farm and Summer's online magazine, they were thriving. Their days were full, but so were their hearts. Sure, some days went by a little too quickly, or the to do lists were a little too long, but they made it work.

"I hope you're still reminding her how lucky she is," Phoebe said.

"Just like she reminds me," Carter grinned, sipping his coffee.

There had been times in the not-so-distant past that Carter had wondered if he'd ever find the light again or if his scars, both physical and mental, were too deep. And then along came Summer. A breath of fresh air, a hit of sunshine.

"She's five years cancer-free today," Carter told them. The notification in his calendar had surprised him this morning. But Summer was already at work, and he was wrestling the twins into the car for daycare.

"Five years?" Phoebe shook her head. "It feels like yesterday when she showed up on the farm interrogating you."

"How are you celebrating?" Elvira asked.

"Well, since you mentioned it..."

~

"I'M SO, SO SORRY," Summer gasped, shoving through the screen door of the kitchen, her rescued Great Dane Valentina on her heels. "I got caught on this conference call. And the advertiser was on the west coast, so of course they have all the time in the world. Granted, the package they're agreeing to will pretty much cover college for Meadow or John."

Meatball the beagle waddled out from under the dining table and plopped down at her feet. Summer gave him a stroke between his silky ears before he led Valentina on a lazy jog around the first floor.

She paused to take a breath and notice the quiet of the house. Carter, her devastatingly handsome husband that she never got tired of looking at, was grinning at her while he finished up the dishes in the sink.

He tossed the dish towel over his shoulder and managed to look sexy doing it. Carter nodded toward the glass of wine waiting for her on the island. "How about you take that wine, and I take this beer, and we go enjoy them outside?"

"Where are the twins?" Summer asked, cocking her head and listening for three-year-old chaos that usually echoed through the house.

"Mom took them overnight."

"Really? What's the occasion?" Summer asked, following Carter's fine denim-clad ass through the door onto the porch.

He slung an arm over her shoulders and pulled her in close, guiding her toward the backyard. She loved the smell of him—all fresh air and sunshine—the feel of him against her. Everything about Carter Pierce made her feel safe, protected, loved.

"Beautiful night," he commented.

Summer gave the beauty of the night sky a cursory glance and frowned at his evasion. "I feel bad when Phoebe and Franklin take them overnight. The kids aren't exactly a walk in the park, and Meadow's been waking up before six this week." Mentally she began to tick down the reasons why she should have gotten her ass off the phone at a more reasonable hour.

"Mom raised three boys. One of them being Jax. I think she can handle Meadow and John for a night. Besides, you have plans tonight."

"I do?" She was ready to launch into the questions when Carter stopped.

He'd plugged in the string lights they'd strung from the back patio to the huge oak. A fire crackled in the fire pit he'd put in last summer. Tucked behind the house and next to the garden, it offered up an unobstructed view of rolling meadows and tidy fence rows. There was a patchwork quilt spread over the grass next to the fire. The rest of her bottle of wine was tucked inside an ice bucket. Music, something soft and low, played from a wireless speaker.

"Carter! What is all this?" She looked up at him trying to read what had gotten into her husband.

He took her hand and kissed her knuckles. "I was feeling lucky today."

"Stuff like this makes me feel lucky every day."

He led her to the quilt, and together they sat, Summer with her back to his chest, his arms around her. She took a deep breath of the night air and exhaled slowly.

"And there's my girl," Carter said, nuzzling her neck.

Her husband had dedicated himself to finding creative ways to force Summer's Type A mind into relaxation mode. He was ingeniously good at it.

"It's so beautiful out here," she sighed, the tension and energy of the day slowly seeping out of her muscles. Fireflies danced over the dark fields while crickets sang. The sky, a moody navy, was filled with the twinkle of stars and the silver sliver of moon. An owl hooted from the tree line.

"Why don't we do this every night?" she asked, sinking back against Carter's warmth.

"Because we have two three-year-olds."

"And two dogs," Summer added.

"Four cows, a goat..."

"A very large extended family..."

"Two-hundred acres and an online empire."

She shifted, resting her head against his shoulder. "It's pretty perfect, isn't it?"

"Honey, everything with you is..." Carter searched for the words.

Summer turned against him, slipping her legs over his thighs and wrapping her arms around his neck. "I know exactly how you feel. Thank you for all of this."

"Do you know what today is?" he asked, skimming lips over the line of her jaw.

"My lucky day?" She felt Carter go hard beneath her and relished the ache that ignited within her. "Because I think every day I get to wake up next to you and all your home-grown hotness is my lucky day."

He gripped her hips, big hands digging into the fabric of her skirt.

"Five years," he said, his voice low. "Cancer free."

She grinned at him, scooting higher on his thighs. "God, I love that you keep track of things like that."

"Things like that?" he asked gruffly. "There isn't much bigger than that."

"Oh, yes there is, Carter Pierce," she argued. Summer laid a hand over his heart. "This right here is bigger than that."

Ever so gently, he brushed a strand of her stick-straight blonde hair back from her face.

"This," she said, grinding against his rigid length, "is much bigger than that."

She opened her arms wide and tilted her head up to embrace the darkness. "This, is much bigger than that." Their life, complicated and messy and full of barely controlled chaos, was a bigger dream than she'd ever dared to allow herself.

"There is nothing more important to me than you, Summer," Carter breathed, pulling her back into his arms. And with those words, he single-handedly destroyed her. Steadfast, loyal Carter was a ruthless lover.

Her mouth found his in a greedy kiss, tempered only by the tenderness with which Carter held her. He made her feel treasured, worshipped, desired. And Summer knew that no matter what happened in their life together, she could always count on Carter to be by her side. And right now, she wanted to show him exactly how he made her feel.

"I want you right here, Carter," she said, breaking contact with his lips just long enough to whisper the words.

She felt his mouth curve against hers.

"I was hoping you'd say that."

Summer sent her hands racing over her husband's chest, over the soft cotton of his worn tee, and lower to the button of his jeans.

He stilled her hands with his own. "Honey, we have all the time in the world tonight."

She laughed softly. "I forgot. I'm so used to naptime sex or the-kids-aren't-awake-yet sex."

"Well, allow me to remedy that," Carter said, sweeping her off his lap and onto her back on the quilt. Her hair spilled out beneath her like a pillow.

Summer shivered when his fingers slipped under the hem of her sleeveless cashmere shell. He trailed them over her belly, taking his time to slowly raise the fabric higher and higher on her ribs. Goosebumps. The man gave her goose-bumps with the wisp of a touch. If twins hadn't murdered their sex life, Summer was confident they could enjoy this for the rest of their lives.

"So, beautiful," Carter said, leaning down to press a kiss to the flat of her stomach.

Summer shivered.

"Are you cold?" he asked, stroking up the sides of her ribs until his hands came to rest just beneath her breasts.

She shook her head. "So warm," she promised.

He returned to his purpose, sliding her shirt over her head and tossing it onto the corner of the quilt. The man knew her well enough that she'd yell over cashmere in the dirt.

"Mmm." He approved her purple satin La Perla with a rasp of breath.

Reverently, he skimmed his hands over the satin, over the curves of her breasts. She loved his hands on her. Loved the way he looked at her. Hungry. Craving.

"I want to make love to you all night, Summer," he said. "I want to feel you come until you've got nothing left." His hands abandoned her breasts for her thighs where he nudged the soft jersey of her skirt up to ride on her hips. More of the same purple satin welcomed his gaze there.

"Lose the shirt, Carter. I want to touch you," Summer demanded, her pulse skittering. She needed something to anchor her here before her husband's hands carried her into oblivion. With one swift move, he pulled the shirt over his head and, without missing a beat, flicked open the front clasp of her bra.

She gasped as those rough hands took their fill of her breasts.

Just a few years ago, if someone had told her she'd be on her back under the summer night sky on a farm being seduced by her farmer husband, she'd have laughed until she fell out of her Jimmy Choos. She still had the Jimmy Choos, but she'd gotten a lot more by walking away from New York and the empty promises of a fashion magazine.

There was nothing empty about here. About Blue Moon.

With a burst of strength, she pushed Carter over onto his back, covering his bare torso and its scars with her body. Bullet holes could heal. So could cancer. And fear. And they healed with the kind of love they'd found in each other.

Summer reached between their bodies and opened

Carter's fly. Anticipation zinged through her veins as her fingers found him iron hard. She was already wet for him, already needing him inside her.

Carter stroked his thumb lazily over the damp spot on her underwear, drawing a shiver of pleasure from Summer. Determined to slow them down, Summer leaned over and captured his lower lip between her teeth.

The blur of a shadow caught her eye on the path behind the
barn.

"Oh, sweet Jesus! What the hell is that?"

Carter rocketed up, sweeping her off his lap and shoving her behind him. He always put himself between her and whatever threat materialized, a nerf gun wielding three-year-old, a muddy enthusiastic Great Dane, a runaway goat...

"Fucking Clementine," Carter groaned, flopping back down onto the quilt.

"How did she get out this time?" Summer wondered, staring after the departing shadow. The damn goat was basically Houdini reincarnated.

"Who knows? Maybe she ate a power saw and cut through her stall doors when no one was looking."

"She's headed toward the stables," Summer said, squinting in the dark.

"Probably going to scare the piss out of Jax," Carter predicted.

Summer hid her smile. Clementine the goat had an agenda where Carter's youngest brother was concerned. It was a hate-hate relationship between the two.

"I should probably go catch her before she eats another pair of jeans," he sighed, but he wasn't looking at Clementine anymore. He was looking at Summer's naked torso.

"Probably should," she agreed, biting her lip.

"Of course, Jax doesn't know that we know that she got out."

"Plausible deniability."

"And it's dark. We can't be sure it was her."

"So, maybe we have some time?" Summer asked, slipping her hand back into Carter's jeans. She wrapped her fingers around him, gripping his thickness.

"What goat?" Carter breathed.

AUTHOR'S NOTE TO THE READER

Dear Reader,

I hope you enjoyed your introduction to Blue Moon. I sure did! Without any intention of mine, the town itself became a character in the story. And what a character it is. Blue Moon Bend only gets crazier and sweeter and funnier in the next books, so I hope you'll read on.

So what did you think of Carter and Summer? Ever read a vegetarian hero before? I liked the idea of coming in on Carter's story when he'd been through hell and walked out again with the help of his family. He got to be the rock for Summer, which brought his healing full circle.

The Pierce men are good, heart-of-gold heroes that make you want to marry them and spend every Sunday naked in bed with them. Check out Beckett Pierce next and the trouble he gets himself into over a crush on the sexy, sweet, scatter-brained, yoga instructor who is renting his guesthouse.

Thank you again for reading! If you loved *No More Secrets*, please feel free to leave a review. If you think there's a possibility that I'm as awesome as my books, sign up for my news-letter or follow me on Facebook and Instagram. I'm super cool. I swear!

Xoxo,
    Lucy

ABOUT THE AUTHOR

Lucy Score is a *Wall Street Journal* and #1 Amazon bestselling author. She grew up in a literary family who insisted that the dinner table was for reading and earned a degree in journalism. She writes full-time from the Pennsylvania home she and Mr. Lucy share with their obnoxious cat, Cleo. When not spending hours crafting heartbreaker heroes and kick-ass heroines, Lucy can be found on the couch, in the kitchen, or at the gym. She hopes to someday write from a sailboat, or oceanfront condo, or tropical island with reliable Wi-Fi.

Sign up for her newsletter and stay up on all the latest Lucy book news.
And follow her on:
Website: Lucyscore.com
Facebook at: lucyscorewrites
Instagram at: scorelucy
Readers Group at: Lucy Score's Binge Readers Anonymous

LUCY'S TITLES

Standalone Titles

Undercover Love

Pretend You're Mine

Finally Mine

Protecting What's Mine

Mr. Fixer Upper

The Christmas Fix

Heart of Hope

The Worst Best Man

Rock Bottom Girl

The Price of Scandal

By a Thread

Forever Never

Things We Never Got Over

Riley Thorn

Riley Thorn and the Dead Guy Next Door

Riley Thorn and the Corpse in the Closet

Riley Thorn and the Blast from the Past

The Blue Moon Small Town Romance Series

No More Secrets

Fall into Temptation

The Last Second Chance

Not Part of the Plan

Made in the USA
Monee, IL
09 December 2023